Wanting You

NEW YORK TIMES BEST SELLING AUTHOR

SAMANTHA CHASE

Cover Design: Kari March Designs

Edits: Jillian Rivera

Praise for Samantha Chase

"If you can't get enough of stories that get inside your heart and soul and stay there long after you've read the last page, then Samantha Chase is for you!"

-NY Times & USA Today Bestselling Author **Melanie Shawn**

"A fun, flirty, sweet romance filled with romance and character growth and a perfect happily ever after."

-NY Times & USA Today Bestselling Author **Carly Phillips**

"Samantha Chase writes my kind of happily ever after!"

-NY Times & USA Today Bestselling Author **Erin Nicholas**

"The openness between the lovers is refreshing, and their interactions are a balanced blend of sweet and spice. The planets may not have aligned, but the elements of this winning romance are definitely in sync."

- **Publishers Weekly, STARRED review**

"A true romantic delight, A Sky Full of Stars is one of the top gems of romance this year."

- **Night Owl Reviews, TOP PICK**

"Great writing, a winsome ensemble, and the perfect blend of heart and sass."

Chapter One

Chloe: Hey! Do you want to meet up for lunch?

Ash: Oh, damn. Sorry! I can't.

Ash: Wait…I thought you were seeing Evan this weekend?

Chloe: Um…long story. But that's over.

Ash: WHAT? When? Why didn't you tell me sooner???

Ash: Reid surprised me with a weekend away, but we can totally turn around and come home if you need me!

Sighing with disappointment, Chloe Donovan stared down at her phone.

Chloe: No worries! I'm fine. I promise. Have fun!

Ash: Thanks! I'll call you Monday!

She was about to put her phone down when she decided to reach out to her older sister and see if she was available.

> Chloe: Hey! Do you want to meet up for lunch?

> Billie: Hey! Thought you were seeing Evan this weekend?

Damn. She really did tell her sisters pretty much everything about her life.

> Chloe: We decided to end things. And before you ask, I'm fine. Really. It's all good.

> Billie: Damn. I'm sorry.

> Chloe: I'll tell you all about it over lunch.

> Billie: I'm sorry, I wish I could. I'm on my way to Richmond to look at some new baking equipment for the coffee shop

> Chloe: Oh, no problem! Good luck! Maybe I'll see if Jade is available...

> Billie: She's with me. Levi and Silas are having a boys' day

> Billie: Isn't that sweet?

> Billie: Did you ever imagine our brother being a dad and doing stuff like that?

Another sigh was out before she could stop it because... well, yeah, it was sweet, and she was totally happy for her brother, but it also made her sad. Everyone was busy having a life and she...wasn't. Okay, maybe that was a bit dramatic, but it seemed like her siblings were all involved with great people or had jobs they were passionate about or were doing things that had them moving forward in life while she was just standing still.

"As usual," she murmured before putting her phone down.

A few weeks ago, she thought she was going to be just like them—at least the part about being in a serious relationship. She had been dating Evan King casually for a couple of months and that had just ended—not that she was surprised. Evan was a super successful lawyer from a very wealthy family. He was worldly and handsome, and ultimately they had nothing in common. Still, it was flattering that he'd been interested in her at all, but now that was over and while she wasn't surprised, she was bummed. Outside, it was a beautiful summer day and all she wanted to do was go outside, walk around, and simply enjoy it.

She just didn't want to do it alone.

The plan had been to go on a picnic with Evan before going up to the ski resort, Summit Ridge, for dinner. Now she had zero plans and it sucked.

School was starting again in a few weeks, and Chloe had really been looking forward to enjoying the rest of her summer vacation with Evan.

The sigh was out before she could stop it. It wouldn't be hard to fill her time if she really tried. There was always so much to do before the school year started. And this year, that was really true. With all the growth happening in Sweetbriar Ridge, the elementary school was expanding. Mobile classrooms had been set up on campus for grades four and five, and an additional class was being added for each grade because of the influx of residents. She'd been teaching kindergarten for three years and had been the only kindergarten teacher for that entire time. Now there was going to be a second kindergarten class, which meant a new teacher—a new partner—and she was excited about all the possibilities.

She'd met Kimberly Fairmont on a Zoom call and they had a lot in common. They had already started talking about joint projects and new curriculums, and Chloe actually found herself looking forward to going back to work.

But I'd also been looking forward to spending time with a nice guy…

A nice guy who found her to be too boring, too sheltered, and too committed to her small town. Again, it wasn't anything new. Chloe had always been the quiet Donovan, the shy Donovan.

The boring Donovan.

Maybe no one said it to her face, but she knew they were all thinking it.

At least…no one until Evan.

"We're just too different," he'd said. "You have to admit that we don't have much in common. Every time I try to convince you to come to Baltimore, you're not interested. There's nothing to do in Sweetbriar. Things are growing, but there's no real…culture. I don't understand why you don't want to broaden your horizons, but…I need more. I'm sorry."

The conversation had been brief and mildly crushing, but he was right. And as much as he said he needed more, so did she. She wanted someone who shared her passion for the simple things in life and who didn't feel like they had to be on a constant adventure to be happy.

So far, she hadn't met anyone like that.

Her sister—her fraternal twin—Ashlynn, had a wonderful fiancé, a new hair salon of her very own, and was constantly out doing fabulous things. Her brother Levi recently married Jade and was in the process of adopting her son Silas. And her big sister Billie was living her dream of baking. She'd left the stress-filled world of finance and bravely moved on to something she was passionate about, and she didn't care that she had to take a major pay cut to do it.

Actually, all three of her siblings had gone through major career crises and boldly moved on to bigger and better things.

"And I'm still gluing popsicle sticks together and finger painting."

Okay, that was the last negative comment she was going to make about herself today. Just because her family was busy didn't mean she had to sit around feeling sorry for herself. There were plenty of things she could do—even by herself—that would put her in a better mood than she was currently in.

Standing, she walked over to the massive window in her living room and looked out. There was a small park directly across the street and right now, a couple of families were over there laughing and playing and having fun. Moving into the renovated craftsman bungalow had been a major thing for her last month because she was tired of apartment living. She was only renting it, but was working on her finances to figure out a way to eventually buy it.

Technically, she could get approved for a mortgage thanks to the teacher home loan program, but she didn't want to just make enough to cover her monthly payments; she wanted to be able to actually live and enjoy her life too.

"Baby steps," she said with another sigh, thinking of her little side hustle. Art was something she'd always been good at and lately she'd been creating paintings that she sold in an Etsy shop as well as custom costumes for cosplay. She didn't tell anyone about it—not even her family—but that was only because she knew they'd encourage her and tell her everything was great. And while that was one of the things she loved most about them—their unwavering support—sometimes she wanted to try something on her own and test the waters first. So far she hadn't put a whole lot of stuff out there, but maybe if she upped her inventory in her online shop, she could buy her house sooner rather than later!

Inspiration hit and she made her way to the smaller of her two guest rooms that she turned into a craft room and began rummaging through her supplies in search of inspiration. Thirty minutes later, Chloe decided on her theme for her classroom this year—Pixar's *Inside Out*—and discovered that she needed to order more fabric for some half-finished costumes as well as more paint and canvasses. That led her to happily strolling back out to her living room and sitting down with her laptop to shop online.

"I should probably reach out to Kimberly and see if she wants to share classroom themes. I can easily make double of everything I'm going to use." And after she did all her shopping, she quickly tapped out an email asking her new coworker what her plans were for her classroom. Knowing she wouldn't get a response right away, she closed the laptop and found that all she'd managed to do was kill an hour.

There was still an entire weekend to get through.

"Drats." But she refused to simply sit home alone and let the beautiful day pass her by. "I can do some shopping and maybe run into someone in town to have lunch with."

Changing out of her yoga pants and sweatshirt, Chloe chose something a little trendier—dark skinny jeans, a sleeveless floral blouse, a pair of hot pink strappy sandals, and matching crossbody purse. The colors were a little bolder than her usual palate, but she was excited to finally wear it.

Smiling at her reflection, she felt good about herself, confident even. She felt like someone who could go out and spend a day on her own without feeling self-conscious about it.

"At least...that's what I'm hoping to do!" she cheerily reminded herself. "But only after I fix my makeup." Slipping her purse off, she walked into the bathroom and decided to actually do more than her usual minimum. Ashlynn always said that wearing a full face of makeup made her feel like she could do anything. As much as she loved her sister and her advice, Chloe lacked the skills to pull off that kind of artistry.

A little more concealer, a touch of eye shadow, bronzer, blush, a hint more of mascara, and some soft pink lip gloss had Chloe smiling at her reflection. "Okay, I might not conquer everything, but I kind of feel sassier. Yay me!"

And with that, she walked back out to her bedroom and pulled her purse back on. Grabbing her phone, keys, and sunglasses, she headed out the door and was ready to tackle the day.

The drive into town was short and she opted to park in the first available spot so she could take her time, walk along the street, and take in all the new shops that had opened up. Two years ago, this street looked very different. There were empty storefronts and nothing exciting to see. Now, besides Jade's new shop, Books & Beans, there was a nail salon, a craft store, a wine bar, and a bougie little bath shop filled with every kind of sweet-smelling soap and bath bomb you could imagine. Most of the owners were locals and there was something incredibly charming about walking down

Main Street and seeing all the growth while still keeping the original vibe of their small town.

She stopped at the corner shop and smiled at the window display. Very Vintage was the newest addition to the local businesses. The thrift shop had everything Chloe loved—lots of antique jewelry, clothing, and furniture. Sometimes she swore she was an old soul who was born too late.

At least, that's what many people had told her for most of her life.

Not that she took it as an insult, but it certainly made her feel a little like she didn't fit in.

Stepping into the shop, she pushed all the negative thoughts aside and decided to embrace her old soul self and simply browse to pass the time.

"Hey, Chloe!" Abby Winters called out from behind the jewelry display case. "We just got a bunch of really cool stuff from an estate sale Dave and I went to last month. I'm setting up the jewelry now, but there's some great furniture in the back room, if you're interested."

"Thanks, Abby! Ever since moving from my apartment and into the house, things are still a little sparse. I'd love to look for some new stuff for it." Glancing at a few dresses as she made her way over to Abby, she smiled. "It's been a long time since I've had to buy any furniture, and I'm not sure what exactly I'm looking for, but it can't hurt to look, right?

"Ooh...I didn't know you bought a house! How exciting! We moved into our first place last year and I love it. We lived in apartments for the last ten years, so it was a real treat to be in a house of our own. You're going to love it."

"Well, I'm just renting it for now," Chloe replied. "My cousin Marissa, well...she's actually my cousin's wife, but I consider her to be my cousin too...she convinced me to rent first while I figure out my finances so I can make an offer to buy."

"Marissa handled our house too! We adore her. I'm sure she'll help you find some great financing deals. What kind of house are you looking for? Or did you mean you were going to buy the one you're renting?"

"Um..."

"Who's buying a house?" someone called out from the back room.

Chloe looked around for a moment and then spotted her friend MacKenzie Holland walking toward her. "MacKenzie! Hey!"

They hugged for a moment before MacKenzie pulled back and gave her a huge smile. "You're house hunting? Why didn't you mention it the other day when we were hanging out?"

"Oh, uh...it's actually the house I'm renting. Ultimately, I'd love to buy it. Renting first seemed like a way of testing the waters and all that. Marissa thinks I can get financing because I'm a teacher, but I'm afraid to take that step."

MacKenzie's eyes went wide. "Wow, seriously? This is huge! And, no offense, a little out of character for you. I never pegged you for wanting to take on such a big responsibility."

With a small shrug, she said, "I never thought I would either, but the apartment walls were closing in on me. It was time for a change. I know we've talked about that."

"Devin and I were talking about looking at houses just the other day. His place is awesome, and he's put a ton of work into it, but it's small if we decide to start a family right away."

All Chloe could do was nod.

Another person living the dream while I'm basically house hunting solo...

"From everything he's told me, Sweetbriar Auto Care has doubled its profits this year," MacKenzie went on. "I love working with him and being a part of the success—even though I've only been there for less than six months—but I'd like to find something of my own so I can contribute to a house. You know, when the time comes."

Yeah, MacKenzie was still new around here, but she totally fit. It had practically been love at first sight for her and Devin, and they'd been inseparable from the moment they met.

The sigh was out before she could stop it, but fortunately that's when Abby came over to show them both a beautiful beaded purse she was about to put on display. If there was one thing Chloe had gotten good at this last year, it was smiling even when she didn't feel like it. She was always optimistic and always the first one to offer congratulations or an encouraging word. Basically, she was a happy person.

It just felt like more of an effort lately.

"Hey, any chance you're free for lunch?" she asked MacKenzie.

Her friend smiled as she studied her. "Wasn't Evan supposed to be here this weekend?"

Inwardly, she groaned. "It's a long, boring story. How about we talk about it over lunch?"

"Absolutely! But let's shop first!"

* * *

"We're sorry, but the position has been filled."

Tanner Westyn forced himself to smile—even though it

was a phone conversation—and thanked the woman for her time.

Right before he threw his phone down hard on his sofa and began to pace.

Seriously, how was it this difficult to find a job he was qualified for? It had been three months and not one teaching position had opened up for him.

Okay, that was kind of a lie. Technically, several positions were available; they just weren't what he was looking for. People had warned him it might be like this, but he'd been too arrogant—some would say mildly cocky—to believe them. He'd never had a problem achieving a goal before, and he'd be damned if that was going to start now.

As if on cue, his father walked into the room. "So? How'd the interview go? Did you wow them?"

For a moment, Tanner pinched the bridge of his nose while he silently told himself not to snap. Letting out a long breath, he turned and faced his father. "Actually, Dad, the position was already filled."

With little more than a nod, Nate Westyn went and made himself a fresh cup of coffee before coming back and joining Tanner. "Where's the next school on the list?"

No judgment, no lectures, just a show of support.

That was his dad.

"I'm thinking that I should just skip this year and try again for next fall. Obviously all the positions everywhere are filled." Dropping down onto the couch, his head lolled back as he sighed. "Teaching elementary school has been something I've wanted to do for a long time. I know I took a bit of a detour while I was competing with my skiing, but it feels like so many of these schools are holding it against me."

"Have any of them specifically mentioned that?"

"Well, no, but..."

"Has your skiing career come up in any of the interviews?"

"No, but..."

"Tanner, I realize that you've always been an over-achiever," his father reasoned. "And there hasn't been any obstacle you haven't overcome. But out in the competitive job market, you have to accept that there may be applicants who are more qualified than you."

"Dad, I graduated with honors. I have dozens of recommendations from former teachers and the school where I was a student teacher. Everyone loved me there!"

His father slowly sipped his coffee while making eye contact. It was his go-to reaction to force Tanner to dig a little deeper with whatever he was dealing with.

"Okay, if they had really loved me, they would have offered me a position somewhere," he admitted. "And the principal told me I was sometimes a little overzealous and rubbed some teachers the wrong way. But that's only because I'm passionate about teaching and everyone else was way too laid back!"

Placing his mug down on the coffee table, Nate smiled serenely. "Were they too laid back, or were you trying to show off? Because I think we both know..."

Groaning, Tanner shut his eyes. "I hate it when you do that."

"What? Tell the truth?"

Forcing himself to sit up, he looked at his father. "I just...I want to be the best teacher I can be. Just like I wanted to be the best student, the best athlete, the best skier..."

"You were your high school's valedictorian, graduated college with honors and in the top one percent of your class, and you were one of the top Alpine skiers in the country. By now, you should know that you excel at everything you do."

"Not at getting a teaching job," he mumbled.

"You waited until a month ago to finally get serious about applying," his father gently reminded him.

"I sent out my first application three months ago."

"And you only sent the one because you were so certain they were going to hire you."

"I put my resume up online too."

"Okay, that's true. But you were so busy with endorsement opportunities and doing promotional events that finding a teaching position became an afterthought. Are you really surprised when most schools start up in two weeks?"

"Dad..."

"Fine," he said with a hint of humor. "I've said all I'm going to say on the subject." Reaching for his mug, he picked it up and stood. "Your mother and I are going to dinner with the Nicholsons tonight, so you're on your own for dinner."

Hearing that made him feel like a child, and he hated it. He'd moved back in with his parents six months ago because he'd been traveling a lot for his endorsement appearances. Being a professional athlete had made him a decent amount of money, but he was smart about how he spent it. As much as he hated having to move back into his old room, it meant he wasn't tied down to any neighborhood, city, or state in his quest to get a full-time teaching gig.

If only someone would hire him!

Once his father was out of the room, Tanner straightened in his spot, flipped open his laptop, and challenged himself to find a school, any school, and have a lead on a job by dinnertime.

Dinner that he'd be eating alone, but that was another story.

"Focus," he murmured before giving himself a good, long stretch and cracking his knuckles. "Let's do this."

He'd been completely prepared to start scrolling through all the top hiring sites, but Tanner came up short when he spotted a new email with the subject, "Interview Request." Opening the email, he saw it was from a school in the western part of Virginia, in a town called Sweetbriar Ridge.

"When the heck did I apply for that?"

Not that it mattered. He'd posted his resume online as well as reached out to several school districts in the last month, and if they were reaching out to him, that meant there was a position available!

"Dear Mr. Westyn," he began, before scanning the first paragraph. "Your resume was impressive and if you would like to set up an interview, please call..."

The phone was instantly in his hand and he quickly tapped out the number indicated before crossing his fingers and saying a quick prayer.

"Thank you for calling Sweetbriar Elementary! This is Susan. How may I direct your call?"

"Hi, Susan. This is Tanner Westyn. I just received an email from Principal Kincaid and wanted to set up a time for an interview," Tanner said smoothly.

"Hold on for one moment, Mr. Westyn, while I check his calendar," she replied.

"Take your time," he told her before re-reading the email.

There was no mention of anything specific about the school or the community, so he opened another tab and did a little research himself while he waited.

14

"Sweetbriar Ridge is a town in...blah, blah, blah...population 1,200. Yikes. Currently going through a bit of a renaissance with the re-opening of the ski resort...interesting..."

"Mr. Westyn?"

Clearing his throat, he said, "Yes?"

"Principal Kincaid is actually available to speak to you right now if you have the time," Susan told him, and Tanner had to hide his delight.

"That works for me," he said evenly. "Thank you."

"Hold on while I transfer you, and good luck!"

He thanked her again before the line went quiet. Letting out a slow breath, he prepared himself to give the best damn job interview of his life.

"Good afternoon, Mr. Westyn. Thank you for being so agreeable and speaking with me on such short notice. I'm Steven Kincaid. It's nice to meet you."

"Thank you. It's nice to meet you too. I just received your email and figured I'd call and make an appointment."

"That's normally how we do things, but I was in between appointments and figured there was no time like the present." He paused. "Your resume is very impressive, but I see this would also be your first full-time teaching position."

"That is correct. I realize I may have started applying a little late for this school year, but I was hopeful to find a district that needed a fifth-grade teacher."

"Tell me why you're drawn to that particular grade. Most early educators are a little more open to where they get placed, except for kindergarten teachers. They are the most passionate about teaching that grade. So tell me your story."

"My story?" Tanner repeated, shifting a bit in his seat.

"Well, I feel like that age is on the verge of moving on to middle school and really figuring out what subjects they like or dislike, and a lot of times, they're just discovering who they are. It's an amazing age that's filled with so many possibilities, and I love the challenge of helping to guide them into that next phase of their education."

"I see," Principal Kincaid murmured, seemingly unimpressed.

"Um..."

"Would you be open to perhaps starting out the year as a substitute in another grade? We have a situation where we just lost a teacher—not to anything dramatic, but she had a family emergency and took a position in a school closer to them. We're getting ready for school to start back and we only have the one classroom available."

Well...shit.

"So this would only be a short-term position?"

"Well...we haven't had any other applications for it, so there's a very good chance it would be for the entire school year. Then, once you're in our system, any openings for a fifth-grade teaching position, you'd be given first consideration."

"First consideration? Even after proving myself as an excellent teacher in another grade, the position still wouldn't go automatically to me?"

Steven Kincaid laughed softly. "We haven't seen how you are as a teacher yet, so I really couldn't commit."

"I guess that's fair," he reasoned.

"Our town has been going through a bit of a transformation, Mr. Westyn. I see on your resume that you were a competitive skier. Our resort, Summit Ridge, is gearing up for its inaugural season. It's located less than twenty minutes from the school. We work with the local real estate company here to help our teachers relocate, if you need that sort of service. I can send you our information packet on the town with everything you'd need to know. You'd be moving here from upstate New York, correct?"

Tanner nodded. "Yes."

"And considering your skiing career, I'm guessing the cold weather isn't an issue for you."

Tanner chuckled. "It's safe to say that I'm used to it."

"Excellent! Do you have any questions for me?"

"I do," he told him. "You haven't mentioned what grade the position is for."

"Kindergarten. We already have one kindergarten teacher, Chloe Donovan, and she's amazing. She was our Teacher of the Year the last two years. Because of all the growth our town has been seeing, the school has expanded a bit and now we have a need for a second kindergarten class."

The frown was firmly in place, and his entire body tensed. Kindergarten? Did he really want to teach kindergarten? He loved kids and loved teaching, but he really enjoyed it when the students were a bit older and settled into school life. Could he honestly switch gears like that?

"I understand it's not exactly what you're looking for, but I'm hoping you'll consider it. I truly believe you'll be a perfect fit in Sweetbriar Ridge. And if things keep expanding the way they have in the last year, I'd like to say that we'll be needing more teachers in the next few years. If you're patient, you can potentially get that fifth-grade class you're looking for."

Just not right now...

Sadly, his initial reaction was to say thanks, but no thanks. Tanner knew what he wanted and didn't want to settle for something else.

However...

Could he really afford to pass up the opportunity?

"I want to thank you for taking the time to speak with me today, Principal Kincaid," he began, "but I'm going to need to think about this. I've got a few other offers to consider."

"I completely understand. Feel free to call me back if you have any other questions. In the meantime, I'll send you that informational packet I mentioned along with information about the position including salary, benefits, and all the other boilerplate stuff."

"Thanks. I appreciate it. I'll be in touch soon." And with that, they said their goodbyes and hung up.

That's when the guilt set in.

He lied.

And Tanner never lied. It was something he prided himself on, but in the moment, it seemed like the only way to save face.

Immediately pushing all thoughts of the conversation aside, he settled in for a deep dive into finding the perfect position for him.

At some point, his parents left to meet up with their friends, the sun went down, and he found himself sitting in the dark with nothing but the light of his laptop screen. Still feeling determined, he got up and ordered himself some Chinese takeout before continuing his search. Then, he accepted the dinner delivery and ate while still searching.

He must have fallen asleep because the next thing he knew, his father was waking him up and gently telling him to go to bed.

The next morning, he started his search again.

It took another entire day before he realized he only had

one option, and by then, it was too late to call Sweetbriar Elementary and accept the position.

If it were still available.

So that night, over dinner, he went over the information packet with his parents. It would be a nine-hour drive from his home to Sweetbriar Ridge, and there were several homes for rent that were well within his budget. His father offered to drive a U-Haul with all of Tanner's belongings and help him get moved in, and his mother agreed to come along and make sure his home was well-stocked with food and every necessity he would need so he could focus on his new job.

He'd hit the parent jackpot with the two of them. They'd sacrificed so much for him and were always ready to lend a hand wherever he needed it.

"Do you think I'm doing the right thing?" he asked them. "Should I wait and try again for next year?"

"Tanner," his father began. "The position is a good one. The town sounds like the kind of place that's perfect for you, and everyone has to start somewhere. Most people don't just step into their dream job on the first day. You're getting your foot in the door and that's the most important part. If it's not a good fit, then you give proper notice, and then move on. No one expects you to stay if you're miserable. It wouldn't be fair to you or the students."

"I know, but..."

"And you said the other kindergarten teacher was Teacher of the Year? Sounds like she'd be a great person to work with! You'll learn a lot from her, and before you know it, you'll be getting a classroom of your own with the age group you really want."

Nodding, he looked over at his mother. "Mom? What do you think?"

Michelle Westyn smiled before reaching for his hand

and squeezing it. "I think you're going to do a wonderful job. You've always been a great leader and someone who has a heart for teaching. I think those kids are going to love having you as their teacher!"

He felt himself blush at the praise. "Thanks."

They finished dinner and cleaned up together before Tanner found himself in his room alone. Picking up the latest Steve Berry book, he got comfortable on his bed and settled in for a relaxing night of reading. Talking with his folks really put his mind at ease and as much as he had been putting pressure on himself to find the perfect job, they were right. It would come in time, and this was only the first step.

So tonight, he could relax. Tomorrow morning, he'd make sure that he was up early so that he could hopefully be the first person Principal Kincaid talked to.

Sweetbriar Ridge might not be a place he'd ever heard of before, but he had a feeling it was going to be a great place to spend at least the next year.

And who knows? Maybe Sweetbriar Elementary was ready for a new Teacher of the Year.

"It's always good to have a goal," he said confidently as he opened the book to chapter one. "And it's even better to achieve it."

Chapter Two

School was going to start in a little over a week, and Chloe was totally ready to go. She still hadn't heard back from Kimberly, but she was going to talk to Principal Kincaid later today when she went in to start setting up her classroom.

In the meantime, she was meeting Ashlynn for breakfast over at Books & Beans.

She arrived early—because she was always prompt—and went inside to chat with Billie and Jade and see what kind of goodies were in the bakery case today.

"Hey, Chloe!" Billie called out as soon as she walked through the door. "I thought you were starting work on your classroom today."

Moving over to the counter, she smiled. "I am, but Ash and I are having breakfast first. Do you have time to take a break and join us?"

"Um...maybe? I've got some stuff in the oven, but once it's all out, I'll try to come sit for a little while." She pointed to today's cakes and cookies. "What are you in the mood for today? A muffin? Pound cake? Scone?"

"Hmm..." Leaning in, she looked at everything and wished she could sample it all. "I think I'm going to go with a chocolate chip muffin please. And some tea."

"You got it!"

The bell over the door jingled, and Chloe turned and saw Ashlynn coming in with a big smile. They hugged before her sister frowned at the bakery case. "Still no chocolate croissants? Seriously, I've been lobbying for them for like...a year! Come on, Bill!"

Their older sister gave her a stern look. "You are literally the only person in this entire town who has ever asked for chocolate croissants. Everyone else loves what's on the menu. If you want one so bad, maybe you can figure out how to bake it yourself!" Then she spun away and stormed off to the kitchen.

"Wow, someone got up on the wrong side of the bed this morning," Ash murmured. "Jeez, I mean...it was just a suggestion."

"You didn't even say good morning or even hello to her. You just started complaining about croissants."

"Because chocolate croissants are delicious! And if other people were given that option, they'd rave about them too! It's like nobody listens to me!"

"Okay, let's change the subject," Chloe suggested before frowning. "Although now we need someone to finish our order. Billie was making mine..."

Just then, Jade stepped out of the kitchen, smiling at them both. "Hey! I'm guessing one of you pissed off the baker?" she teased.

"Um..."

But she waved them off. "It's okay. She's been a little tense today, and I'm not sure why."

"So it really wasn't my fault," Ash reasoned.

"Well..."

"Can you please just order something?" Chloe prompted. "And don't complain about what they *don't* have."

"Ugh...fine! Can I get a slice of the pound cake and a caramel Frappuccino?"

"You got it," Jade said. "Why don't you guys go and sit down and I'll bring everything over?"

"Thanks!" Chloe said as they made their way to their favorite table in the romance section of the books part of the store. "I just finished a fantastic book last night. A holiday romance. Well...more like a family reunion holiday story with some romance thrown in."

"You read a holiday romance in August?"

"There's never a wrong time to read a holiday romance, Ash. Trust me. You should totally check it out. They're a huge family and the father—who's now a grandfather—plays matchmaker with everyone." She sighed happily. "I'm telling you; it gave me all the feels. I can totally lend you my copy..."

"Sure! Bring it over with you when you come for dinner Friday night!"

"Done!"

Jade walked over with their food and placed the tray on the table. "Here you go!" Then she straightened. "So? Anything new and exciting going on?" She paused and glanced over her shoulder. "Anyone have any idea what's got your sister in a mood?"

They both chuckled, but Ash answered first. "No clue. We've learned to just give her space and not ask too many questions." Then she shrugged. "I guarantee she'll join us in a few."

The bell over the front door sounded again, and Jade excused herself to go help customers.

"Do you really think something's wrong with Billie?" Chloe asked, breaking off a small piece of her muffin. "She doesn't normally snap like that."

"Are you serious? That's the first sign that something's wrong in her personal life. If you ask me, she needs to get a personal life. And a romantic life." Stirring her drink, she added, "We may have to set up a dating profile for her and find her a man."

But Chloe was already shaking her head. "No way. Absolutely not. We are not getting involved like that."

"Why not?"

"Because dating is very personal! I know I wouldn't want anyone doing something sneaky like that and then setting me up with some stranger I know nothing about."

"I hate to break it to you, Chlo, but that's what dating is usually like. You go out with someone you've never met before, that's just the way it is."

She hated when her sister used logic like that.

"Still, it should be Billie's decision when she's ready to go out with someone, not ours."

With a dramatic groan, Ash relented. "Ugh, fine. I won't set up a dating profile. Sheesh."

"Thank you."

"Okay, so what's up with you? Are you setting up your classroom today?"

The smile was on her face instantly. "I am! And I'm so excited about it too! I'm going with a Pixar theme and using the characters from *Inside Out*! It's going to be super cute and colorful!"

"I'm sure! And is the new kindergarten teacher going to

do it too so both classes have a cohesive look or is she doing something different?"

"Honestly, I have no idea," she replied as her smile faded. "I've reached out to her several times in the last week, and she never responded. I'm going to talk to Principal Kincaid when I get to the school. I really thought Kimberly and I hit it off, but now she's ghosting me. I hope I didn't offend her in some way."

"Stop," Ash said firmly. "You're not capable of offending anyone. You're like the nicest person on the planet. Maybe this Kimberly person is just super busy moving here or getting ready to start her new job." Reaching across the table, she squeezed Chloe's hand. "I'm sure it's all going to be great and the two of you will be friends."

"I hope so. I was kind of upset at the thought of there being another kindergarten teacher. Everything's growing around here, so I realize we need more teachers and more classrooms, but...I was just really hitting my groove with everything and now things are changing."

"Change can be a good thing. You know you're an awesome teacher. Hell, you were Teacher of the Year for the last two years! All you need to do is keep being yourself and you'll be fine. Trust me. This year is going to be amazing for you."

If only she had that kind of confidence.

Not that she expected to always be Teacher of the Year, but with six new teachers coming in—and not knowing any of them—Chloe had no idea how things were going to go. And she really wished Kimberly would have called her back so at least she could have gone into the school today with a bit more...clarity.

"You're frowning," Ash said. "And you need to stop.

You're awesome and that's all there is to it." She took a sip of her coffee. "Are we cutting your hair before school starts? Want to do it Friday night before dinner? You can swing by the salon and then we'll head to my place. What do you think?"

Chloe ran a hand over her hair and nodded. "I didn't think it was ready for a trim, but I guess it can't hurt."

"And highlights? Can we please refresh your highlights too?" her sister asked excitedly. "I have a new color and technique I want to try that would look absolutely stunning on you!"

"If we do all that, we'll never get to eat. Let's just stick to the trim. I'll swing by the salon at four. Will that work?"

"That's perfect!" Before Ash could say anything else, her phone dinged with an incoming text and as soon as she swiped the screen, she frowned. "Dammit."

"What's wrong?"

"A delivery showed up early and I need to go." She immediately began collecting her things. "I'm sorry to cut our breakfast short, but I'll see you Friday and good luck today!" Waving, Ash turned and all but sprinted out the door.

Letting out a soft sigh, Chloe reached for her coffee and was about to take a sip when one of Jade's customers came strolling over to scan the bookshelves in the romance section. Normally that wasn't a big deal, but this was a guy and one she'd never seen around here before.

Although, with the way Sweetbriar was growing, that was happening a lot more often lately. There was a time when she swore she knew everyone's name and where they lived. But now it was totally different, and that's not necessarily a bad thing.

And this guy in particular was definitely not a bad thing, she thought and felt her cheeks heat.

Forcing herself to focus on her tea and nothing else, she silently reminded herself that it was rude to stare. But really, that was all she wanted to do.

He was tall and lean, but in an athletic way. The black t-shirt he was wearing showcased some impressive biceps and she found herself studying them as covertly as she could.

I could casually look up and maybe smile at him politely...

Shifting slightly in her seat, she smoothed her hand over her hair again and slowly looked up. As fate would have it, he turned his head at the same time and smiled, and Chloe's heart felt like it skipped a beat.

Wow...

It had been a long time since any guy gave her that fluttery feeling in her belly—the kind that felt like a swarm of butterflies were taking flight there—and that's how she felt right now. His dark hair, dark eyes, and a bit of scruff on his jaw had her staring more than was polite.

Don't look like a weirdo...

And so, tucking a strand of hair behind her ear, she averted her gaze and once again focused on her tea. The next time she looked up, he was gone.

"Drats," she whispered. Not that she would have been brave enough to strike up a conversation with a handsome stranger, but it might have been nice if he had said hello or even commented on a book to her.

"Where'd Ash go?" Billie asked as she joined her.

"Oh, some delivery arrived early at the salon and she had to go and meet them." Smiling, she asked, "Everything okay with you? You seemed a bit tense earlier."

But Billie waved her off. "I got an invitation to a friend's wedding and I'm on the fence about going. It's nothing."

She took a sip of the coffee she'd brought over with her. "Do you have everything you need for your classroom this year?"

It was obvious she wanted to change the subject, so Chloe obliged. "I do. My car is completely loaded and I should have it all done by the end of the day today. I'm probably going to go in and tweak things throughout the week. I'll have to do a quick inventory on some of the basic supplies, but once I send home our classroom wish list with the students, we'll definitely have everything we need."

Nodding, Billie gave her a small smile. "I'm so proud of you. You really found your calling and you're out there doing such a great job."

Chloe felt herself blushing again. "I love what I do and I'm glad it's appreciated. It would be awful if I loved the job and was actually terrible at it." She laughed softly. "I'm a little nervous about all the new teachers coming in. Maybe they'll all be the ones who are really doing a great job and I only looked like I was doing a good job because..."

"I'm going to stop you right there. You're doing a great job, Chloe. Don't think about the other teachers and what they're doing. You just keep doing your thing and everything will be just fine."

"Billie?" Jade called out. "One of the ovens is beeping!"

"Good luck today!" Billie said as she quickly got to her feet and made her way to the kitchen, leaving Chloe alone again.

"I think that's my cue to head over to the school," she murmured before popping the last of her muffin into her mouth. After clearing off her table, she grabbed her purse and tea and headed out to her car. The drive to the school was short and it made her smile to see so many cars in the parking lot. Apparently she wasn't the only one getting her classroom ready.

Pulling her collapsible wagon from the trunk, she opened it and began piling all her supplies into it. She'd worked it out at home so it would only take one trip from the car, but it was definitely overflowing, and that didn't even count the giant duffel bag she had slung over her shoulder and her purse. All the struggling would be worth it when she had it all in her classroom.

After awkwardly making her way through the front door, she pulled her wagon up to the front office and left it there so she could step inside and hopefully speak to Principal Kincaid.

"Hey, Susan!" she said cheerily when she spotted the front office administrator. "How was your summer?"

"Very peaceful," Susan replied. "Unlike how today is going." Then she chuckled. "How about you? Did you have a good summer?"

"I did. A little boring, but it was good." She glanced around. "Is Principal Kincaid in?"

"He is, but he's in the office with one of the new teachers. Is there anything I can help you with?"

Her shoulders sagged. "Maybe? I had been talking to the new kindergarten teacher, Kimberly Fairmont, but she hasn't responded to me in more than a week. I'm curious if maybe I did something that offended her, or...?"

But Susan smiled as she shook her head. "I'm sorry, I should have reached out to you. Ms. Fairmont had a family emergency and opted to take a teaching position close to her parents."

"Oh, so...is there someone replacing her?"

"That's who Principal Kincaid is in with right now. We couldn't find anyone who specifically wanted to teach kindergarten, so technically he's a substitute..." Then she paused to think about it for a moment. "Like a long-term substitute? Maybe? Either way, Tanner Westyn will be teaching the other kindergarten class for the time being."

That didn't sound good. It was going to be a bit difficult to make it feel like a team if this Tanner person wasn't truly committed to the position, which is what she said to Susan.

"I wouldn't worry about it, Chloe. He's a certified early education teacher and he seems genuinely excited to be here. He relocated from upstate New York so clearly he's taking the job seriously."

"Maybe..."

"Why don't you head down to your classroom and I'll make sure Principal Kincaid brings Mr. Westyn down to meet you first?"

"Thanks, Susan. That sounds good!" And even though she was smiling, all sorts of crazy scenarios began to play in her head. What if she didn't like this guy? What if he didn't like her? What if he just took this job to get his foot in the door and expected her to do all the work? Or worse, what if he was a terrible teacher who ended up quitting, leaving her with twice as many students?

As she pulled her wagon full of supplies to her classroom, one other crazy thought came to mind.

What if he's awesome and completely outshines me?

By that time, she was at her classroom and forced herself to push all those negative thoughts aside and focus on her task at hand.

Making her classroom fun, inspiring, and welcoming.

First, she set up her decorative border on her main corkboard, and then moved on to the border that would go around the entire room. She'd made it herself and it was a labor of love; the further she went around the room with it, the bigger her smile grew.

"Knock, knock!" Principal Kincaid happily called out, and Chloe turned to face him and instantly froze.

The handsome guy from the coffee shop was standing right beside him.

* * *

So far, Tanner was mildly impressed with everything he was discovering in Sweetbriar Ridge. He'd moved two days after accepting the position and was renting a craftsman bungalow that was newly renovated. What the town lacked in things like restaurants and some basic conveniences, it more than made up for in charm.

And Summit Ridge was seriously impressive.

Not only was the resort building beautiful and the property amazing, their pro shop carried the line of skis and snow gear he endorsed. The manager had gushed over him and begged him to sign a bunch of items that they could display and then asked if he'd come back at the opening of ski season and do a promotional event with them. Of course he'd said yes and put the date on his calendar. Now all he had to do was wait for it to snow.

Today he was getting the tour of the elementary school and Principal Kincaid was probably the most personable and sincerely nicest guy he'd ever met. After filling out paperwork and simply talking to get to know each other, they were heading to the classroom he'd be using.

"Before we get to your room, I'd like to introduce you to the other kindergarten teacher."

"Donaldson, right?" Tanner asked, trying to remember the name. "She was Teacher of the Year...twice?"

"It's Donovan," the principal gently corrected. "Chloe Donovan, and yes, she is a two-time winner of Teacher of the Year here in Sweetbriar. Parents and students adore her. She actually went to school here, so obviously you can tell she's a native to the area. If there's anything you need to know about the town or the school, Chloe is the perfect person to ask."

Tanner nodded as they walked, but he was already envisioning some sort of snooty know-it-all with a bit of an over-inflated ego because she grew up here—not that it was anything to brag about. It was the smallest town he'd ever seen and there might be something wrong with her if she never left. So...maybe not snooty, perhaps she was mousy and quiet and never left because she was too afraid to try. Pfft...he was someone who enjoyed taking risks and beating odds. In his mind, he was already determined to be the next Teacher of the Year and prove you didn't have to be born here to be the best.

Actually, he was more determined than ever to make it through the entire year of teaching kindergarten just to achieve that goal.

"Knock, knock!" Principal Kincaid called out when they reached the classroom at the end of a short hallway. He was smiling and, if anything, looked almost giddy that they were here to talk to this Donovan woman.

Whatever.

Stepping around his new boss, Tanner stepped into the room and looked around. Was she even in here? "Um..."

"Principal Kincaid! Hi!"

That's when Tanner spotted her on a small stepladder in the corner of the room. She was petite and a little nondescript, in his opinion—almost like she blended into her surroundings. But when she climbed down and walked toward them, he had a moment where he thought he'd seen her before. Of course it was possible that they'd passed each other on the street, but...

"Chloe! The room is already coming to life!" the principal exclaimed. "And look at that border! You did that yourself, didn't you?"

She blushed as she nodded and Tanner took a moment to look a little closer at said border and had to admit that she definitely had some artistic talent. So did he. And if this was the level she was bringing, he knew he could match it.

Hell, I can surpass it...

"Chloe Donovan, I'd like to introduce you to Tanner Westyn. Tanner's going to be teaching our new kindergarten class!"

"It's nice to meet you," Tanner quickly said, holding out his hand to her. He gave her an amiable smile and watched as she just stared at him for a long moment. "Um...?"

"Oh, sorry," she blurted out before shaking his hand. "It's nice to meet you too." Then she turned her attention back to Principal Kincaid. "I heard that Kimberly Fairmont took another teaching position. We had been talking to each other online and making plans for our classrooms until a few weeks ago. Ultimately, we were going to try to keep a common theme between the two so the students had a sense of familiarity when we got together for different projects."

"That sounds wonderful!" Kincaid gushed, and Tanner had to fight the urge to roll his eyes. "I'm sure you and Tanner can find some time to get together and talk about all that. We realize he hasn't had as much planning time, so any help you can give him would be greatly appreciated."

Chloe looked over at him and smiled. "I'm more than happy to help you with your room. I made extras of most of my decorations in case Kimberly had wanted to use them. You're more than welcome to..."

"Thanks," he interrupted. "But I have some ideas of my own that I'd like to implement. I'm sure what you're going to do in here will be awesome, but I'd really like to put my own stamp on my classroom."

You could have heard a pin drop in the room, but Tanner wasn't the least bit deterred, so he continued.

"I appreciate the offer, but this is going to be my first classroom and I've been working on my own themes."

Her smile faded slightly. "I completely understand, Mr. Westyn. And if you have any questions about the curriculum or the best way to organize your room…"

"Thanks," he said firmly but with a smile before facing the principal. "Am I in the room next door?"

To his credit, Principal Kincaid looked mildly uncomfortable, but kept whatever opinions he had to himself before nodding. "Yes. Why don't we go on over and check it out?" Then he looked over at Chloe. "We're going to have a faculty meeting on Thursday, Chloe. I'm sure you got the email. But I was wondering if maybe you could pick up some refreshments from Books & Beans?"

"I can definitely do that," she assured him. "I'll get a wonderful variety so that…"

"You know what?" Tanner interjected. "Why don't you let me pick up the refreshments? As the new guy, maybe it will help break the ice a bit. You know, show a bit of good-will toward my new coworkers!"

"Um…"

"My sister-in-law owns Books & Beans, and my sister is the baker there," Chloe told him, her tone going a bit frosty. "I've been bringing the refreshments from there since it opened, so…"

He shrugged. "Doesn't mean it has to all be on you. I

34

can just as easily go in and pick some muffins and cookies up. I'm just trying to be part of the team."

Now she was looking at him with open hostility.

"Tanner, we appreciate the offer," Principal Kincaid gently said. "But maybe you can bring refreshments another time."

"Or maybe I can pick up something from somewhere else? Or perhaps bake something from scratch at home?" he suggested. "Either way, I've got this covered." He smiled at Chloe before taking a step toward the door. "And my room is...?"

"Chloe, why don't you stop by my office before you leave today?" the principal asked quietly, but Tanner still heard. Undoubtedly, they were going to discuss her stepping aside on this one and letting the new guy have a shot at winning some favor with everyone.

When they stepped out of her classroom and went to the room before it, Tanner was...

Horrified.

The room was rather grim and plain and bare.

Slowly, he walked around and took it all in, trying to hide his disdain. "There's nothing here," he said after several minutes.

"Our teachers tend to stock the room to get the year started and then send home wish lists to the parents for the rest of the necessities."

"I get that, but..." Again, he glanced around. "There is seriously nothing here. No books, no posters, just...nothing."

Chloe's room had a reading nook that was overflowing with books. There was a colorful carpet on the floor and her cubbies were painted in bright colors. This room looked like it could have been a supply closet except all the supplies were missing.

"I understand that this is the first year that you're having a second kindergarten classroom, but maybe Chloe can share some of those supplies. I mean...if the district supplied them to her..."

"Oh, the district didn't supply 99% of what's in Chloe's room. The rest is all hers. There are some boxes in our storage room that you can go through and take whatever you'd like, and obviously we'll be supplying everything you'll need curriculum-wise, but the rest is really up to you, Tanner. I thought you understood that."

Raking a hand through his hair, he seriously began to doubt his ability to pull this off. He had five days to decorate, stock, and plan. With the move and everything happening so quickly, he just assumed there'd be more for him to work with.

And he'd gone and turned down Chloe Donovan's offer for help.

Nice work, genius...

Yeah, sometimes his ego got the better of him.

Like now.

"Okay," he said after letting out a long breath. "Why don't you show me what's available and I'll take it from there?"

Several hours and several dozen dusty boxes later, Tanner stood in the doorway to his classroom and was only slightly less horrified. Things were coming together, but the room lacked that bright, cheery tone he knew was important. There was no way he could paint the entire room, even if that was allowed, and he was feeling overwhelmed at all the things he needed to get just to cover the essentials. There was still the curriculum to look over and lesson plans to make.

So maybe he should take Chloe up on her offer and sit

down with her and get a little...guidance. He didn't need help—at least not in the traditional sense—but he certainly needed a little something to make everything come together.

Turning off the classroom light, he walked next door to Chloe's room and stood in wide-eyed fascination. Now that he'd spent some time in his own room, he realized just how bright and clean her room was. Everywhere you looked, there was something that would make a young child smile. Her reading corner had books that were neatly organized, she already had cubbies labeled with her students' names, and it looked like an entire class could walk in here right now and start learning.

His hands ran through his hair again and he realized he had messed up.

"Grovel," he murmured. "Grovel if you have to so you can hopefully get whatever extras she has to offer."

Walking out of the room, he made a beeline to the main office in hopes of catching her there. Susan wasn't at her desk and no one was around, but he definitely heard voices coming from the principal's office.

"I understand what you're saying, Steven," he heard Chloe saying. "But I just don't see myself working with someone like that. He was rude and condescending. I'll be professional, but I'm going to focus on my room and my students." Then she paused. "Unless a student really needs me because I won't let them suffer because their teacher is an arrogant egomaniac."

Okay, wow...that was a little harsh.

"I'll admit he was a little...um...abrasive," Principal Kincaid said diplomatically. "But he's new here, to both the school and the town, and we need to extend a little grace. We haven't had any applicants for the position, so really, he's all we have."

And double wow because that stung!

"You know I'm going to always put the students and the needs of this school first," Chloe said. "But I'm not going to be walked all over by someone who is desperately seeking approval. There are a lot of new teachers here this year, and none of them have behaved like he did."

"Did you meet the new art teacher, Dana Perry?"

"I did! And she was such a delight! She loved the artwork I did for my room!"

"It really was impressive, Chloe," he told her. "Such a fun and inviting atmosphere!"

"The unit where we work on emotions will really make the room come to life," she explained. "It sort of inspired me."

"You could teach a class on creating an environment that encourages learning. In fact, maybe at next year's teaching retreat, you could!"

There's a teaching retreat?

"We can talk about it more in the spring," she told him. "But I hope we can make things work now with this whole... current situation. You know I never complain..."

"I know, I know, Chloe, and believe me, I'm going to talk to Tanner and explain how things work here at Sweetbriar Elementary. You don't have to worry. I've got it under control."

"Thank you so much. I really appreciate it."

Tanner glanced around and knew he had to hide, otherwise they'd know he'd been eavesdropping on their conversation. If he went out the door, they'd hear it and there was no place to hide in the hallway, but it was that or crawl under Susan's desk.

And yeah, he glanced at it for longer than he should have before quietly sneaking out the door and sprinting down the hall and counting to ten. Then he'd casually stroll toward the office like he hadn't been there since his meeting earlier.

Brilliant!

At the door of his classroom, he stopped and took a moment to glare at how awful the room looked, and then turned and slowly walked toward the office. When he turned the corner, he spotted Chloe walking out while still chatting with Principal Kincaid. They both paused when they spotted him, and he saw the apprehension on the principal's face and thinly veiled annoyance on Chloe's.

"Tanner!" Principal Kincaid said after a moment. "How's the room coming along?"

"I believe I'm making progress," he said carefully before focusing on Chloe. "I may have been a little quick to turn down your generous offer. Would it be possible to perhaps get some of the extra decorations you prepared?"

The look on her face said she wanted to turn him down and that she didn't like him—her face was incredibly expressive—but he saw her glance at their boss and knew she would be nothing but gracious.

"Of course," she said begrudgingly. "I had already packed it all up and put it in my car, but if you'd like to follow me out, I'll get it for you." Then she turned and walked out the front door without another word.

Tanner was about to follow when Principal Kincaid stopped him.

"A word of advice, Tanner," he said sternly. "We're a tight-knit community and everyone that works here treats one another like family." Placing a hand on Tanner's shoulder, he continued. "No one expects you to come in here and do it all yourself. So if anyone offers you help or advice, take it. And lastly, don't try so hard. You're going to make great friends here if you take the time to sit back and observe."

"Thanks. I appreciate the advice. I didn't mean to step on anyone's toes."

"No worries. Now go and get those supplies from Chloe and let me know if there's anything else we can help you with."

With a nod, Tanner went to walk away, but stopped and shook the principal's hand first. He found Chloe out in the parking lot by her Honda sedan with the trunk open. Jogging over, he made sure to smile.

"Hey! Sorry to keep you waiting," he said and was relieved when she actually smiled back at him. She didn't respond right away and that just had him staring at her for longer than was probably polite. "I know we just met today, but...I feel like I've seen you around town."

She ducked her head slightly and combed a wayward strand of hair behind her ear. "Um...it was at Books & Beans this morning," she said shyly. "I was in there having coffee with my sister and you were checking out the books."

It took a moment and then it hit him. She had been sitting alone while he was scanning the books in the romance section—not that he read those books, but he was just taking in everything the shop offered.

"Oh, right!" Then he slid his hands into his pockets and leaned closer. "I don't really read romance; I was just seeing what kinds of books they carried there. You know, like...all the different genres and all that."

"It's a great shop, and Jade makes sure she carries an eclectic selection of titles. Did you happen to get any coffee or baked goods?"

"Just coffee. I don't really eat a lot of sweets," he told her.

And it was true. All his years as an athlete made him adapt to a strict and healthy diet. Even though his competitive years were behind him, he still favored eating that way. Especially as a spokesperson for athletic wear and equipment.

"Well, if you ever decide you want to try some cake, I would highly recommend the glazed lemon pound cake. It's my grandmother's recipe, and it's legendary around here."

"I'll keep that in mind."

Then there really didn't seem to be anything else to say. He had the decorating supplies and even though the principal's words were still fresh in his mind, Tanner wanted to head home and come up with more ideas on his own. If by Friday he was still floundering, he'd reach out, but for now, he was set.

Taking a step back, he said, "Thanks again for all of this." He held up the bag of supplies she'd given him. "I appreciate it and, again, I apologize if I appeared ungrateful earlier. I look forward to working with you."

She smiled—and this time he could tell it was genuine because it completely transformed her face. She had dark brown hair with honeyed highlights that the sun just seemed to emphasize, dimples when she smiled, and the biggest blue eyes he'd ever seen.

If she wasn't his direct competition, he'd consider asking her out, but...she was. Tanner was all about making a name for himself no matter what the playing field. And that included teaching kindergarten.

Chapter Three

Thursday morning, Chloe stopped at Books & Beans to pick up her order of goodies for the meeting. She'd called Billie Monday night and told her what she needed, otherwise she'd end up wiping out their bakery case.

"Hey, Chloe," Jade said when she walked in. "Your sister's boxing everything up for you. How's classroom setup going?"

"Amazing!" she gushed because...well...it was. "I think I outdid myself this year. I've coordinated everything in the room so the theme is consistent. I swear, I could get a job working for Disney at this point." Grinning, she added, "Principal Kincaid thinks I can teach all about how to turn the classroom into a creative and inviting space at the next retreat!"

"That's awesome! Good for you! Do you have any pictures?"

"Of course!" Pulling out her phone, she tapped on her photo app and then handed it over to Jade. "I'm telling you, the only thing missing are the students. Tuesday can't get here soon enough!"

Jade chuckled. "Silas is not feeling as excited as you are about school starting next week. We finished all of our back-to-school shopping last night and he's been groaning ever since about how he wants just one more week of summer." Laughing some more, she shook her head. "And if he got that, he'd want another, and then another, and it would be endless!"

"Aww...I hate that he feels that way, but I know it's completely normal. Once kids reach the age where they're almost done with elementary school, they start getting like that. And this is a big year for him. Fifth grade, his last year at Sweetbriar Elementary, and then moving on to middle school and the unknown. Who's his teacher this year?"

"Mrs. Allen. She emailed a welcome video to all her students and I thought it was very sweet. Silas was only mildly impressed, but I'm hoping once he gets to school on Tuesday and sees all his friends—and most of them are also in Mrs. Allen's class—he'll have a better attitude."

"He definitely will," Chloe assured her. "I've known Mrs. Allen for years; she's a great teacher. I met the new fifth-grade teacher and she seems very nice too, but I can personally vouch for Mrs. Allen."

Nodding, Jade poured her a cup of tea and handed it to her while they waited for Billie to bring her order out. "There are a lot of new teachers this year, huh? I know they brought those trailers to use as classrooms for the fourth and fifth graders. Mrs. Allen did a tour of hers in her video. I have to admit that I wasn't thrilled with the prospect, but I understand it was necessary."

"They're portable classrooms—or modular buildings—and I get it, but they're actually nicer and newer than most of the ones in the school. Plus, the ones we're using have eight classrooms and a couple of bathrooms. I believe they're only using six of the rooms for actual classes and the other two will be used as a teachers' lounge and an office. It's a great option for us until they figure out when they can realistically renovate the school."

"I suppose. What about the new teachers? Have you met them all? Are they nice?"

Chloe inwardly groaned. "Um...most of them are," she said and cringed at her negativity.

"Most of them?" Jade asked with a hint of amusement. "Are you telling me there's somebody you don't like already? I didn't think that was possible! You get along with everyone!"

"Yeah, well..."

"Okay, come on. Out with it. You have to tell me what this person did to make your face scrunch up like that."

Ugh...did she really want to get into this right now when she was feeling so happy?

"It's nothing," she lied. "Just...the new kindergarten teacher isn't the one I had been communicating with. She ended up taking a teaching position elsewhere. So they hired this...guy, who is kind of...I don't know...icky."

Jade's eyebrows went up. "Icky? I'm sorry, but did you really just describe another adult as icky?"

Sighing loudly, she said, "I know! It's the only word that came to mind! He has a very high opinion of himself and was kind of abrasive when we met. I offered to help him since he was coming into all of this late, and he acted like my offer was beneath him!" She took a sip of her tea before continuing. "And then...then he accepts part of my offer and took some of the extra decorations I made and has kept his classroom door shut since!"

"O-kay..."

"And I've knocked on the door just to see if he needs anything, but he just steps outside so I can't see in! I mean... how childish is that? This is his first year teaching! You'd think he'd appreciate some input, but does he? No! Such a jerk!"

"Icky and a jerk," Jade said carefully. "This is going to be interesting."

"Who's icky and a jerk?" Billie asked as she stepped up to the counter and put several boxes down. She smiled at Chloe. "A dozen assorted muffins, six slices of marble pound cake, six slices of lemon pound cake—and I did them both gluten-free so Dave Scholl can eat them—plus a dozen pieces of caramel crumb cake, a dozen oatmeal raisin cookies, and a dozen croissants." She let out a dramatic breath. "Do you think that's enough for everyone?"

Chloe couldn't help but laugh. "It better be! Luckily, Susan's handling the coffee, tea, and juice; otherwise, I'd need ten extra hands to carry it all!"

"I know Sweetbriar Elementary isn't a big school, but there are enough teachers that could lend a hand," Billie said before shaking her head. "Now who's icky and a jerk? You never told me."

"Um..."

"The new kindergarten teacher," Jade replied instead. "According to Chloe, he thinks he's a bit of a hotshot, even though this is his first year of teaching."

"Ah...young and cocky. Got it," Billie said as she poured herself a cup of coffee. "He's fresh out of college, Chlo. Cut him some slack. He'll find out soon enough that he's got a lot to learn."

"He's actually two years older than me," she murmured, and when both Jade and Billie stared at her expectantly, she knew she had to explain herself. "Okay, so after the whole awful first meeting, I went home and...you know...did a little research."

"You Googled him. Got it," Billie confirmed. "And?"

"And...he graduated several years ago but didn't start teaching right away because..." She groaned. "He's kind of famous."

"Famous? For teaching? But how...?"

"Not teaching," she corrected. "Apparently, he's kind of a big deal in Alpine skiing."

Both Jade and Billie pulled out their phones as they asked his name.

"Tanner Westyn," she replied begrudgingly. "He's..."

"Oh my God!" Jade said excitedly. "I've seen some of his stuff up at the ski resort! He's a spokesman for one of the lines they carry! How cool is that?" Then she looked up at Chloe and instantly sobered. "But um...he's a jerk, so...no big deal."

"Too bad he's a jerk," Billie commented. "Because he's kind of cute." Then she glanced at Chloe. "Don't you think he's good-looking?"

"I hadn't noticed. His rude personality was all I could see."

Liar! Liar!! Liar!!!

Okay, fine. She totally noticed it. Hell, she noticed it when she saw him right here at Books & Beans on Monday morning. When Principal Kincaid had walked into her classroom and she'd turned around and saw Tanner, she couldn't believe her good fortune!

Then, he opened his mouth and ruined all her dreamy thoughts.

And she truly had tried to befriend him for the last several days. After he apologized and accepted her room decorations, she thought they were good. But he'd been weird and secretive ever since, and she had no idea what to do with that. All the teachers she'd ever worked with had been open and friendly. Was it just her he was being rude to or was it the entire staff?

Guess I'll find out when I get to the meeting...

Which reminded her that she really needed to get going.

"Ring me up, Jade," she said cheerily. "I need to get there a bit early so I can help set up. We're going to use the new lounge in the portable building, so I don't know where everything is yet."

Handing Jade her credit card, Chloe watched the screen and then signed the tablet before thanking her sister again.

"It was my pleasure," Billie told her. "And don't let this Tanner guy get you down. You have seniority and you're a hometown girl. A few well-placed comments and no one's going to think he's a big deal. You just say the word and..."

Chloe held up her hand to stop her. "As much as I love the fact that you want to do that for me, I can't let you smear someone's reputation."

No matter how much they might deserve it.

"I get it," Billie said sweetly. "And if he's as big of a jerk as you say, he'll smear his reputation on his own." She took a slow sip of her coffee. "Either way, he's going to learn how to behave in a small town."

"His bio says he's kind of from a small town too," Jade commented, and once again looked up and seemed to regret her words. "I mean, yeah! He's going to have zero friends here!"

That made Chloe giggle as she picked up her boxes of

baked goods. "I appreciate the show of support, but I really need to go."

"Call me later and let me know how it went!" Billie called after her. "You know I love the praise!"

She had just stepped out onto the sidewalk when she spotted her brother Levi jogging toward her.

"Here, let me grab those," he said, effectively scooping the boxes out of her arms. "You go open the car door."

"My hero," she said with a grin. "I didn't think about how I was going to open the door with my hands full."

"Then it's a good thing I showed up!" He carefully put the boxes on the front passenger seat before closing the door and giving her a hug. "Teacher meeting today, right?"

Hugging him back, she nodded. "Yup! I need to get there early and set up."

Taking her hand, he walked her around to the driver's side. "Then I won't keep you. We'll catch up tomorrow night over dinner at Ashlynn's."

"Sounds good, and thanks, Levi!"

The entire drive over to the school, she couldn't help but think about Tanner. She realized now that she regretted looking him up online because all it did was make her like him less. It led her to believe that he was arrogant because of his celebrity status and had her questioning why on earth he was now going to be teaching kindergarten. Why couldn't he stick to skiing? There was no report of a career-ending injury or an illness; he simply retired.

But he still had some endorsement deals, so why couldn't he just do that? Not that she knew anything about how much that sort of thing paid, but she had to imagine it was more than a teacher's salary.

"And if he wasn't such a jerk, I could ask him these

things," she murmured to herself. "But I can't. So now my imagination is just going to go wild. *Gah!*"

Fortunately, she pulled up to the school and found a parking spot back by the portable classrooms. Several teachers were walking over and when they spotted her, they came over to help carry everything in.

Inside the new teachers' lounge, Susan was setting up the coffee bar, Terry Murphy, the music teacher, was putting out paper goods, and Principal Kincaid was writing some stuff on the giant whiteboard.

Within minutes, the room was almost full and everyone was sort of hesitating to be the first person to either grab something to eat or drink. She was about to be the one to get things started when Tanner strode in with an enormous foil-covered plate.

"Good morning, everyone!" he called out. "Sorry I'm late, but I had to let the breakfast frittata finish cooking! Hope you're all hungry!"

Son of a...

She met Principal Kincaid's eyes from across the room and hopefully he read the dismay she was feeling. Of all the nerve! They had *both* told Tanner that she was bringing the refreshments and he completely disregarded them!

"A breakfast frittata?" Marcus Brown, one of the second-grade teachers, asked. "That sounds awesome!"

"I've also got a tray of chocolate chip cookies out in the car," Tanner said. "I'll be right back!"

Chloe was about to go after him when Susan walked over and stopped her. "It's being handled," she said quietly before glancing over her shoulder toward the table. "But you have to give him credit. He's determined to make an impression and knows food is always a good start."

"It was rude since he knew I was bringing all the food

this morning," she hissed. "How am I supposed to work with him if this is how he starts off the year?"

"I think he's trying a little too hard, but it's rough being the new guy," she reasoned.

"And yet the six other new teachers haven't been stepping on anyone's toes..."

Before Susan could reply, Dave Scholl, the PE teacher, joined them. "Hey, Chloe! Thanks for getting some gluten-free stuff for me this morning. I appreciate how you always remember."

It was the perfect distraction. "No worries, Dave. I'm happy to do it." A few other teachers came over to thank her and gush over the variety she had brought with her, and it all calmed her down.

Maybe she was being overly sensitive. After all, what was the harm in a bit more food for the meeting? Letting out a soft breath, she decided to stop focusing on the negative and embrace the start of the school year. She and Tanner won't have to interact on anything until the holiday plays and those were three months away. So for now, she was going to forget all about him and his obnoxious and overbearing ways and stay in her own lane.

After all, she'd garnered a reputation for being an excellent teacher and coworker here at Sweetbriar Elementary. And no one was going to take that away from her.

* * *

"I don't understand what the big deal is. It was just breakfast."

"Yes, but it was breakfast we already discussed was being covered. It seems to me like you purposely did this to overshadow Chloe. What I don't understand is why."

Tanner shifted the large plate of cookies in his hands. "It's nothing personal. I was raised to share the burden and also do everything I could to make a good first impression. Chloe's been here longer and she's been Teacher of the Year twice. Maybe I'm trying to take some of the pressure off of her," he said with a casual shrug.

But the look on Principal Kincaid's face said he didn't fully believe him.

"I'm just trying to be a team player and contribute; that's all. I accepted some of Chloe's decorations and I've been working really hard on my room so everything will be ready for Tuesday. Now, I'd love to bring these cookies inside and stop holding up the meeting. I'm sure you have an agenda and schedule you're trying to keep."

Fortunately, that seemed to work. They headed back into the classroom and found everyone making plates of food, getting drinks, and taking their seats. Tanner put the plate of cookies down and smiled at a few people as he walked over to get himself a cup of coffee.

And found himself standing right next to Chloe.

"Good morning," he said, reaching for a cup. "All the baked goods look delicious. And I know they will be. I went into Books & Beans yesterday on my way here and grabbed a blueberry muffin and a slice of the lemon pound cake. I can see why it's famous. Your grandmother must have been a fabulous baker."

She looked at him warily before conceding. "She was. I'm glad you enjoyed it." Then she picked up her coffee and went to sit down.

By the time Tanner had his own coffee made, the only place left to sit was next to Chloe. Rather than make it look like he'd rather sit anywhere else than there—which he did

—he simply made himself a plate of food and then took his seat.

Principal Kincaid stood at the head of the long table—which was really just several tables pushed together—and welcomed them all to the new school year. After that, he launched into introductions where everyone had to say a little something about themselves and share a fun fact about them.

Tanner sipped his coffee and listened to everyone talk about their families, their kids, their hobbies...it was a lot of the same old, same old. Then it was Chloe's turn, and he figured it would be more of what he'd already heard.

"Hey, I'm Chloe Donovan, and this is my fourth year teaching kindergarten," she began. "I have lived in Sweetbriar Ridge my whole life, and other than visiting family along the East Coast, I've never seen the middle of the U.S. or the West Coast!" She laughed softly. "I always thought I'd see it eventually, but I'm getting ready to buy my first home, so...traveling will have to wait." Then she paused before adding, "Another random fun fact about me other than my lack of seeing the country is that I have zero baking skills, unlike the rest of my family, but I love to cook. I make some killer Mexican dishes, so if you're ever in the mood for homemade guacamole or enchiladas, I'm your girl!"

Everyone clapped and several were already asking when they could have a potluck, and Tanner was readily on board with it. He was the last one to speak, and he smiled at the group as he shifted slightly in his chair.

"Hi, I'm Tanner Westyn. This is my first year of teaching and I'm new to Sweetbriar Ridge. I've always wanted to teach, but my goal was for it to be a fourth or fifth grade class." Pausing, he took a sip of his coffee. "I'm starting a bit late because I was a professional Alpine skier and was trying to figure out just how long I could keep doing it." Another pause and he suddenly felt the need to be completely transparent. "The thing is, I could have kept going, but there were a lot of younger athletes who were just starting to make names for themselves and even though I'm far from old, I was starting to feel my age." Staring down at his coffee, he continued. "So rather than keeping at it and risking an injury because I was trying to compete with guys who were younger and more skilled, I thought it was best to go out on top."

It was almost uncomfortably silent for a moment, and he knew he needed to end on a high note.

"So, I thought what better place to be than a town with a brand-new ski resort so I can still embrace my passion while starting the career in my other passion?" Smiling at everyone, he concluded with, "And I'm looking forward to getting to know all of you better and making some lifelong friends." Holding up his coffee in a toast, he said, "Here's to a great year!"

Everyone repeated the sentiment and that's when Principal Kincaid stood back up and went over his plan for the school year, including holidays, vacations, student activities, festivals, and musical programs. After that, the art, music, and PE teachers each took their turns talking about what they had planned for the year for the students. It was a lot of information, but Tanner felt energized. Hell, he couldn't wait to go back to his classroom and do a little more work on it. This weekend, he needed to finish looking over the curriculum, but he needed the room to be done by the end of the day tomorrow.

And he didn't want anyone to see it before then.

"I think we're going to have an amazing year," the principal said when he was back at the head of the table again.

"We're excited about our new staff and all the new students joining us. My door is always open, so if there's anything you need, please don't ever hesitate to stop by and see me." He looked around the table before going on. "We do still have a lot of supplies in storage, so if any of the new teachers need anything, please help yourself. And if you can't find it there, either Susan or myself can help you or point you in the right direction. As you can tell, we're a small school district and our budget is even smaller. If you're still in need of a lot of items, the best ways to go are sending home a wish list with your students or even creating one online through one of the big retailers so you can just share a link to it."

Tanner took a moment to do some inventory in his head and realized that he'd already seen everything that was in storage and none of it fit his needs. He had an order being shipped to him for some last-minute stuff, but the rest he could definitely put on a wish list.

"I'd like to thank Chloe for providing us with all the baked goods this morning," Principal Kincaid said. "And thank you to Tanner, too, for the frittata and cookies. This was a great way to start our day! Everyone, take your time and finish eating, and if you have work to do in your rooms, the building will be open until five today. I appreciate you all coming in. If there's anything else we need to discuss..."

Tanner raised his hand.

"I was just curious if there's a specific time we should be here on the first day and then the mornings afterwards, and what time is typical for us to leave."

"Excellent questions," Vice Principal Pam Russell replied, who'd been very quiet for the entire meeting until now. "The school day goes from 8:55 a.m. until 3:55 p.m.— that is the bell schedule. I would suggest getting here on the first day no later than 8:00. In the afternoons, by the time carpool is done and all the busses are gone, plan on being here until 4:30. Of course, those times are going to vary from day to day. Your arrival time should be based on what you may need to do before your students show up. With departure, you need to stay until all of your students are picked up, whether by bus or parent, and you should straighten your classroom each day before you go."

He nodded. "Thank you."

"Any other questions?" she asked.

But no one had any, and for another hour, it was all just a very casual time to get to know the rest of the faculty. Everyone stood and refreshed their drinks or stood in small clusters talking, and Tanner gravitated toward the fourth and fifth grade teachers to sort of scope out if any of them weren't planning on staying beyond this year.

Keith Holly was in his fifties and had been teaching the fourth grade here in Sweetbriar for over twenty years. He mentioned how he'd like to retire soon multiple times during their brief conversation.

Good to know...

Trina Allen was one of the fifth-grade teachers and had also been here for a while. Ric Carlson was the new teacher in that grade; he was around Tanner's age and seemed thrilled about his position.

So he's not going anywhere, he thought.

The next thing he knew, everyone was cleaning up and making their way out of the building. Tanner collected his plates and was pleased to see the frittata was completely gone and there was only a handful of cookies left. He packed everything up and placed them out in his car before heading back into the school. Opening the door at the rear of the building, he stepped inside and found Chloe standing right there. Her blue eyes went wide when she saw him.

"Oh, um...hey," he murmured. "Sorry. I didn't realize anyone was standing right here."

Nodding, she motioned to the first classroom. "Jenna just went in to work on her room and the lights flickered and then went out. It seems like the entire school has gone dark. She ran down to the office to see who we need to call."

"And you're watching her classroom...why?"

She shrugged. "I wasn't really watching it. I guess I was just lost in thought; that's all." Another shrug, and she turned and walked away.

Knowing she was more than likely heading to her own classroom—which was right beside his—he decided to walk with her. "Has this sort of thing ever happened before?"

"No. Not even when they were setting up the mobile rooms. I hope they'll get it worked out today. My room's ready and I was really just planning on making copies and doing some busywork, but I know everyone's not ready for the first day."

She might not have been directly talking about him, but it sort of felt that way.

"I'm almost done," he said confidently. "It was hard to get anything done in advance. Besides the fact that I only found out that I had the job less than two weeks ago, I had no idea how much was already here for me to work with."

"That makes sense. Plus, you had to deal with moving. I'm sure it's been stressful."

And this time, he knew she was being sincere.

"It has, actually. My folks helped me with the move and getting my house unpacked, but I wish I'd had more time to just get settled in myself before starting a job. I feel like I'm at a bit of a disadvantage."

They were strolling more than walking at this point, and Chloe turned her head and smiled at him. "Well, you don't let it show," she softly told him. "You're very confident and I can't imagine you letting anything bother you."

"Yeah, well..." he shrugged with a small laugh. "Years of competing and being in the public eye taught me to never let anyone see me in any way except a positive one."

"That's got to be tough."

That...wasn't what he expected her to say. "How come?"

"I don't know. I guess that just seems like a lot of weight on your shoulders. I mean...everyone's entitled to letting their guard down and just...you know...having a moment. What did you do when something went wrong? Did you just have to smile through it?"

Another shrug. "When I first started competing, everyone knew exactly what I was feeling, when I was feeling it. As I got older, I realized how unprofessional it looked to have a hissy fit if things didn't go my way. Basically, I wanted everyone to look at me and only be able to say something positive."

Beside him, Chloe made some sort of noncommittal sound that piqued his curiosity.

"Tell me what you're thinking right now," he teased, playfully nudging her shoulder.

Her eyes went almost comically wide. "Um...what? Why? I wasn't thinking anything!"

"Chloe, come on. That little sound you made spoke volumes."

"Then why don't you tell me what I'm thinking?" she said with just a hint of sass that he didn't think she was capable of.

"Okay...you were thinking that me wanting everyone to only say positive stuff meant I must have a colossal ego."

"Hmm..."

They were still walking, and she wouldn't look at him. "I'm right! I knew it! You think I have a colossal ego!" The fact that she wasn't denying it made him laugh and soon she was laughing with him. They stopped at his classroom door and when she turned to face him, her entire face was lit up with pure delight. "I'm gonna need to hear you say it, Chloe. Tell me I'm wrong. Or right!"

She giggled softly as she shook her head. "You're ridiculous."

"What? Me? Why?" But he was laughing too. "Obviously I'd prefer to hear that I'm right..."

"Because you have a colossal ego!" she said right before her hands flew up to cover her mouth.

"I knew it! I knew you thought that! Ha!"

Lowering her hands, she shook her head again. "Fine. You were right. There." It took a moment for her expression to turn thoughtful. "How come you won't let me see your classroom?"

That had him sobering. "Um...what?"

"I've come over here several times in the last couple of days and you refuse to let me in. Why?"

And because he was beginning to relax a bit, he figured he could be at least a little honest with her. "Okay, so not only do I have a huge ego..."

"Tanner..." she whined, but he wasn't listening.

"But I'm also a perfectionist. This is my first classroom and I want it to be perfect. It wasn't just you I wouldn't let see it; it was everyone. I wanted to have everything in its place before I let anyone in."

"I get what you're saying, but...that's crazy! Do you have any idea what my first classroom looked like?"

"Probably spectacular based on the way your current one looks," he murmured and watched her expression soften.

"Hang on," she said, reaching into her bag and pulling out her phone. She scrolled for a minute before turning the screen toward him. "Look familiar?"

"It looks..."

"Just like yours did on Monday," she finished for him. "I started out with nothing and it motivated and inspired me, just like I'm sure it's doing for you. You don't have to do it all alone, though. Maybe that's how it was when you were doing the whole skiing thing, but here? Here we help one another. No one's going to judge your classroom or compare it to anyone else's." Pausing, she gave him a small smile. "We all want you to succeed, Tanner. Because when you succeed, the kids win."

"Chloe, I..."

Her phone rang and the sound startled them both. "Sorry, I need to take this."

"Yeah, sure," he said. "No worries." But when she turned to walk away, he added, "When you're done, why don't you come back over and check out the room?"

This time her smile was slow and sweet and...damn.

"I will," she told him. "Thanks."

As soon as Chloe walked into her classroom, Tanner opened the door and stepped into his. The lights were still out and even though he didn't need them for anything he was going to do, it still would have been nice to have them.

With nothing else to do, he walked to his supply closet and began pulling out the last of his room décor and went to work. He felt better about what he was creating and that maybe he was being a bit too competitive. Perhaps Chloe was right and no one was going to be judging or comparing, but that was a mindset he was going to have to overcome first.

Yeah, it's me. I'm the problem, it's me...

"Great. Now I'm quoting Taylor Swift songs," he groaned before pulling out the stepladder and putting the finishing touches on the bulletin board wall.

Chapter Four

Chloe never got to see Tanner's classroom because the call she'd gotten was from Billie, who said that their mother had been in a car accident. She'd practically run out of the school and didn't stop to talk to anyone. The hospital was a little over thirty minutes away, and she had a white-knuckled grip on the steering wheel the entire time. When she arrived, Billie and Levi were already there, pacing in the main waiting area.

"Oh my goodness," she said breathlessly as she hugged her sister. "What happened? Have you seen her yet?"

"Someone just came out and told us a doctor would come and talk to us soon. Right now they're doing X-rays and scans and whatever else," Billie explained. "As far as we can tell, someone hit her at an intersection."

"T-boned the car on the driver's side," Levi added. "Details are still sketchy. We won't know more until we get to talk to Mom."

"This is crazy!" Then she glanced around. "Is Ash coming? Was I supposed to pick her up?"

"No, no, you're fine," Billie assured her. "She's on her

way. Reid was one of the first responders to the accident and he went to get her once the ambulance left."

They all sat down and Chloe felt herself shaking. She knew she'd been doing that ever since she got the call, but she was running on adrenaline and was too focused on getting here to think about how she was feeling. But now that she could?

"Oh, hey...Chlo, it's gonna be alright," Billie whispered to her and it took a moment for her to realize that she was completely bent in half and sobbing. "Reid said she was alert and talking to him when they were putting her in the ambulance." Her hand was rubbing up and down Chloe's back as she spoke, but it wasn't helping.

"What if she's not okay?" she asked between sobs. "What if...what if something's wrong internally? What if...?" But she never got to finish because her brother was suddenly crouching in front of her and gently urged her to look at him.

"We all need to be strong right now," he said softly. "Think positively. Like Billie said, Reid confirmed that Mom was alert and talking when he saw her."

"Then why won't they let us back there?" she asked, sniffling.

"They have to run tests," he told her. "I'd much rather the doctors be thorough so they know exactly what her injuries are than make them wait so we can go back and talk to her. I know it's hard to be patient, but...we have to be."

Just then, Ashlynn and Reid came running in to join them. "Any word yet?" Ash asked.

Levi stood and hugged her. "Nothing yet. A nurse came and told us someone would be out soon, so..."

Letting out a shuddery breath, Chloe straightened and stood to hug her twin, but they stayed like that for several long moments before Levi suggested they all sit down. Reid excused himself and walked over to the reception desk, and Ashlynn laughed softly.

"I guarantee he's pulling the fireman card to get us information. God, I love him."

"What did he tell you while you were driving here?" she asked. "I know he mentioned a little to Billie, but...did he say anything else about how bad the car looked, or maybe his thoughts on her injuries?"

"Not really. He went on and on and on about statistics and possible injuries sustained in that kind of crash, but he didn't get into anything specific," Ash said with a sigh.

Chloe was about to say more, but Reid was walking back over with someone she guessed was a doctor. "Wow... the fireman card must work."

"Everyone, this is Dr. Barnett," Reid said. "And he's the attending who's taking care of Marie."

"How is she?" Levi asked.

Dr. Barnett gave a curt nod before addressing them. "Your mother suffered blunt force trauma. Her left arm and hip are fractured and she has a concussion, whiplash, and several broken ribs." Pausing, he looked grim. "She's got a long recovery ahead of her, but this could have been a lot worse. Fortunately, she was wearing her seatbelt and her airbags deployed."

"When can we see her?" Billie asked.

"We're waiting for a room to be available, but you can all go back and see her. Just be prepared because she's very banged up and mildly sedated. I'll have a nurse come and take you back."

They all thanked him before he walked away, and then Reid, Levi, and Billie began to talk. Meanwhile, Ashlynn led Chloe a few feet away to talk to her privately. "How are you holding up?"

Tears stung her eyes again. "I'm not," she admitted. "I'm afraid to go back and see Mom looking all...you know, banged up and hurt." Then the dam broke and she was crying all over her sister's shoulder.

"It's okay. I get it," Ash said quietly. "I know Reid was trying to prepare me on the way over, but...I'm not really ready for this either." Hugging Chloe tight, she offered a suggestion. "How about this—until the nurse comes out to get us, let's talk about something else. What do you say?"

Pulling back, Chloe frowned. "Like...what? What could we possibly talk about at a time like this?"

Now Ash led her over to one of the couches so they could sit. "How did the meeting go this morning? Did you get to meet all the new teachers?"

Her shoulders sagged a bit, and now she wanted to cry for another reason. "I love that you pay attention to all the stuff going on in my life and remember it." Squeezing her hand, she continued. "I did get to meet everyone and the meeting was fine."

"But...?"

Ugh...

"But...Tanner brought in breakfast stuff even though he knew I was taking care of it! I mean...he was just doing it to be a jerk!"

"Wait...who's Tanner? One of the new teachers?"

Oh, right. Her sister didn't know about all the drama that had unfolded this week. She gave her the abbreviated version of everything and then sighed loudly. "I think he's just trying to upstage me or something."

"Or..." Ash carefully interrupted. "He was just trying to be part of the team. Maybe like...I don't know...like he was trying to make it like the kindergarten team was providing breakfast. If you look at it that way, it was kind of sweet."

Groaning, Chloe slumped back against the cushions. "I really want to like that theory, but there was just something so...cocky about it." She paused. "Perhaps I'm being overly sensitive..."

"Um...ya think?"

She gave Ash the side-eye before responding. "Everything about him just...irritates me. He's so arrogant and has this colossal ego, and I just can't see him being a good kindergarten teacher."

With nothing more than a tsk, her sister spoke volumes.

"Okay, fine. I'm being judgmental. There. Happy?" she huffed. "We were sort of having a good conversation right before Billie called. Like...we were just talking and it was nice and kind of fun. I was almost seeing him in a new light."

"That's great! Some people just don't make a good first impression. I'm sure you were a little on the defensive because he's not the teacher you were prepared for. Unfortunately, he's the one you got, so you're going to have to learn to play nice."

"Shouldn't he be the one trying to play nice and not come in like a steamroller? Just because he's a little famous..."

"Wait, wait, wait...he's famous?" Ash asked with wide-eyed amusement. "Famous how?"

Pulling out her phone, she showed her the Google search results. "Competitive skier. Apparently his picture's up in the pro shop at the resort."

"Wow! I never met a professional skier! That's kind of cool!"

Chloe shot her a hard look. "Seriously? Now you're dazzled by him?"

"No one said dazzled," she murmured. "But you have to admit that he's kind of good-looking. Are you sure you're not just a little flustered by him because of that?"

It wasn't like she hadn't thought of that, but she just wasn't particularly ready to admit it.

"No. This is strictly because of his personality. At least...it was until about an hour ago. Maybe there's hope for him, but..."

"Chloe, come on! You literally give everyone the benefit of the doubt! Remember that bully, Tad Paulson, in the fourth grade? He was such a jerk and you refused to tell on him!"

"I know, but..."

"He was always knocking your books out of your hands! Everyone thought something was wrong with your arms because you were always picking your stuff up off the floor!"

"Okay, but...you stepped in and got him to stop! It's not the same thing!"

Ashlynn studied her for a moment. "Do I need to show up at the school tomorrow and put this guy in his place? Because I will, you know."

Sadly, she did know this, and as much as she normally appreciated her sister's interference, this was something she was going to have to handle on her own.

"No, but thank you. I'm probably being too hard on him. I'm sure once school starts next week he won't be so full of himself. Once he sees how challenging a room full of five-year-olds is, maybe he'll be humbled and realize that he should have taken some advice from seasoned teachers."

"And you're sure you're not being all weird because he's

hot and you get all weird and uncomfortable around hot guys?"

"Tanner's not hot..."

With Chloe's phone still in her hand, Ashlynn held it up to show a picture of Tanner smiling while holding his skis. "Seriously? How can you even say that? He's obviously hot!"

That was the moment Reid came over to join them. "Who's hot?"

"One of the new teachers at Chloe's school," Ashlynn said teasingly. "And he's going to be teaching kindergarten too!"

Reid looked between the two of them before focusing on Chloe. "So you think he's hot?"

"No!"

Then he glanced at Ashlynn. "So...*you* think he's hot? Do I need to go kick his ass or something?"

Ashlynn laughed before standing up and kissing him soundly. "You're adorable when you're all jealous, but no. You don't have to kick his ass. I was simply pointing out that he's hot because I know Chloe thinks he is."

"But...she just said she didn't..."

"She's lying. Trust me. We're twins and I am the only person on the planet that knows when her pants are on fire. Like now."

"Would you please..."

"Guys," Billie hissed, as if this wasn't the first time she was saying it. "The nurse is here to take us back to see Mom."

And that effectively ended the debate on Tanner's hotness.

Somberly, they followed the nurse down a labyrinth of hallways until they finally came to the room where Marie

Donovan was. Chloe grabbed Ashlynn's free hand as they walked in and the sight of her mother lying so still and her face covered in bruises was enough to bring on a fresh wave of tears.

Ashlynn's grip was just as tight and she squeezed twice as if to say she was feeling it too. For a few minutes, no one spoke; they were all in shock. Levi stood by Marie's head and gently brushed some hair away from her forehead.

"This is worse than I thought," he murmured. "I guess I was expecting to come in here and she'd be sitting up and talking."

"They sedated her because of all the tests and scans," Reid explained. "Plus, until they can set the bones, it's best if she doesn't move around too much. She might be more alert and awake tonight, but I'd say that tomorrow will be the first chance you'll have to really talk to her."

It wasn't the news anyone wanted to hear.

"I'm going to stay tonight," Billie announced before looking over at Levi. "Tell Jade I won't be in tomorrow, and there are plenty of cakes and cookies in the freezer that she can put out. I'll go in at some point and bake for the weekend, but...I need to be here." Gently picking up Marie's hand, she held it in hers. "I just can't believe this happened."

"I can stay too," Chloe said as she slowly stepped closer to the bed. "My classroom is all set up and..."

"No," Billie said, using her free hand to grasp one of Chloe's. "I know how upset you are and I think you should go to school tomorrow and maybe help where you can and then come in the afternoon."

"But..."

"Then I'll stay with you," Ashlynn said. "I have plenty of coverage at the salon and..."

Billie was already shaking her head. "I swear I'm not trying to be bitchy, but...I feel like it will be overwhelming for Mom when she wakes up and the reality of what happened hits her. I think we should save our time away from our jobs and everything until she goes home. That's when she's really going to need people around her. For now, we need to take a step back and see what the doctors have to say."

"I want to argue with you," Levi said solemnly, "but you're right. I think we should all stay until we know she's settled in a room, and then we'll take tomorrow as it comes."

Chloe doubted she was going to get anything accomplished tomorrow at school, but she wasn't about to fight with her siblings about it. She'd handle her feelings on her own. Right now, they had to focus on their mother and her recovery.

* * *

It was crazy, but Tanner was pacing in his classroom on Friday morning and wondering what happened to Chloe yesterday.

Actually, he'd been thinking about it ever since she seemingly disappeared into thin air after walking away to take a phone call.

He'd been tempted to go down to the main office and ask if anyone knew where she was or where she went, but he had a feeling it would come off sounding creepy—especially after the way they'd gotten off on the wrong foot. During their short walk together yesterday, he realized that maybe he did come on too strong and that it wasn't necessarily a good thing. Well, between that and the conversation he had with Principal Kincaid, he felt like he was probably taking the wrong approach here in Sweetbriar Ridge.

And now, the one person he genuinely wanted to impress was nowhere to be found.

"Okay, I need to go to the office and..." Tanner stepped out into the hallway when he spotted Chloe walking toward him. He smiled and was about to call out to her, but the closer she got, the more obvious it became that something was seriously wrong. Again, he was about to say something, but wasn't sure if he was necessarily the person she wanted to talk to.

Ultimately, he couldn't help himself and met her halfway.

"Hey," he said with a sympathetic smile. "Everything okay?"

She shook her head and wouldn't look him in the eye. "Sorry, just...a family thing." When she went to step around him, he let her and then followed her to her classroom.

"Is there anything I can do?" he asked and thought that was a stupid thing to say. They didn't even know each other. What in the world could he possibly do?

Putting her bag down on her desk, she turned and studied him. "Thank you, but...I'll be fine." But the shuddery breath she let out said she wasn't fine right now.

Sliding his hands into his trouser pockets, he slowly walked across the room toward her. "You may not know this about me, but I'm actually an excellent listener."

"Really?" And yeah, that one word dripped with sarcasm. "Because so far you seem to only hear what you want to hear." Her hand flew to her mouth and tears shone brightly in her eyes. "Oh my goodness! I'm so sorry! That was a horrible thing to say! Seriously, Tanner, I apologize."

Instead of being offended, he appreciated her honesty.

"Nothing to apologize for. You were just being truthful. Most of our interactions have been about me primarily talking about myself and disregarding things people were trying to do to help."

Chloe swiped at a wayward tear before frowning. "Um...okay. Thank you."

"So...do you want to talk about it?"

"About you not accepting help?"

That made him chuckle. "No," he said gently. "I meant about whatever's going on with your family."

She sighed as she nodded and sat down. "My mother was in a terrible car accident yesterday. Someone ran a red light and t-boned her car. She's in pretty bad shape—not life-threatening, but she's going to have a long recovery ahead of her. My siblings and I were at the hospital with her until around ten last night. That's how long it took to get her into a room and settled. It was awful."

"That was the call you got when we were talking in the hallway, wasn't it?"

She nodded. "The hospital's thirty minutes away and I don't even remember the drive. I could have caused an accident driving like that, but..."

"Hey," he began, sitting on the corner of her desk. "Yes, that was a genuine possibility, but you don't strike me as the kind of person who makes that sort of thing a habit. There were extenuating circumstances. And I'm sure if there were another emergency, you'd ask someone else to drive you."

Another nod. "I should have called Ash, but I was too focused on getting there as soon as possible."

Ash? Is that her husband? A boyfriend? What kind of name is Ash?

And was now the time to even ask that?

He decided it wasn't.

71

Glancing around the classroom, he asked, "So, what are you doing here today? It looks like the room is ready. If you need the time to be with your mother, then you should be there."

"That was my plan, but everyone told me I needed to be here today because I got too upset last night while we were sitting with her. I guess this was supposed to distract me." Then she looked around. "I'm not sure it's going to work."

"Well, maybe not, but I know something that might."

She looked at him warily, but didn't say anything.

"I'd like it if you came and checked out my classroom. I just put some finishing touches on it right before you got here and I'd really like your input."

"Tanner..."

"I know, I know...I was rude and secretive every time you tried to see what I was doing, but..." He paused and tried to figure out the best way to say this. "The thing is, I'm used to doing everything on my own. If I ever shared what I was thinking or doing, opponents would use it against me."

"We're not opponents," she told him, her voice so soft it was practically a whisper. "We're coworkers."

"I know that here," he said, pointing to his head. "But I've spent a lot of years as a competitive athlete. Some things are going to take time. It's not personal."

"It felt personal," she murmured.

"I'm trying to make things right, Chloe. If you want to know the truth, I'm a little intimidated by you."

And the crazy thing was, he wasn't lying.

With a small snort, she got to her feet and moved to look out the window. "You know, I can handle your arrogance, Tanner. I don't like it, but I can handle it. But don't patronize me. It's just insulting."

Wow, clearly he'd made a huge first impression and it wasn't the least bit favorable.

He stood and followed her. "I'm not, but I get why you don't believe me." Pausing for a moment until she looked at him, he continued. "Look at it from my point of view. I'm a brand new teacher and the only other teacher in my grade has been Teacher of the Year for the last two years! I mean... what chance to do I have of beating you out?"

Her eyes went wide. "Oh my God! You did not just say that!"

"Wait...say what? I'm not sure what I said that was so bad."

"The only thing you're worried about is being the best! You're not really worried about it because you want to make an impression on your students, but just for your own self! That's awful! How could you possibly want to be a teacher? It makes zero sense!"

Okay, he was clearly messing up—again—and he wasn't sure how to make things right.

"Whether or not you choose to believe me, I've always wanted to teach. Why? Because I had some great teachers when I was growing up and I've always enjoyed learning new things. Other than skiing, my favorite hobby is reading. I read all the damn time! One of the rooms in the house I'm renting is a library! My parents couldn't believe how many books I have."

"Oh."

"I remember how excited I used to get learning new subjects in school and the thought of being able to maybe help others feel that way? It freaking thrills me! I would have started teaching sooner, but I was still competing and I couldn't do both."

"So why'd you stop?"

"Competing?"

She nodded.

"Like I said, I was feeling a bit past my prime and I wanted to go out on top. I had never heard of Sweetbriar Ridge before getting the email from Principal Kincaid, but I'm psyched to be here because now I get to teach and I'm close enough to a resort so I can ski on the weekends. It's the best of both worlds."

For several moments, neither spoke, but he heard Chloe's soft sigh.

"Look, I think we just need to accept that our personalities aren't particularly compatible. I don't look at my position here like it's some sort of competition and I have a feeling that's the only way you're going to see it. Obviously we're going to have to work together—not only because we're both teachers, but because we're both teaching the same grade. There are several units we'll be working on together and I'm already dreading it because you're going to bully me to get your way and not listen to the fact that we have a perfectly fine curriculum that works."

"Chloe..."

The laugh she responded with was mirthless as she shook her head. "My sister would be amazed that I'm being this blunt with you. Normally I'm quiet and reserved and afraid to speak up. I'm the least confrontational person in the world, but something about you just..."

Tanner held up a hand to stop her because he knew where she was going with it, and this wasn't a great conversation for either of them. He hated the fact that he had her acting so out of character, but more than that, he hated that she possibly wasn't the only person who felt this strongly about him.

In a negative way.

"I guess we're just going to have to wait and see," he said finally. "But in the meantime, I'd really appreciate it if you came and looked at my room." When she didn't respond right away, he said the one thing he knew would help change her mind. "It's going to be the perfect distraction because I kind of went in a direction a little different from yours."

She groaned softly before conceding. "Fine..."

"Awesome! Come on!" Tanner led the way out to his room and at the door, he stood back and let Chloe go in first. She went all of three feet before she simply froze.

"Um..."

Stepping into the room, he came to a stop beside her. "So? What do you think? I realize I didn't have a lot of time, but..."

He'd used the border and characters she'd given him, but he made his room into a Pixar character ski camp. All of the characters were in action, he'd made mountains out of construction paper, rigged up several old pairs of skis and goggles and other random equipment on the walls and used an almost obscene amount of cotton to make snow.

"I realize it doesn't snow here year-round, but...it's a mountain town and I thought it would still be a cool effect." He paused and waited for her to say something. "So? What do you think?"

"It's...it's...definitely different," she said carefully. "And it's a wonderful use of...um...your ski equipment..."

"I have a lot of it," he admitted. "And before you ask, I spoke to Principal Kincaid about using it, and the entire room got a safety inspection, so everything's safe. I didn't want anyone to see the room, but I'm smart enough to know that the safety of the students comes first."

Nodding, Chloe stepped further into the room. There

were books on the shelves, but not a lot, and his reading corner had a big, white shag carpet. Glancing over her shoulder at him, she said, "White was a bold choice. You realize how messy five-year-olds are, right?"

Actually, he hadn't. He walked over to her. "I was going with the snow theme and didn't think about it."

"You could always go with brown or green and make this like a reading forest."

"Of course! That's brilliant! I can get another carpet before Tuesday, no problem. And as for the rest? It wouldn't be hard to do with some construction paper and cardboard..."

He caught her looking around again. "You're very artistic," she told him, and he had a feeling it wasn't all that easy for her to give him a compliment. Turning her head, she smiled. "Is there anything you're not good at?"

It would be wrong to say no, but...

"I heard I'm not good at being a team player," he said with amusement. "But I swear I'm going to work on it."

Groaning, she walked toward him. "I never should have said anything. You're new here and I was being judgmental. That is not who I am, like ever. You have to believe me."

And the thing is, he did.

"Look, I get it. And to be fair, I can see why you were completely turned off by me."

Her face turned the tiniest shade of red. "I didn't say I was turned off..."

That's when he realized how that all sounded and felt his own face heat. "Sorry! Oh, God...that came out wrong! I meant...you know...like...rubbed you the wrong way...or... dammit!"

When did I get so bad at having a normal conversation?

"Chloe, honestly, all I meant was..."

The sound of her phone ringing interrupted him and he could honestly say he was saved by the bell.

"Excuse me a moment, Tanner," she said, pulling her phone out of her pocket. "Hey, Bill, is everything okay?"

Tanner went over to his desk so it didn't seem like he was hovering or trying to listen in on her conversation, but when he heard her gasp, he decided the hell with it and walked back over to her.

"Okay, okay," she said shakily. "I'm on my way!"

"Is it your mom?" he asked, and when she nodded but couldn't seem to talk, he knew what he had to do. "Let's get your stuff, and I'll drive you to the hospital."

"What? No," she objected, but there was very little fight in her. "I'll call Ash to come and get me. You don't have to..."

"Chloe, don't be ridiculous. I'm right here and I'm done for the day. We can be in my car in less than two minutes. Please. Let me do this for you."

She nodded, but still didn't seem thrilled about it. "Thanks. Just...let me go get my purse from my room."

"I'll meet you by the front door," he told her and watched her leave. After locking up his room, Tanner quickly jogged to the front office and told Susan what was going on.

"Oh my goodness! I hope everything's alright!" Then she paused. "And it's very nice of you to offer to drive Chloe to the hospital. If you'd prefer, I can do it. I know the two of you don't know each other very well..."

"No time like the present to rectify that," he said, spotting Chloe standing outside the office. "I'll keep you posted on what's going on."

"Thanks, Tanner!"

Stepping out of the office, he gently placed his hand at

the small of Chloe's back and guided her out the door. "You ready?"

"I think so."

In the parking lot, he helped her into his Toyota SUV before jogging around to the driver's side and climbing in. "Tell me the address and I'll plug it into the navigation app."

"That's not necessary. Just turn left when you pull out of the parking lot, and then right at the light. The hospital is on that road. It's a fairly straight run."

With a curt nod, he pulled out of the parking lot and did as she said. He wasn't sure if he should try to start a conversation or not and decided to follow her lead.

He just hoped it wasn't going to be a silent drive.

Chapter Five

Trembling, Chloe sat in the passenger seat and tried to calm herself down. If she had called Ash, she'd probably be feeling stronger right now. But with Tanner sitting beside her, it just made her feel...awkward.

"Do you want to talk about it?" he asked after they'd made that right turn. "You don't have to. I just thought that maybe..." Then he shrugged and added, "If you'd rather me just sit here quietly, I can do that too."

Somewhere in the back of her mind, she seriously doubted that, but she probably should talk to him so she didn't run into the hospital and completely freak out on everyone.

Letting out a long breath, Chloe forced herself to speak calmly. "My older sister called because our mom had a seizure. Actually, she had two of them." Pausing for a moment, she let that sink in. "She's never had one in her life and the doctors are saying it's because of the accident."

Beside her, Tanner nodded.

"Last night, they said she had a concussion, but no one mentioned that something like this could happen. So now they're worried that there's a more significant brain injury than they originally thought, and...it's terrifying. I mean...I can't believe this is happening."

"That's totally understandable," he said softly before going quiet for a moment. "When I was in my early twenties and competing, I had a teammate who had an accident while skiing downhill." He paused, and Chloe saw him swallow hard. "He'd done that run a hundred times and used to brag he could do it with his eyes closed. But that day...something went wrong. He lost his balance or just...I don't know. All I know is I was waiting to follow him down on our practice run and he just fell and then kept falling. Our coaches and pretty much everyone held our breaths for what felt like forever because we didn't know if he was alright. When he finally came to a stop..."

Unable to help herself, Chloe reached over and placed her hand on his thigh. He didn't have to say what happened; she could already tell.

"At some point in the fall, he'd hit his head on a tree and..." The breath he let out was shaky before he glanced over at her. "The recovery was rough and there were so many times we all swore he wasn't going to make it." The smile was small, but it spoke volumes. "But I can tell you that miracles are real because Benny is still here. He doesn't ski competitively anymore, but he is skiing. There were dozens of us on the slopes the day he first came back, and I don't think I've ever cheered so hard in my life when he reached the bottom. It was...it was amazing." His voice cracked and she felt tears stinging her eyes.

"Thank you for sharing that," she said quietly. "It gives me hope that my mom can overcome this. I know it's too soon to really know, but...this really helped."

They stopped at a traffic light and Tanner turned his

head and smiled at her and she felt that same fluttery feeling in her belly that she felt that morning at Books & Beans.

So not the time for this...

"We don't have to just talk about trauma stuff," Tanner said after a moment. "Tell me what the first day of school is going to be like. What's your favorite part of it?"

That was the perfect distraction question.

"I love getting to meet all my students for the first time. They come in with their parents and you get some who are excited to be there and some who are totally scared and I make sure I take the time to greet each of them and show them to their seats. It's an easy transition from holding their mom's or dad's hand to walking with me."

"What do you do if a bunch of families come in at the same time?"

"I greet them all and then just work my way through all of them until everyone's in their seats. Most of the time, the parents distract their kids by walking around the classroom with them and showing them something they think is fun. That's why I always make sure the room is fully decorated. This way, they have a lot to look at."

"And...that's not distracting when you're trying to get them to focus?"

She shrugged. "Sometimes, but...that's normal. They're only five, and for most of them, this is their first time in a classroom environment. Getting them to focus on the work takes a little time, but they get there."

"That's kind of why I wanted to teach in the older grades. In fourth or fifth grade, they're more grounded and know the rules. I'm not sure how good I'm going to be at guiding them when they're so young."

Color me surprised...he's admitting that he doesn't know it all.

And just thinking like that made her cringe. It was like she didn't even know herself this last week.

"I'm sure you're going to do great," she assured him. "As long as you're smiling and excited for them to be there, they'll be fine. If you're uncertain or uneasy, they can sense it and have a hard time."

Nodding, he continued to drive. "So basically, fake it until I make it, huh?"

"Maybe..."

Her phone vibrated in her pocket and she pulled it out to see a text from Ashlynn.

> Ash: Where are you? Are you almost here?

> Chloe: On my way. About ten minutes out.

> Chloe: How did you get there so fast?

> Ash: Was already on my way up with a change of clothes for Billie.

> Ash: Is Levi with you?

> Chloe: No. I didn't even think to call anyone.

> Chloe: Have you seen Mom or talked to her doctor?

> Ash: Only for a minute with Mom. They were taking her for some scans.

> Chloe: I hate this. I hate this so much!

> Ash: I know. Me too.

> Ash: Wait…if you're not with Levi, how are you texting me? You don't have voice command set up.

Crap.

> Chloe: Oh, one of the teachers offered to drive me because I was so upset.

> Ash: Aww…that's so nice. I was worried about you driving alone again.

> Chloe: It's all good. I promise.

> Chloe: I'll see you in a few minutes.

> Ash: Sounds good. I'll meet you in the lobby.

> Ash: Love you!!

> Chloe: Love you too!

"Everything okay?" Tanner asked when she put her phone down.

"What? Oh, um…that was my sister. She was asking when I was going to get to the hospital."

He nodded again. "Do you just have the one sister and a brother? I thought I remember you saying that your sister bakes for Books & Beans and your sister-in-law owns it, right?"

"I actually have two sisters and one brother. My older sister, Billie, is the one who bakes, and Ashlynn and I are twins."

"Really?" he asked with a bit of wide-eyed interest. "That's very cool. My older brother passed away when I was five. He had a heart condition that no one ever diagnosed and died while playing JV football in school."

"Oh my goodness, Tanner! I'm so sorry!" And again, her hand went to his thigh. "I...I don't even know what to say to that. Do you have any other siblings?"

He shook his head. "My parents were devastated and..." Shaking his head again, he let out a soft, mirthless laugh. "Sorry. We're supposed to be distracting you and not talking about sad and depressing things." Another pause. "Is that the hospital up ahead?"

It was and the rest of the ride was spent with mindless chit-chat about the town, the roads, and eventually, the parking. When Tanner actually pulled into a parking spot, Chloe was a little perplexed. "Um...you can just drop me off up by the door. I'm sure..."

"I'd feel better if I walked you in," he told her as he climbed from the vehicle, leaving her no choice but to follow. Tanner walked around and opened the door for her and then placed his hand at the small of her back again as they made their way to the main entrance. She spotted Ashlynn as soon as they walked in.

"I'm so glad you're finally here!" Ash said as she came over and hugged her. When she pulled back and spotted Tanner, she smiled. "And I want to thank you for making sure Chloe got here safely. I'm Ashlynn."

"Hey," he said. "I'm Tanner." He shook her hand and looked between the two of them in mild confusion.

"We're fraternal twins," Ash explained. "People get confused all the time because we really don't look anything alike."

"No, but there's definitely a resemblance there," he confirmed. "So, um...is there anything you guys need? I can go and grab food or coffee or..."

"Thanks," Ashlynn replied. "But I think we're okay for now. My fiancé's on his way up and so is our brother. And honestly, I don't think I could eat or drink anything until we have some answers about our mom."

Chloe nodded in agreement before facing Tanner. "I can't thank you enough for getting me here, but I know you have things to do back at the school. We're going to be here for a while and I can get a ride home from one of my siblings, so..."

"No problem," Tanner said graciously. "I'm glad I could help. If you want, I can..."

He never got to finish because Levi and Reid walked in and then Billie stepped out of the elevator and called to them. "They're bringing Mom back to the room and the doctor is going to talk to us! Come on!"

Before joining her siblings, Chloe turned and faced Tanner. "I...I really am thankful for everything you did today, Tanner. I guess I'll see you on Tuesday."

Nodding, he slid his hands into his pockets. "Glad I could help. And I hope your mom's okay."

"Chloe!" Billie called out again, her impatience clear.

"I need to go. Thanks again." And with a small wave, she ran to join everyone in the elevator.

"Who was that?" Levi asked as the doors shut.

"Oh, um...he's the new kindergarten teacher. Tanner Westyn."

"Wait," Billie interjected. "That was Tanner? The guy you called an icky jerk? What was he doing here?"

She inwardly groaned before explaining the situation.

"Well, I think it was very nice of him to do that," Ashlynn said before giving her a sly grin. "Very nice indeed."

This time, her groan was outward. "He was just being a

decent human being because he saw I was too upset to drive."

"You could have called me," Levi murmured, but she was saved from responding when the elevator doors opened up on the fifth floor. They all filed out and followed Billie down the hall toward the ICU. They stopped in the waiting area, where there were several chairs and sofas.

"Wait, this wasn't where she was yesterday," Chloe said out loud. "Why did they move her here?" She and Ashlynn moved toward one of the doors, hoping it was Marie's, and fortunately, it was.

"Is it just me or is Mom not moving? Like at all," Ash whispered so only she could hear.

"She's not," Chloe confirmed, and that had her trembling and on the verge of tears again.

"Guys," Reid quietly said as he joined them and guided them back to the waiting area just as a nurse stepped out of the room. "We can't just go in there." Then he turned toward the nurse. "Do you know when we'll be able to go in and see her?"

"Dr. Barnett and Dr. Manning will be down to speak to you in a few minutes," the nurse said as she made her way past them.

"Um...she's just sleeping, right?" Ashlynn asked her before she went too far.

"She's sedated right now to help with the seizures. Dr. Manning will explain it all to you." And before anyone else could ask, the nurse was walking into another patient room.

"Rude much?" Billie asked no one in particular. "I mean, this is all scary and we're just concerned. Would it have killed her to just stay until the doctors got here?"

"Maybe she doesn't have all the information and doesn't want to tell us the wrong thing," Levi countered. "And you have to admit, there's far too many of us up here and we can be overwhelming."

Billie mumbled something under her breath before sitting down on one of the sofas.

"I hate this," Chloe quietly commented. "I hate that we're all here, I hate that mom's hurt, and I hate not knowing what's going on."

Levi moved to her side and wrapped his arm around her. "We all feel that way, but we have to stay strong and positive and believe that everything's going to be okay."

Easy for him to say...

The two doctors came down the hall, and after introducing themselves again—like they had the day before—they took turns explaining all of Marie's injuries and how they had placed her in a medically induced coma because of the swelling to her brain. It was only temporary and they were optimistic that they could wake her up within the next day or two, but that was why they had moved her up to the intensive care floor.

After that, it was a lot of medical jargon that Chloe didn't fully understand, but it sounded like there was going to be a lot of waiting around with very little results.

And now I hate this more...

"You can reach us at any time," Dr. Manning said. "We understand that this is all very upsetting for you, but our primary concern is making sure Marie is kept sedated and monitored. I wish we had better news for you, but the next forty-eight hours are going to be critical. There isn't much you'll be able to do here, but you're more than welcome to stay until visiting hours are over."

"Please remember that you can only go in and sit with her one at a time," Dr. Barnett added. "Any of the nurses at the desk can help you with going in and out of the room, but we ask that you not stay too long. What your mother needs right now is to let her brain and body rest."

"Isn't that why you put her in the coma?" Billie asked. "I can't imagine us sitting there and doing anything to disturb that."

Both doctors nodded. "That's true," Dr. Manning replied, "but patients can still hear noises around them while in a coma. We just ask that you keep that sort of thing to a minimum."

"Can one of us stay the night?" Levi asked. "I understand about visiting hours, but my sister stayed last night, and I planned on being here tonight. Of course, that was when she was in a regular room, but..."

"You can," Dr. Barnett responded. "Just let one of the nurses know, and she'll make sure you have a blanket and pillow. The chair beside the bed pulls out to a sleeper. It's not the most comfortable, but it beats sleeping sitting up."

They talked for a few more minutes, but all Chloe wanted was to go in and see her mother. That took another thirty minutes because she somehow ended up being the last one to go in. All the time she sat waiting, she wondered what she was going to do or say when she went in, but all she knew was that she had to be strong and not cry.

It didn't quite work out that way.

Once she was standing beside the bed, she broke down crying and hated herself for it. "I'm sorry, Mom," she quietly sobbed. "I know I need to be strong, but I can't. Not right now. I want to talk with you and tell you about my classroom and share crafting ideas." Resting her head on the edge of the bed, she let the tears fall. There was nothing she could do, nothing she could say, and she had no idea how long she had even been sitting there when Ashlynn opened the door.

"Chlo? You okay?"

All Chloe could do was shake her head.

"Come on," her sister said softly as she helped her to her feet. "Let's get you out of here for a little while."

A nod was her only response.

Stepping out of the room, Chloe was surprised to see Tanner standing with her family. He was passing out bottles of water and cups of coffee and snacks.

What the...?

"Maybe he's not such an icky jerk," Ashlynn whispered before walking over to join everyone.

* * *

Tanner knew he could have left when Chloe and her family went in the elevator, but he felt like maybe they wouldn't mind if he stayed. Right now, they might not think they need anything, but wouldn't it be great if they didn't have to do anything for themselves right now? So he went and scouted out the cafeteria and decided the selection wasn't great before going out to his car and finding the nearest coffee shop and buying a variety of things to tide the Donovans over for a little while. He grabbed bottles of water, coffees, and an assortment of cookies, cakes, and chips.

He knew they wouldn't be as good as what they had at Books & Beans, but he figured it would be okay.

When he stepped off the elevator a few minutes ago, everyone had been in the waiting area except for Chloe. Ashlynn had introduced him to everyone before heading down to her mother's room, and after thanking him, they had all settled into some casual conversation about his move to Sweetbriar Ridge. He was telling them about his house when he spotted Chloe coming down the hall looking utterly devastated, and he had the strangest urge to just walk over and wrap her in his arms. Of course, her twin was comforting her and then the rest of her family, so Tanner simply stood back and tried not to be too intrusive.

It was mildly fascinating watching them. Everyone took turns hugging Chloe—including her future brother-in-law, Reid—and then her brother was the one to put his arm around her and lead her back to the waiting area. She gave him a weak smile and accepted the bottle of water he offered to her.

"I have coffee too, if you'd prefer," he lamely offered, but she simply shook her head. Then he sort of stood back and tried to stay out of everyone's way, even as he listened to what was going on.

Apparently, their mother was put into a medically induced coma because of some swelling in her brain. Part of him wanted to share the story he'd shared with Chloe—but in more detail—but he honestly didn't want to intrude.

Every once in a while, one of them looked over at him and probably wondered why he was still there, and it made Tanner wonder too.

Yeah, what am I still doing here?

And the answer was...he wanted to help.

Billie got up and went into their mother's room, and ten minutes later she came out and then Levi went in. They kept up that routine for a couple of hours and still Tanner didn't leave. Sure, he'd gone and refreshed coffees, and called the school to give Susan an update, but other than that, he sat off to the side and casually played on his phone until he heard someone mentioning a need.

That's when he ordered lunch to be delivered.

Nothing fancy, just a variety of sandwiches from the local café.

"Tanner, you really didn't have to do all this," Levi said before clasping him on the shoulder. "But we really appreciate it. Thank you."

"No worries. Glad I could help."

They all ate and talked about visiting schedules and questions they wanted to ask the doctors, but all along, Chloe sat quietly next to Ashlynn and just seemed lost in her own thoughts.

"I hate to say it, but...I really need to go home and nap for a little while and then go and get some baking done," Billie said when they were all done eating. "Jade has everything under control and we could probably get by with what we have in the freezer, but it will do me good to leave for a little while." After she hugged everyone, she thanked Tanner for everything and left.

An hour later, Reid was the one to stand up. "I have a shift starting in a couple of hours and need to go home and do a few things." He looked at Ashlynn. "Are you staying?"

She glanced toward the rest of her family and sighed. "I want to say yes, but...I think I have to agree with Billie. It will do me good to leave for a little while. Sorry, guys."

"Not a problem," Levi said. "There really isn't anything any of us can do. Go check on the salon and we'll see you later."

After they left, Tanner figured he probably should go too. Slowly, he got to his feet. "Um...I guess I should get going too." He looked at Chloe. "Can Levi drive you home or do you want me to take you back to your car?"

Levi looked at the two of them for a moment. "I'm planning on staying through the night. I don't want Mom to be alone." Then he glanced at Tanner. "If you wouldn't mind...?"

Chloe quietly cleared her throat. "I can go get my car

and then come back. You shouldn't be here by yourself either."

But her brother stopped her. "Honestly, Chlo, we're all going to be taking turns, so why don't you go home and tomorrow night will be your night here? Get a good night's sleep and take care of anything you need to."

"But..." She looked around nervously, and Tanner could tell she didn't feel right about going. "Ash said she was coming back, and so did Billie. Why can't I...?"

Levi moved in closer to her and hugged her. "We both know Billie's going to go home and crash hard and probably be up baking half the night. Ash is going home and then checking on the salon and when she calls, I'll tell her not to come back too. There seriously isn't anything we can do here. You take tomorrow night, Ash will take Sunday night, and hopefully by then, Mom will be awake and we can start looking at when she can go home."

Her shoulders sagged. "I guess you're right."

"Just...promise me you're going to eat. You barely touched your lunch. We need you to be strong, so..." Then he turned to Tanner. "I hate to ask because you've already done so much today, but..."

"I'll make sure she eats dinner," he assured him.

"I'm right here, you know," Chloe huffed. "And I'm not a child."

Levi hugged her again. "I know, but I worry. Humor me, okay?"

She let out another huff, but nodded. "Fine." Then she glared up at Tanner as if he'd betrayed her, but he could take it. When she stood, she only looked at her brother. "Please send some updates, even if it's to say nothing's changed. And if anything does change..."

"I'll call. I promise." Kissing her on the forehead, Levi

gently turned her toward Tanner while mouthing, "Thank you."

All he did was nod at the acknowledgment.

They rode down in the elevator in complete silence that carried them all the way to the car. It wasn't until he was ready to start driving that he decided he'd had enough.

"Look, for what it's worth, I get it. You're upset because Levi essentially forced you to leave, but...that's not my fault. I'm simply trying to be helpful. If you don't want to eat with me, that's fine. You're a grown woman and I'm sure you know that you need to eat and keep up your strength."

"I do," she mumbled.

"Okay, then. I'll just take you back to your car and...say goodbye."

"Thank you."

He was totally prepared to drive in silence, so it was a complete surprise when Chloe spoke.

"I was really surprised when I saw you sitting with my family earlier. I thought you'd left."

Shrugging, he pulled out of the parking lot. "I had a feeling there was going to be a lot going on and I know from personal experience that we tend to overlook things, like eating, when we're in high-stress situations. It just didn't feel right to leave."

He could feel her staring at him, but decided to wait it out and see what she was going to say.

"You're turning out to be not quite what I expected," she said shyly. "After the way things went when we met..."

Yeah, he knew where she was going with this.

"I come on strong. I know. And abrasive," he added for good measure. "But believe it or not, my heart's in the right place. As for today, after our conversation on the way to the hospital, it reminded me of what it was like when my friend was brought in. His wife and parents were so overwhelmed that they stayed up in the waiting room for days until his wife nearly passed out because she hadn't eaten."

"Food was probably the last thing on their minds. I know it was for me. And it was very kind of you to not only take care of one meal, but two."

He shrugged again. "Coffee and snacks were really just a distraction; the sandwiches were a necessity. I could tell that Billie was exhausted, and Reid mentioned that he had to work a shift tonight, so it made sense that for everyone's well-being, they needed to eat." He let that statement sink in before adding, "Is there anywhere you can recommend for dinner? I haven't really tried any of the restaurants in town yet."

"The café is very good, and there's a steakhouse that's also pretty good. What are you in the mood for?"

Chuckling, he shook his head and knew he couldn't exactly say what he was thinking.

"Tanner?"

"Hmm?"

"Oh, come on!" she said with a small laugh. "I can totally tell you're thinking of something. Just say it!"

Groaning, he said, "Mexican. After hearing you talk about it yesterday at the meeting, all I can think about is guacamole!"

Fortunately, she laughed. "Wow! That was not what I was expecting you to say at all! I figured you'd want to know where to get the best pizza or burgers!"

"That's a little sexist," he teased, but immediately laughed. "My parents and I went to the steakhouse last weekend and it was good, but there is something about chips and guac that is too hard to resist!"

"I totally agree, and if I had the ingredients at home..."

"That wasn't what I was hinting at, Chloe. I swear. But if there's a good Mexican restaurant nearby…"

"There is. It's on the other side of Sweetbriar, so after you drop me off at my car, it will be another ten-minute drive."

"Awesome." He paused before deciding to be a little bold. "Any chance you'd like to join me?"

Her soft gasp was the initial response, but then she ducked her head and played with her hair a bit. "Um… thanks, but…I'm a little emotionally exhausted. I'm going to make myself some soup and maybe a sandwich and just try to relax. I'll probably call Ash and see if she wants to join me after she checks on the salon."

It was crazy how disappointed he was. And it wasn't just because he didn't know anyone in town yet, but because he was genuinely starting to like Chloe.

A lot.

Probably more than he should, considering the fact that they were coworkers and he was planning on putting up a fight to win the Teacher of the Year award this year. Was he willing to give all that up?

No, he told himself.

Right now, he was just feeling like this because of the situation with her mom. He was certain that under other circumstances, he wouldn't think of her as anything but a fellow teacher.

Liar.

Okay, yesterday he had started softening toward her, but…how could he not? She was sweet and pretty and had a great laugh and…

Tanner inwardly groaned because having any kind of feelings for Chloe was not good, especially right now. With no other choice, he had to go back to thinking of her as the competition and nothing more.

With that decision made, they drove back to the school while discussing some of the other places to eat, both right in Sweetbriar Ridge and the surrounding towns. By the time he came to a stop in the parking lot next to her car, he felt like he had a good grasp on at least the restaurants in the area.

"I know I've already said it," Chloe said as she reached for her door handle, "but thank you again for everything."

"Glad I could help."

She climbed out of the car and Tanner did the same, following her over to the driver's side of her car. "I hope someday I can return the favor," she said as she unlocked the door. "Seriously, if there's anything you need, just let me know. Whether it's information about the town or help with projects for your students, I'll be there."

"Chloe..."

"And just so you know, we'll have decent weather next week, but around mid-September, it starts to get cold. You might get lucky and be able to ski by the end of October!"

"Oh, well..."

"I hope you have a great weekend!" she rambled on. "The school will be open for the teachers on Monday, so if there's anything you still need to do, you can go in and get it done."

Before he could respond, she was talking again.

"I feel terrible about you losing an entire day because of me, so if there's anything you need help with..."

Okay, he had to put a stop to this because she was clearly nervous and talking just for the sake of talking. "Chloe," he began, placing his hand on her arm. "We're good. I promise. I'm glad I could help today and I'm not keeping a scorecard. Stop worrying about me and what I need to do, and just focus on yourself. Everything's going to be alright. I swear."

The next thing he knew, she was pressed up against him, hugging him tight.

It would be rude not to hug her back, right?

So, not wanting to be rude, Tanner's arms banded around her waist as he held her close. He thought he heard her hum softly, but figured maybe it was just his imagination.

When she pulled back, she stared up at him with those big blue eyes and he swore they were the most beautiful eyes he'd ever seen. Then she whispered his name and seemed to move closer and before he knew it, he was closing the distance between them. The moment his lips touched hers, he was lost.

Chloe's arms tightened around him, and this time he knew he heard her hum. Her body was pressed up against his, her soft lips opened beneath his, and it was possibly one of the most perfect moments of his life. As much as he told himself only minutes ago that this wasn't a good idea, he knew he was helpless to deny that there was a definite attraction between the two of them.

An attraction he wanted to explore.

Now.

He deepened the kiss and held her tighter, hearing her soft intake of breath before she relaxed against him again. It was sweet and sexy all at the same time and he was about to suggest they maybe get in one of the cars or even go to his place, when Chloe broke the kiss and forcefully stepped out of his arms.

"*Ohmygod!*" she whispered, a look of sheer horror on her face. "I...I'm sorry. I need to go!"

"Chloe, I..."

But she wasn't listening. She scrambled into her car and was pulling away before Tanner could even think of something to say.

With nothing left to do, he stood there and watched her drive out of the parking lot and kept watching until the car was out of sight.

"Damn," he murmured, raking a hand through his hair.

Only...he wasn't sure if he was referring to her leaving, his disappointment, or how damn stunned he was by how hot a simple kiss was.

"And I'm not going to figure it out while standing alone in the middle of the school parking lot."

Walking back to his car, a smile crossed his face as he suddenly had another reason to look forward to the first day of school. Not only was he ready to take on this new challenge with a class full of kindergarteners, but he was ready to see where things went with Chloe.

Chapter Six

Tuesday morning, Chloe grabbed her large tote bag from the back seat of her car before facing Sweetbriar Elementary School with a big smile. It was only 7:30 in the morning, but she was beyond energized and ready for the day. With her bag slung over her shoulder, she reached back into her car and carefully grabbed her travel mug of coffee and the bag with a blueberry muffin in it.

Ashlynn had surprised her just minutes ago by showing up with it to wish her a great first day of school.

I love my family.

After a tense weekend, things were taking a step in the right direction. Yesterday, the doctors were able to bring her mother out of the coma and all her stats were looking good. The brain swelling had gone down, and now they could focus on her other injuries and her recovery. It was going to be a long road to getting her back to the way she was before the accident, but they now had hope.

Locking the car, Chloe made her way into the school, greeting and waving to everyone she saw. She knew she was one of the first to arrive, but she didn't mind. Having some peace and quiet to set up her room and to mentally prepare was her favorite time of the day. But the closer she got to the classroom, the louder things got.

"Is that music?" she murmured. And sure enough, when she got close to Tanner's room, she heard some very loud music. If she wasn't mistaken, it was *The Final Countdown*. It certainly wasn't something she would have expected of him, and honestly, it made her laugh a little bit. The door was closed and, as curious as she was, she wasn't sure she wanted to knock on his door and ask any questions. She was still reeling from the way she had essentially thrown herself at him on Friday. All weekend, she'd played that scene over and over in her head and cringed every time.

What was I thinking?

It was one thing to hug him to thank him for sacrificing almost an entire day to help her and her family. It was another to kiss him and rub up against him like some crazy sex fiend. The thought of having to face him today was overwhelming, but considering it was the first day of school, there were going to be plenty of other things to keep her busy.

And she was looking forward to all of it.

Walking to her classroom, she turned on the lights and smiled at how welcoming and cheery the room looked. At her desk, she put all her things down, pulled out her chair, and got comfortable. Taking a sip of coffee, she hummed with appreciation. It was going to be a good day—a great day!

"And a great year," she said softly, sighing with relief when Tanner's loud music ended. With another sip of her coffee, Chloe allowed herself one more moment to relax before getting started. First, she would eat a bit of the muffin her sister was kind enough to bring over at such an early hour, and then...

"Knock, knock..."

Crap. Tanner.

He smiled as he walked into the room, heading right for her, looking incredibly handsome and charming. And the closer he got, the better he smelled.

Ugh...do not smell him! Bad Chloe!

"Good morning," he said smoothly. "How's your mom doing?"

And he has good manners? How am I supposed to even look at him without flinging myself at him again?

"Good morning," she said, her voice a combination of a squeak and a croak. Clearing her throat, she nodded. "And thank you for asking. She's awake and doing well. The swelling has gone down and now the doctors can focus on her recovery."

He slid his hands into his pockets and nodded, still smiling. "That's great! I'm sure you're all relieved."

"We are. She's got a long road ahead of her, but I think we're heading in the right direction." Forcing herself to look away, she took a casual sip of her coffee before speaking again. "Are you ready for your first day?"

His smile was positively beaming. "I am! I spent the weekend getting everything ready and came in yesterday to finish my room and all that's missing are the kiddos!"

She had to admit that she loved his enthusiasm. "You're going to do great, I'm sure."

Tanner nodded again before taking a step closer. "So, um...I was wondering if you'd like to grab an early dinner with me tonight. You know...we can talk about the first day and get to know each other a little more."

"Um..."

101

Oh, God...is he asking me out as a coworker or like...a date?

"I really wanted to call you this weekend, but realized I didn't have your number. After the way you left, I wanted to make sure you were alright."

The look on his face said he was hoping for her to say something, but she didn't have a clue how to respond to that.

"And I know you were just thanking me," he went on, "and the kiss maybe wasn't planned, but I really enjoyed it and thought that we could spend some time together and..."

A date. He's definitely asking as a date. What do I do?

"Um..."

"We don't have to do dinner," he told her. "Maybe we could go to Books & Beans and just have some coffee and talk about our day? What do you think?"

He looked so handsome and sounded so sincere, but...

"Thank you, Tanner," she said primly. "But I already have plans for after work. The first week of school is usually exhausting and between that and dealing with my mom, I'm really not going to have a lot of free time. I'm sure you could reach out to any of the other teachers and they'd be happy to have coffee with you after school."

And yeah, she hated saying the words because she saw the disappointment on his face.

Same, she thought with an inward sigh.

With a curt nod, he took a step back. "No problem. I get it. And hey, have a great first day and I guess...I'll see you around."

Chloe nodded too. "Yeah, you too, Tanner. And if there's anything you need with the..."

"I got it," he said before turning and walking out.

Groaning, she slouched down in her chair. "Well, that

was awkward." Then she sighed loudly. "And it's for the best. Getting involved with a coworker is wrong and... ugh..."

It took all of sixty seconds before she reached for her phone and texted her twin.

Chloe: Okay, so...weird question.

Chloe: Wait, are you awake or did you go back to sleep after the muffin drop?

> Ash: Is that the weird question or is there another one?

Chloe: There's another one.

Chloe: And I didn't think that was a weird question. I felt bad about maybe waking you up.

> Ash: Once I got up and drove around town, I was awake. What's going on?

Where do I even begin?

Chloe: Tanner just asked me to go out with him after school and I turned him down

> Ash: Um...that's not a question

Chloe: I was getting to it! Sheesh!

> Ash: Did you turn him down because you still think he's an icky jerk? Because I'm gonna have to disagree with you on that one

> Ash: He was so freaking nice at the hospital. Totally delightful

The eye roll she couldn't stop practically had her seeing her own brain.

Chloe: It's not because of the icky jerk thing. It just feels wrong to go out with a coworker

Ash: You went with that teacher guy to our reunion last month.

Chloe: As a friend! I was dating Evan at the time and he couldn't go, remember?

Ash: Okay, yeah. And you think Tanner wanted this to be like a date?

Chloe: Yup

Ash: Hmm…I feel like there's something you're not telling me.

Ash: When I saw you Friday night you were acting a little weird but I blamed it on all the emotional stuff with Mom.

Ash: Did something happen between you and Tanner that you're trying NOT to tell me?

She seriously hated how well her sister knew her. It was virtually impossible to keep anything to herself.

Ever.

Chloe: Never mind. I have too much to do to be getting into this right now

Chloe: Just…forget I texted. Go back to sleep!

Ash: Well I'm wide awake now!

> Ash: You can't drop a bombshell like this and think I'm just going to forget about it!

"I didn't drop a bombshell," she hissed at her phone, even though her sister couldn't hear her.

> Chloe: I have to go. The kids will start to arrive soon.

> Ash: Did you kiss him?

> Ash: Did he kiss you?

> Ash: You didn't do it in one of the hospital rooms, did you?

Growling, she tried to strangle her phone.

> Chloe: What is wrong with you? Who does that?

> Ash: LOL! Just checking.

> Ash: But it was a kiss, right?

> Chloe: Ugh! If it will make you shut up, yes, it was a kiss. Happy?

> Ash: GIDDY! YAY!!

There was an almost obscene amount of smiley face emojis followed by balloons and noise makers that just fueled her embarrassment.

> Chloe: Please stop.

> Ash: Fine. But I'm coming over after work with a pizza and I want to hear all about it.

It was pointless to argue. Ashlynn tended to do whatever she wanted.

> Chloe: I'll see you later.

> Ash: Love you!

> Chloe: Love you too, even though you're a brat!

And with that, she tossed her phone back into her purse and took a huge bite of her muffin.

It was going to be a long day.

* * *

It was a good thing Chloe hadn't accepted his invitation to coffee or dinner, because Tanner had never been more exhausted in his life.

How was it possible that a class of eighteen 5-year-olds could sap so much of his energy?

"It's because they never stopped," he murmured as he wandered around his classroom like a zombie. The last student had just been picked up and he relished the silence. "And this was only the first day."

Shit.

It didn't matter how prepared he thought he was; clearly, he wasn't prepared at all. His confidence—or arrogance—made him believe there wasn't anything he couldn't handle. Who knew it was a room full of kindergarteners that was going to bring him down?

Hard.

Still, he forced himself to walk around and straighten everything up before grabbing his own satchel and shutting off the lights. When he stepped out into the hall, he looked toward Chloe's room and saw that the light was still on. He considered going over and asking how her day went, but...he didn't. She had effectively cut him down this morning, and it bothered him way more than it should have.

In his years of competitive skiing, he'd had his fair share of women chasing after him, and he'd done more than his fair share of kissing them. But it stung having Chloe kiss him and then run off. And then having her essentially treating him like it never happened stung even more.

"I'm pathetic," he mumbled and headed down the hall toward the exit. All he wanted was to go home, crash on the sofa, and maybe order a pizza. "I'll probably be asleep by 8:00 too."

And yeah, that made him feel even worse.

But as he climbed into his car and made his way home, Tanner reasoned that he was only feeling like this because it was the first day. Tomorrow would be easier. And the day after that, it would be even easier. By the end of the week, he would start to settle into this new norm and everything would be alright.

There hadn't been another challenge in his life that broke him, and teaching kindergarten wasn't going to either.

"I refuse to let this be the thing that breaks me."

Tomorrow, he was going to go into that school with his usual confidence and he was going to be the best damn teacher Sweetbriar Elementary had ever seen. He was going to kill it at his first year of teaching, of that he was certain. And even though he didn't regret helping Chloe and her family, since she wasn't interested in him—even though her kiss said otherwise—he now had zero conflict with beating her for the Teacher of the Year title.

And it wasn't about being spiteful; it was about doing what he always did—striving to be number one.

Even if it meant isolating himself and maybe having a smaller circle of friends.

"Doesn't matter. I've got all the friends I need."

But...did he?

Pushing the thought aside and attributing it to exhaustion, he turned on the radio and spent the rest of the drive letting his mind go a little blank. At home, he kicked off his shoes, went to the kitchen and grabbed himself something to drink before going to the living room and collapsing on the couch.

The glass barely made it to the end table before Tanner closed his eyes and fell asleep.

* * *

As expected, the rest of the first week went well.

The second week went even better.

And week three went great.

Tanner was totally hitting his stride and people were noticing.

Including Chloe Donovan.

It was Friday afternoon and he knew her students were in art class when she came to a stop in his classroom doorway. He gave her a polite smile and a small nod, but noticed she didn't seem in a hurry to leave. His class was finishing the counting sheets they'd been working on, and as he walked to the door, he called out, "When you're done with your work, turn it over and take your spot in our reading forest!"

There were some cheers that he thought were adorable, and apparently Chloe did too because she was smiling.

"What can I do for you?" he asked casually, doing his best not to notice how her blue sweater matched her eyes.

"Sorry to interrupt, but next week we'll be starting our fall unit and thought we could do some of it together. You know, merge our classes for some of the activities. What do you think?"

"Um..."

"Mr. Westyn! Mr. Westyn! Jackie knocked all the books off the shelf!" one of his students cried.

Turning his head, he glanced into the room and sure enough, there were a lot of books on the floor.

"I know you're busy," Chloe stammered. "Maybe you can meet me at Books & Beans after school and we can discuss it?"

He nodded. "Yeah. Sure. Thanks." And then he walked away to deal with the mess before anything else got too wild. Crouching down next to the pile, he smiled patiently at the culprit. "What do you say you give me a hand cleaning this up, Jackie?"

The little girl nodded solemnly and began picking the books up one at a time and placed them back where they belonged. As much as he wanted to make her clean it all up, he had a lesson to get to. It wasn't until they were done and he picked up the book he planned to read for story time that he realized he'd agreed to meet Chloe for coffee.

He silently admonished himself, but knew it all didn't mean anything. It was just coffee between two coworkers for the sake of their students. No big deal.

Except...he suddenly couldn't wait for the end of the day.

It wasn't like he had been pining away for her or anything, but...he genuinely liked her and just wanted a chance to get to know her better.

Probably shouldn't be so petty about competing for Teacher of the Year then...

But he really wanted the title.

Like...a lot.

A conversation he'd had with his father a month ago came to mind.

"And the principal told me I was sometimes a little overzealous and rubbed some teachers the wrong way. But that's only because I'm passionate about teaching and everyone else was way too laid back!"

"Were they too laid back, or were you trying to show off? Because I think we both know..."

"I hate it when you do that."

"What? Tell the truth?"

This continuous quest to be number one was possibly ruining his life more than he realized. Why couldn't he just be good at what he did? Why did being the best have to consume him?

And that was something he vowed to work on if today's coffee maybe led to dinner.

Or maybe I should work on it because it's the right thing to do...

"Mr. Westyn! Mr. Westyn! Are we going to hear a story?"

He looked up and realized his class was sitting on the floor waiting for him. Smiling, he moved to his spot and sat down. "You bet we are! Who's ready to read about the little pug who thinks he's a superhero?"

There was an excited round of "Me!" that made him chuckle, so he opened the book and began to read.

When story time was over, he took his class down the hall for PE and opted to hang out in the teachers' lounge instead of in his classroom. He found Chloe doing the same thing. She smiled up at him and he looked around and saw they were the only two in there.

"Hey," he said. "Hope I'm not interrupting your break."

"Not at all," she said as she looked up from the book she was reading. "I just felt like relaxing in here while the kids are at PE instead of my classroom."

That made him smile. "Great minds think alike. That's exactly why I'm here." Then he held up the curriculum binder he'd brought with him. "I was going to look over the unit we're going to talk about after school. I'll admit I haven't really allowed myself to get too far ahead in planning. I'm just trying to master everything for the current week."

She nodded. "Nothing wrong with that. My first year, I probably read that binder front to back about a hundred times because I was so afraid of missing anything. Then I realized I just had way too much free time on my hands." Laughing softly, she added, "Although now I practically have it all memorized, so...there's that."

That didn't surprise him. "Hopefully you'll be patient with me. That's why I brought the binder in here. I was hoping I wouldn't sound unprepared when we met for coffee."

Her shoulders sagged. "Tanner, I really hope you don't think I'm some sort of judgy person. That's the last thing I want to be."

It was on the tip of his tongue to remind her of her initial opinion of him, but he had a feeling that would only make him look bad.

Again.

Shifting a bit in his seat, Tanner tried to choose the right way to respond. "You have to see it from my point of view," he began. "You've been here much longer than I have, and you've been Teacher of the Year twice."

Rather than smile, she frowned—which seemed like an odd reaction.

"Okay," she said quietly, leaning in a little closer as if sharing a secret. "Here's the thing, while it was an incredible honor to be...you know...Teacher of the Year, they've only been doing it for those two years." Shrugging, she continued, "And they only did it to boost morale because we were one of the poorest districts in the state. I got a certificate and a $25 gift card to an online store. It's really nothing compared to winning a skiing competition."

That put some things into perspective, but...

"Still, Chloe, even if the prize wasn't great, they obviously chose you for a reason."

Another shrug. "I was the newest teacher, the youngest teacher, and the most excited about pretty much everything. I seriously think they did it to reward my enthusiasm so I didn't get jaded."

"Damn."

"I know." She sighed. "That makes me sound ungrateful. I'm sorry, I'm really not. I never should have said anything. I just didn't want you thinking that I did anything so spectacular to deserve the award."

If he were being honest, he'd admit that he really thought there was more to it.

"I appreciate you sharing that with me, and yeah, it does take a little of the pressure off."

A grateful smile was her only response, and it was damn near dazzling. Did she have any idea how pretty she was?

And to stop himself from asking that question out loud, he picked up the binder and smiled back at her. "So...the fall unit. What do we do?"

"It's a lot of fun," she told him. "We talk about the weather and we go out and pick up leaves and make some cute art projects for them to give to their parents. Last year, I got a batch of tiny pumpkins that they painted and we had a scarecrow in the classroom where I would put our sight word of the day on."

"O-kay..."

"You don't have to do any of that," she quickly interjected. "I just thought it was fun to have the room decorated for the season. But I'm open to suggestions."

He was about to open the binder when the alarm sounded on his phone that it was almost time to get his class. Chloe's chimed right after his and they both laughed softly.

"I guess we'll talk about it more over coffee," he said with a lopsided grin.

Chloe nodded and began collecting her things. "Does 4:30 work for you, or will you need more time?"

"That will work."

"See you then!" And with a little wave, she left the lounge.

Tanner stared at the door for several moments and questioned what was going on with him. Why was he suddenly so drawn to her? The first time he saw her, he didn't think there was anything particularly appealing about her. If memory served, she sort of blended into her surroundings. But now he realized just how wrong he was and couldn't seem to stop thinking about her.

That's when it hit him: he hadn't been involved in a relationship or even out on a date in several months. So it wasn't that Chloe was anything special, he was just...lonely? In a rut? Horny?

"Ugh...no. Just...no," he murmured before picking up the binder and heading out of the lounge.

As he made his way back to his classroom to drop the binder off, he thought about all the people he'd met so far in

Sweetbriar. Of course, there were all the Donovans—including the one who helped him with his home rental—and every time he'd gone into Books & Beans, Jade and Billie introduced him to pretty much everyone who was in there. He'd grabbed a beer with Will from the automotive repair place and played poker with him and his boss, Devin. Ashlynn's fiancé Reid had been there, along with a couple of other guys from the firehouse, and it was nice to have a new group of friends.

And they'd all offered to introduce him to some of the single women around town, but because he really needed to focus on his job, he'd turned them down.

Is that why I'm attracted to Chloe? Because it's convenient that we work together?

Okay, that was something he was going to have to examine a little more, too.

But...later.

Like, after they had coffee this afternoon.

For now, he needed to get his students and finish the day and the week strong. Then he could put all his attention on this new unit Chloe was talking about and figuring out what he was feeling for her and why.

It was either going to make him really happy or feel like a total jerk.

Chapter Seven

"Oh my goodness! I'm so glad you're here! It's like our twin telepathy is totally synced today!" Ashlynn gushed as she hugged her. Chloe had barely made it through the door of Books & Beans before her sister ran over to her. "I was going to call you, but wasn't sure what time you were going to get out of school today."

Pulling back, Chloe glanced around and almost sagged with relief that Tanner wasn't there yet. "Um...what's going on?"

Shrugging, Ashlynn smiled. "I just booked a bridal party! Like they're going to come to the salon—all eight of them!—so we can do their hair and makeup for the wedding! How cool is that?"

"Uh...very! Yay you!"

"I stopped in here to get myself some celebratory brownies that I was going to take home and eat by myself, but now you're here! We can totally share them and catch up!" She took Chloe's hand and began to lead her toward the counter.

"No!" Chloe hissed. "You have to go! I'll pay for your brownies, but you have to leave!"

"What? Why?" Frowning, she moved in close. "What's going on with you? You're acting weird." Then her eyes went wide as she gasped. "Do you have a date? Are you meeting a guy here?"

Oh God...

"I don't have a date," she whispered. "I'm just...I'm meeting Tanner here to go over our fall unit that we start next week. I had some ideas about our classes doing some activities together and rather than stay late at the school, we decided to come here."

Her sister's first response was to yawn loudly.

Then roll her eyes.

"That was the most boring thing I've ever heard," she said. "And what's the big deal? You said you told him you weren't interested, so this is just a work thing. I don't see why I have to leave. It's not like..."

Ashlynn's eyes went wide again.

"Sooo...you're secretly interested in Mr. Tanner Skier McHotty! I *knew* it!"

She hated the theatrics her sister used in situations like this. "If you knew it, then why are you just figuring it out?" And though she thought she was being smug, she realized too late what she had just admitted.

"You lied to me!" Ash said with a bark of laughter. "You sly thing! I can't believe you pulled one over on me!"

"Okay, fine! I think he's hot! He kisses so damn good and he's a total distraction whenever I see him at school! Now can you please just *go*? I can't deal with you being here watching and judging me!"

It took Ash several long moments before she sobered and nodded. "Fine. I'll go. But not without my brownies."

"Ugh..." Taking Ash's hand, she dragged her over to the counter and smiled at Jade's mom, Cora. "Ashlynn needs all the brownies," she said firmly. "To go. Please box them up and you can add them to my order."

"Chloe's treating me because I booked a bridal party for the salon today!"

"Oh, how wonderful! Good for you, Ashlynn! Let me get those brownies for you!"

As soon as she walked away, Chloe noticed Tanner's car pulling up out front. "Tanner's here," she murmured. "Say hello and please just take the brownies and go. I promise to call you tomorrow and tell you everything, okay?"

"Why tomorrow? Why not when you get home?"

"Ashlynn..." she whined.

Huffing with annoyance, Ashlynn relented. "Tomorrow. But only because I'm probably going to be in a sugar coma and I plan to jump Reid when he gets home. Sex and brownies! It's gonna be a great night!"

Tanner walked in and spotted her, smiling. Chloe waved before moving in close to Ashlynn's ear, "If you say one thing to embarrass me, I'll tell Reid all about how you're afraid of the Muppets."

"What is a Snuffleupagus, Chloe?! And why is he just living on Sesame Street?" her sister whispered anxiously.

"I will call Reid right *now*, so help me!" Pulling back, she smiled brightly.

"Tanner! Hey!" Ashlynn said when he joined them. "How's teaching going?"

"Better than I expected," he told her. "There are days the kids are a little overwhelming, but I think we're all getting used to each other."

"Here's your brownies, Ashlynn!" Cora said, handing her the box. "And congratulations again!"

"Ooh...what are you celebrating?" Tanner asked.

"I'll let Chloe tell you. Apparently, I need to go," Ash said with a frown in her sister's direction. "I'll talk to you in the morning." Then she smiled at Tanner. "Have a great weekend!"

"Um, yeah. You too," he said. Once she walked out the door, he looked at Chloe. "Did I interrupt something? I kind of got the impression she didn't really want to leave."

"Really? I didn't get that from her at all," Chloe lied. "I was just getting ready to order. What would you like?"

"Oh, um...I think just a regular coffee with cream and sugar and a slice of the pound cake. But...I got it. You don't have to...I mean, you weren't offering to..."

It took her a second to realize what he was saying, and she laughed softly. "I mean, I wouldn't mind treating you to coffee and cake. After all, I was the one who invited you."

He was shaking his head. "Absolutely not. I've got this."

"I still owe you for all you did that day at the hospital..."

"We've been over this. You don't owe me anything."

"Are you two ready to order?" Cora asked.

Tanner repeated his order and then Chloe ordered a hot tea and a sugar cookie. Tonight, she was making herself a little Mexican feast just because, and she didn't want to fill up too much. When they had their orders and turned to find a place to sit, it was the first time she noticed just how crowded the shop was. She'd been so distracted by her sister and then Tanner that she hadn't been paying attention.

"I hope we can find someplace to sit," she said.

"Follow me," he told her, and she did. It took longer than she thought it would to find a table, but ultimately they did. It was in the corner of the non-fiction section, but at least it was clean and had two chairs.

"Whew! I wasn't sure we'd find anything. At least we

didn't have to stand around and stare at people until they left!"

He chuckled. "Luckily it didn't come to that." They got situated and he stirred his coffee while she did the same with her tea. "So, how was the rest of your day?"

"Pretty uneventful. The kids were a little hyped up after PE, but..."

"Hey, you guys!" Billie said as she walked over. "Cora told me you were here! And how did I manage to miss seeing Ashlynn?"

Chloe inwardly groaned. "She was in a hurry. She was going home to celebrate with brownies because she booked a bridal party today."

"That's amazing! I'll call her when I get home. I mean, I was going to anyway—you too—to give you an update on Mom. I talked to her care team today and they've made arrangements with the rehab facility. They're going to move her next week."

"Oh, wow...and that's better than sending her home with a full-time nurse?" Chloe asked.

"Definitely. She needs way more specialized care still. The plan is for her to be there for a couple of weeks and then she can come home with a full-time caretaker. I know we can all help some, but we all work. Levi said he could work from home at her house, but it's not ideal." She then talked about all the possibilities and ways they could divvy up some of the responsibilities, and it was more than Chloe was prepared to deal with right now.

"There you are!" Jade said as she came closer. "Hey, Chloe! Hey, Tanner! Mom just told me you guys were here!"

"Hey, Jade," Chloe murmured.

"Billie, I just got the email that the new mixers are

coming next week! That's a month sooner than we were expecting! Isn't that great!"

"That's awesome! Oh, I can't wait to use them and..."

Chloe tuned them out and gave Tanner an apologetic smile before leaning over slightly. "Maybe we should have stayed at the school."

He waved her off. "It's not a big deal. I'm sure they're eager to head home after a long day and we'll be able to work on our stuff."

"Mom! Mom! Grandma said I could have two snicker-doodles because I got an A on my math test!"

Yup, Jade's son Silas ran over to join them now too.

"Great job, buddy!" Jade said as she hugged him.

"Hey, Aunt Chloe! Check it out, I got an A on my math test! And you know how much I hate math!"

"I know you do," she said with amusement. "But you're a natural at it. I'm proud of you!"

"Thanks!" And then he ran off.

"What are you guys up to?" Jade asked them. "We're not interrupting anything, are we?"

"Well, um...we need to go over a unit we're starting next week," Chloe began. "I thought this would be a good and quiet place to do it, but..."

"Oh, this time of day is usually chaos," Billie explained. "Once all the schools let out and the cars are through with carpool, a lot of the families stop here for a snack and to get a jump on homework. You would have been better off staying at the school."

Note to self...remember that.

"Anyway, I need to go. I'm heading up to the hospital to see Mom. I'm going to stop at home first. I've got a pot roast cooking in the slow cooker that I'm going to bring up and share with her. She hates the hospital food. I'll talk to you over the weekend!" Waving, she turned and walked away.

"I don't know how she does it all," Jade said with a sigh. "Or when she sleeps. It's crazy how much she does every day. Levi and I really worry about her."

Chloe nodded before taking a sip of her tea.

"Who do we worry about?" Levi asked as he came up behind Jade and kissed her on the cheek.

You have got to be kidding me! Chloe quietly fumed.

"Hey, kiddo," he said as he stepped over and kissed her too. "How's school going?"

Rather than be annoyed that she and Tanner were clearly never going to be alone to talk about anything, she simply smiled at her brother and told him how much she was enjoying her new class. Then he asked Tanner the same thing and he replied the same way.

"You guys are genuine heroes," Levi told them. "I have trouble doing homework with just Silas every night. I don't know how you do it all day, every day, with so many kids." Laughing, he shook his head. "All I'm saying is that I'm thankful for teachers."

"Yes, we know, honey," Jade said with a grin as she patted his arm. "Now how about we take our boy out for pizza? He got an A on his math test!"

"That's amazing! Let's do it!" Smiling at Tanner and Chloe, he wished them a good night as Jade waved and did the same.

Chloe let out a long breath. "I think that should be all of my siblings," she said with a weak smile. "I'm so sorry. I know we're a lot."

"Nah, I think it's awesome. I'd like to think if my brother were still alive, we'd want to hang out whenever we ran into each other." He took a sip of his coffee, and all

Chloe wanted to do was hug him. As much as she was just majorly annoyed by her family, she was incredibly thankful for them.

"Mr. Westyn! Look! My mom bought me the pug book that we read today in class!"

Both she and Tanner smiled at the little girl who ran over to their table.

"That's great, Evie! Are you going to read it to your mom?"

She giggled. "I can't read, Mr. Westyn!" Then she giggled some more. "But Mom said she'll read it to me tonight before I go to bed!"

That's when Evie's mom came over to gush at how much her daughter loved school and how she talked about Tanner all the time. Chloe smiled as she listened, and she truly was happy that he was connecting with his students. It was a far cry from how she thought things would go, so this was a pleasant surprise.

"Have a good weekend, Mr. Westyn!" Evie said as she and her mom walked away.

And then two more students came over to talk to them—both of them from Tanner's class—and after that, one of Chloe's former students came over to do the same. By the time they were done talking to everyone, her tea was luke-warm and it was getting dark out. She pulled out her phone and gasped.

"What's the matter?"

"It's almost six o'clock!" Sighing, she shook her head. "So much for planning next week's unit."

Tanner took a sip of his coffee and grimaced. "That's cold." Pushing the cup to the side, he frowned. "Next time, we'll stay at the school and maybe order takeout."

That was all fine and well, but it didn't help them right now.

"Would you like to join me for dinner?" she blurted out.

His eyes went a little wide and it was kind of adorable. "You mean...now?"

She nodded. "I'm making some chicken enchiladas and fresh guacamole. It's nothing special, but if you give me an hour, you can come over and I can guarantee no one's going to interrupt us."

At least...she hoped they wouldn't—not after she just finished talking to her entire family.

"That sounds great! Can I bring anything?"

"Um...maybe some wine?"

Ugh...did I make this sound like a date by saying that?

"Perfect! I just need your address and let's say 7:00? Will that be enough time?"

Another nod. "Absolutely." She gave him her address and collected her things, eager to get home and have some time to get ready. It would be nice to change into comfy clothes and just embrace the silence for a little while, but... she'd have to see how that went.

They walked out to their cars together, and Tanner seemed genuinely excited about the invitation. He drove away first, and as soon as his car was out of sight, Chloe pulled out her phone and called Ash.

"Well, well, well...this isn't tomorrow," she said coyly.

"Oh, hush! Put your brownies and sex aside; I have a crisis here!"

Fortunately, Ash didn't make a joke or do anything like she normally did. "Alright, talk to me."

"I invited Tanner to my house for dinner! I did it because no one left us alone at the coffee shop and we didn't get to do any of our work stuff. So I asked him to dinner and told him to bring wine!" She groaned. "I made it a date, didn't I?" It wasn't a question.

"Okay, first, relax. Nothing wrong with asking him to bring wine, just like there's nothing wrong if this is kind of a date. Are there rules against dating a fellow teacher?"

"No."

Ash snickered. "You answered rather quickly. I'm guessing you looked into this already."

"Maybe."

"Fine. So...no rule against it. You have to think positive. People date one another all the time and sometimes it works, sometimes it doesn't. If it doesn't, it might be awkward for a little while, but ultimately, it's not a big deal. You're not prone to drama, so...be positive. This could be a good thing!"

"I don't know..."

"Way to be positive," Ash murmured.

"Could you *please*...?"

"Look, go home, get comfy, and remember to breathe. It's all going to be okay. And if you start to get twitchy, text me and I'll talk you through it, okay?"

It wasn't ideal, but it was her only choice.

"Okay. Thanks. I love you."

"Love you too. And good luck!"

* * *

At 6:59, Tanner pulled into Chloe's driveway and let out a long breath. She only lived two blocks away from him. How crazy was that? And her craftsman bungalow looked a lot like his. Well, like a lot of houses in the area, but hers looked newly updated too.

Grabbing the bottle of wine and his curriculum binder, he felt oddly conflicted. Was this just a dinner between colleagues or...a date? He clearly remembered what she told him on the first day of school, but...what if she changed her mind? What if this was her way of letting him know she changed her mind?

He glanced down at himself and suddenly hated the jeans, t-shirt, and sneakers he opted for. Was he too casual? Did he have anything in his car to change into?

"And where would you change, genius?" he mumbled.

"Tanner?" Chloe was standing in the doorway watching him. "Do you need help with anything?"

Yeah, not freaking myself out...

"Nope! I have everything. Just making sure I had my keys!" Fortunately, he did, and as he walked up her front steps, he noticed she was dressed super casually too.

So...maybe not a date?

For crying out loud, enough!

"Hey," she said softly as she stepped aside to let him in. "Thanks for coming over."

Smiling, he stepped into the living room. "No problem. Apparently I only live two blocks away so it wasn't hard to get here." They both laughed and he followed her into the kitchen. "Dinner smells amazing!" And when they reached the kitchen, he saw she had the table set and there was a bowl of fresh guacamole and another with salsa beside a huge basket of tortilla chips. "Wow! This all looks delicious!"

"Thanks," she said and he noticed that she blushed. "I'll open the wine. Have a seat and help yourself."

He sat, but he forced himself not to taste anything until she joined him. A minute later, she handed him a glass of wine and took her seat. Once she was settled, Tanner lifted his glass to her. "Here's to some creative planning, good food, and an enjoyable evening. Cheers!"

Chloe tapped her glass to his. "Cheers."

For a moment, he feared things were going to be awkward—mainly because Chloe seemed like she was going shy on him—but she surprised him by launching into a description of what she made and how long it would take for the main course to be served.

Helping himself to some of the guacamole and chips, he took a bite and moaned with pleasure. "Damn, Chloe. Even if the enchiladas burned and we couldn't eat them, I could make a meal out of the chips, guac, and salsa! They're delicious!"

She smiled. "Thank you. I was thinking about this meal all week. I like to make a big dinner on Friday nights so I can have the leftovers during the weekend. Although Billie sort of made me think that I should make stuff and bring it up to the hospital when I go to visit my mom. I never would have..." She stopped abruptly. "Sorry. No more Donovan family stuff tonight. It was too much while we were at the coffee shop, and I don't want to subject you to any more of it."

"I honestly didn't mind. It was good to get an update on how your mom is doing, and listening to all the other stuff just makes me feel a little more connected to the town."

"I heard you played poker with my brother and some of his friends last weekend," she said as she made a small plate for herself.

Nodding, he explained how it all came about because he met Will at the pizza place and struck up a conversation. "Because of my skiing career, I'm just used to talking to everyone I meet and making friends."

"Do you miss it? The competing?"

"Not really," he admitted. "It stopped being fun, but I was happy that there were companies that still wanted me to endorse their products. It helped me make the transition from competitive athlete to...well, teaching."

"They're just so drastically different. Like...I still can't figure out how you went from such a high-profile career to teaching in such a small town."

He believed in being honest and hoped it didn't make her think less of him. "Well...moving to a small town really wasn't part of the plan. Most of the schools I applied to were all in big cities. Unfortunately, I waited too long to put applications out and by the time I did, most of the positions were filled. Plus, my goal was to teach fifth grade. When Principal Kincaid offered me the kindergarten teaching position, I didn't jump at it." Pausing, he took a sip of his wine. "But, I knew I needed a job and being that the town had a ski resort so close by, it seemed like a good fit."

"What if a position became available for a fifth-grade class someplace else? Would you leave?"

Shaking his head, he told her, "I am committed to this year. Principal Kincaid believes that now that I'm here in the district, I'd be considered if a position for one of the older grades opened up. But for now, I'm happy where I am. I'll admit, I never considered teaching kindergarten— because those teachers are the ones with the hardest jobs— but so far, I'm not hating it."

"Why do you think they're the hardest jobs?"

"Because you're teaching them everything they're going to need to prepare them for the next twelve years of their life and beyond! Remember that book, *All I Really Need to Know I Learned in Kindergarten?* It's the truth! Every foundation about being out in the world and in school, you're the one teaching them that. I think what you do is amazing and...it's all still a little terrifying to me."

The look she gave him said she didn't quite believe him. "Oh, come on, Tanner. You're the most confident person I've ever met. You know you're doing a great job. Your students love you and the parents are impressed too."

He took another sip of his wine before leaning forward a little. "I've told you before; it's all about appearing to be confident. It doesn't mean it's how I feel. All the years I competed, I had to look confident. I had to believe in myself. Even when I was scared or not feeling my best, I still had to go out there and do my job." He shrugged. "Now it's just the way I live."

"Is that how you want to live?"

Frowning, he paused. "What do you mean?"

"I mean...I get the idea of believing in yourself and putting on a brave face even when you don't feel it, but...do you allow yourself to just feel? Do you accept that some days you're just not at your best, or do you beat yourself up for it?"

"Um..." He laughed softly. "That was a pretty heavy question."

"You're right. Sorry. There's just something about you that fascinates me. Like I can't figure you out."

Putting his glass down, he met her gaze. "Do you want to figure me out?" It was a bold question, he knew that, but he was also dying to know the answer.

All she did was nod.

Okay, so that meant...?

"I'm going to be fully transparent here, Chloe," he said carefully. "I like you. I thought after the kiss we shared that maybe you liked me too and wanted to get to know me. But you sort of cut that down quick and I respected that."

"I know," she quietly admitted. "The whole thing kind of freaked me out and you have to know that I don't normally do that sort of thing. Ask anyone and they'll tell you that."

Reaching across the table, he placed his hand on top of hers. "I'm not asking anyone anything because it's no one's business but ours. I like that you felt like you could do something like that with me and...I wouldn't be opposed if you wanted to do something like that again."

The blush was back in full force as she looked down at their hands.

"Either way, I'm just happy to be here. If you want us to just be colleagues who are friends, then I'm fine with that, but I wanted you to know how I feel too. So if you'd rather we just have dinner and discuss the curriculum, it's okay. I'm not going to be offended, and I'm certainly not going to put any pressure on you."

She didn't say anything right away, but as she slowly pulled her hand out from under his, she said, "I'd like to just see how the night goes. No plan, no agenda. Just us taking the time to get to know each other and talk about...whatever." Then she laughed softly. "I mean, I really do want to talk about the curriculum, but it's not the only thing. Is that okay?"

"More than." And that's when Tanner felt like he could finally relax. Scooping up some guacamole on a chip, he asked, "So...why Mexican? How did this become your specialty?"

And for the next hour, they discussed her love of cooking, his lack of knowing how to cook anything other than the basics, favorite books, movies...everything you would cover on a first date.

When the enchiladas were ready, Chloe served them,

129

and they talked about Tanner's career in skiing and his spokesperson responsibilities.

"When the season opens, I'll go up to the lodge and do some sort of opening ceremony with them and then sign stuff in the pro shop," he explained. "My sponsors haven't organized anything else for me recently, but I let them know about this event."

"Would they ask you to travel to different events?"

"They have in the past, but they know I'm teaching now, and my schedule isn't as flexible as it used to be."

"But...won't that be a deterrent to them? Like...why would they keep you on if you weren't able to be where they want you to be?"

Good question.

But he shrugged. "We'll cross that bridge when we come to it. I knew I wasn't going to do that sort of thing forever, but for as long as they still want me, I'll do my best to appear wherever they'd like." He took a bite of his dinner. "Do you ski?"

She laughed. "Um...no. I'm completely uncoordinated and really okay with it. The last time I tried to ski, I was fifteen and I broke my arm, so..."

"Gotcha. It's good to know your strengths."

"And weaknesses," she teased. "But...I'm a great spectator and love sitting with a cup of hot cocoa and watching my friends and family ski. Sometimes I go sledding, though. That's always fun."

"It looks like there are some great hills around here for it."

Nodding, she agreed. "I think you're going to enjoy winter here in Sweetbriar."

Looking up at her, he smiled. "I believe you're right."

And it had nothing to do with the weather.

"Okay, so Billie loves to bake, you love to cook. What about Levi and Ashlynn?"

The bark of laughter was unexpected. "Oh my goodness. Ash doesn't cook at all. I mean...she can do some basic stuff, but Reid is definitely in charge of their kitchen. But she does hair and makeup like no one else and has a flair for decorating. And Levi...well...he tries." She grinned. "And we weren't going to talk about my family anymore, remember?"

"You're right, you're right. I just like figuring out the dynamics of a big family. Mine is small, so..."

"Tell me about them," she softly prompted, and Tanner didn't even hesitate.

"I swear I won the parent lottery. They are...they're amazing and probably the strongest and most supportive people I've ever known."

Chloe picked up her wine and shifted in her seat. "How did they feel about you leaving skiing behind to become a teacher?"

He chuckled. "They wondered why I waited so long to look for a teaching position." Then he shook his head. "No, they always wanted me to chase after my dreams. And from the time I was in middle school, I knew I wanted to teach. But I was heavily involved with skiing, even at that age, and it was always a rule that I had to go to college and get a degree. I couldn't simply rely on competing. There were times when school and competition schedules made things difficult, and sometimes my folks hired a tutor to travel with us to keep me from falling behind."

"That's very impressive."

"Education is important. I always knew that," he said solemnly. "They wanted to give me every opportunity to succeed. Especially after my brother passed away. Believe me when I tell you, I've been to more doctors and had more scans of my body than you can ever imagine."

"They just wanted to make sure you were healthy," she commented. "And I'm pretty sure any parent in their situation would do the same thing."

He nodded. "I always understood, but...I hated it. Like..." Sitting back a bit, he raked both hands through his hair. "As an adult, I look back and wonder how they even carried on. We've talked about it some, and all they say is that they had to keep going because they had me. So naturally, I wanted to do everything I could to make them proud and give them joy." He took a sip of his wine. "That's not to say that I think I saved them or anything, but...we banded together and made a life that my brother is hopefully looking down and smiling at."

Tanner saw the unshed tears shining in Chloe's eyes and knew he needed to change the vibe fast.

"Where do you get tiny pumpkins for the kids to paint?" he asked before taking the last bite of his enchilada.

The question flustered her for a moment, but she quickly recovered. "Um...the grocery store gets them for me if I let them know in advance."

"And did you?"

"I did. And for you too. I'm sorry, I know that was presumptuous, but..."

"Are you kidding? I'm thankful! Like I said, I haven't been reading too far ahead in the binder, so..."

She stood and picked up her plate. "Let me just clean this up and we can go inside and look at everything. I'll just..."

But Tanner was on his feet instantly. "I can help!" Then he realized he sounded a little overzealous and had to laugh at himself. "What I meant is that you don't have to do it all yourself. I'm happy to help."

"Thanks, Tanner."

Together, they had everything cleaned up in minutes, all the while chatting about tiny pumpkins.

"They're actually called Jack-Be-Littles," she told him. "And they're the perfect size for tiny hands. You'll be amazed at how creative they can be at decorating them."

"I'm amazed at a lot of things they do and how eager most of them are to learn new things. I thought for sure they'd be easily distracted and hard to keep their attention, but other than a few stragglers, they've been great."

"Would you like another glass of wine before we go inside?"

"Sure!" Chloe topped off their glasses before they went into the living room. Tanner brought his binder with him and saw Chloe's was already out on the coffee table. "You know, from the outside our houses look kind of similar, but your floor plan's a little different from mine. Do you have rooms upstairs?"

"It's unfinished up there. If I buy the house, I think I'd like to get an estimate on maybe making that a master suite."

"That's what mine is," he explained. "It was a huge selling point for me."

"Oh, so you bought the house?"

He shook his head. "No, just renting, but there were a few houses to choose from, and I liked that layout the best. I have a one-year lease, so I'll re-evaluate then."

"I have the lease too, with the option to buy. I really do like the house, but I'm not sure it's my dream house."

"So why not just wait until you find your dream house?"

Rather than answer, she just waved him off. "Other

than the Jack-Be-Littles and leaf collecting, do you have any ideas about a fun fall activity?"

Reaching over, he placed a hand on her knee. "Hey, did I say something wrong? I didn't mean to upset you. I just thought..."

She sighed loudly. "I got tired of living in an apartment. My siblings—who are not going to be the focus of this story, I swear—were all doing these great things with their lives and I kind of felt like I was standing still. My cousin Patrick and his wife Marissa were handling a lot of the real estate around here, and I went to them to see what I could do. Virginia has some great programs for teachers when they buy a home, so I'm obviously eligible for those, but what I consider my dream home and what I can realistically afford are two totally different things."

"Ah. Gotcha. Yeah, I have that too. My place is perfectly fine, but I don't see myself living there like a forever home."

"Well, to be fair, you're still not sure if Sweetbriar is going to be your forever home either."

It was really too soon to tell, but so far, he didn't see any reason to leave.

"Only time will tell," he said quietly. His hand was still on her knee, and he couldn't take his eyes off of her lips, and as much as he was enjoying talking with her, what he really wanted was to kiss her. He was just afraid that he'd make it awkward if he just came out and said it.

"Tanner?"

"Hmm?"

"It's okay, you know."

"What is?"

"If you want to kiss me," she whispered.

His eyes went wide. "Oh God. Did I say that out loud?"

She giggled. "No, but you've been staring at my lips, and I just thought..."

He didn't let her finish. Instead, he leaned in and pressed his lips to hers, and they both seemed to relax almost immediately. Her lips were just as soft as he remembered, and this time he felt like he could take his time and savor the taste of her. As if of one mind, they each moved a little closer, and his hand skimmed up from her knee to her waist. She was warm and curvy and tasted a little like their spicy dinner, and it all equaled a very desirable package.

Chloe let out a faint little hum as her arms went around him. He took the kiss deeper—tracing her bottom lip with the tip of his tongue—and then it was like they both were so damn thrilled to be there. His arms wrapped around her until he was almost lifting her into his lap, and the kiss went on and on.

At some point, they shifted positions until they were lying down on the sofa and it reminded him a little of being back in high school and secretly making out with his girlfriend while his parents were upstairs reading. If anything, it made the moment even more remarkable because this made him feel happier than he'd been in a long time. He was enjoying himself—enjoying just simply kissing this beautiful, desirable woman—and he knew it wasn't going to go any further than this tonight. It didn't need to. They were just getting to know each other, and with the way she kissed and moved against him, Tanner knew he was going to enjoy every minute of it.

It could have been minutes, it could have been hours, but when they finally broke apart, they were breathless. "Wow," Chloe whispered as she ran her hand through his hair. "That was..."

"Yeah, it was," he said, resting his forehead against hers.

"But it's probably getting late, and..." He moved to sit up and reached for his phone. Sure enough, it was almost midnight. Then he said something he never thought would ever come out of his mouth. "I hate to say this, but...it's late and I'm exhausted. You have no idea how lame that makes me feel, but..."

She sat up beside him and promptly yawned.

And then laughed.

"Obviously, I get it. I know I was up at six, so...it's been a long day."

Turning his head, he smiled at her. "I had a really great time tonight. I know we still need to talk about the curriculum, but...maybe you can come to my place tomorrow for lunch? I'll order sandwiches from the café and the weather's supposed to be great, so we can even go and walk in the park and you can show me some of the places you like to take the kids to."

Her eyes shone bright with unshed tears again, and he didn't know why.

"Did I say something wrong?"

Leaning in, she kissed him again, and when she pulled back, she cupped his jaw. "That was possibly the most perfect thing you ever could have said. I'd love to join you for lunch tomorrow."

Relief washed over him. Kissing her palm, he reluctantly let her go.

And yawned.

And then laughed.

After he picked up his phone, binder, and keys, he faced her. "I hope there are no regrets this time," he said carefully. "Because I would hate it if you still felt that way."

"Tanner, I can't apologize enough for that whole situation and giving you the cold shoulder that day. I just...I got scared. You make me feel things that...well...weren't great at first. And I was afraid that you weren't as into me as I was into you, and..." She sighed. "I'm not the kind of woman that ever attracts a guy like you."

Were the men in this town stupid? Did they not see what an amazing woman Chloe was?

Their loss...

"I'm not sure what to say to that except that I am most definitely as into you as you are into me." He grinned and kissed her softly on the lips. "And you can set the pace with how things go from here. I'm just happy that you're willing to give me a second chance to make a first impression."

Then they kissed again before he wished her a good-night and left, already looking forward to tomorrow.

Chapter Eight

The weekend was amazing.

On Saturday, she and Tanner had taken their lunch to the park and had a picnic. Then, they'd simply walked some of the many paths and thought of activities to do with their classes with all the different colored leaves. It was so nice to have something like this in common! It made her realize just how much of a struggle it had been dating someone like Evan, who she had nothing in common with.

Lunch had turned into dinner and a movie—which they missed most of because they were more interested in kissing on his sofa. Then on Sunday, they worked on their weekly lesson plan together at her place before ordering a pizza and letting it get cold because they were more interested in kissing some more.

Chloe could honestly say she'd never been happier. And for all her worrying about what it would be like at work if they got involved, it was awesome! They shared their lunch break together and ate in either his classroom or hers, and they'd talk about how their days were going. He was really settling in to teaching and she was very proud of him. They'd worked on several joint projects this week with their classes, and it was the most fun she'd had teaching since she started. Every day was just so enjoyable and gave her so much more to look forward to!

She particularly loved the secret little flirty smiles they shared whenever they saw each other, and just how much fun it was to sit and talk with him about lesson planning—which was possibly the least sexy thing in the world, and yet with Tanner, it stimulated her in a way that sex never had.

Ugh...what is wrong with me?

Nothing, she reminded herself. There was something very satisfying about connecting with someone on a physical level, but she was finding that having the intellectual connection was just so much more.

Maybe some people would think it was weird that she found the intellectual connection...well...sexy, but she didn't care. Tanner Westyn was turning out to be the total package, and she never even saw it coming.

But for all the fun she was having, it made her feel a little guilty. Every day after school, she went to spend time with her mother. They had moved her to the rehab facility on Wednesday, and it just broke her heart to see her there. Her bruises were healing, but for a woman who took great pride in her appearance, Chloe could tell how self-conscious her mother was about how she looked. Their conversations had been a bit stilted, and she didn't want to mention her relationship with Tanner because she felt like it would sound like she was bragging. Still, she was thankful for the progress her mom was making and couldn't wait until she could come home. Every night when she left, she would cry all the way home. Most of the time she'd call

Ashlynn, who would calm her down, but it was like being on an emotional rollercoaster.

Now it was Friday, and her last student had just been picked up. The plan was to go home and relax for a bit, and then she and Tanner were going up to Summit Ridge for dinner. She knew he was excited to show her a bit about his life outside of teaching and she was looking forward to learning about it.

"Hey, beautiful," he said as he strolled into her room. Pausing, he looked around. "Everyone picked up?"

She nodded. "Madison and her mom just left." As soon as the words were out of her mouth, Tanner had her in his arms and was kissing her. When they broke apart, she smiled up at him. "I really like ending the school day like that."

He grinned. "Me too." Taking a step back, he looked a little uncertain.

"Is everything okay?"

He hesitated for a moment. "I wanted to throw something out there, and if I'm being too presumptuous, please let me know."

"O-kay..."

"We have dinner reservations tonight at seven up at Summit Ridge, but...I was wondering if you might...I mean...I just thought..."

"Tanner?"

"Hmm?"

"Just say what you want to say."

After letting out a long breath, he looked at her, his expression serious. "I thought maybe we could...reserve a suite for the night," he said gruffly. "Maybe it's too soon, and the last thing I want to do is pressure you, but..."

"Let's do it!" she blurted out. "I mean...the room. Let's

reserve a room. I think that would be a wonderful thing to do! Can we check in before our dinner reservation? Would that be enough time? Ooh...do you think we could order room service in the morning?" Pausing, she laughed softly. "Sorry, but I've always wanted to do that."

Moving in close, Tanner rested his hands on her hips. "Beautiful girl, we can order room service for dinner if you'd like and then again for breakfast."

Her eyes went wide and her heart raced because this sounded like the best thing ever.

And not really because of the room service, but because it meant a whole lot of time alone with Tanner, where neither of them had to leave at the end of the night.

"I'm going to go home and pack right now," she said before giving him a quick kiss. "Wait...what if they don't have any rooms available? What if...?"

Pulling his phone out, Tanner scrolled a bit and then put the phone to his ear. "Yes, good afternoon," he said smoothly. "I was curious if you have any suites available tonight?" He paused and smiled at her. "You do? Fantastic!" Another pause. "Westyn. Tanner Westyn." Then he hummed happily. "That's me! I used to compete." And yet another pause. "Well, thank you! That would be incredibly generous of you!" He gave Chloe a thumbs up. "Oh, one night or two?"

He looked at her for an answer and she decided to be bold. "Two," she whispered.

"Two nights, Micah. Thank you so much and we'll see you soon." After another minute of conversation, he hung up. "Well, Miss Donovan, you and I will be staying in one of Summit Ridge's VIP suites this weekend. Pack your bathing suit because our suite comes with a hot tub." Then he wrapped his arms around her. "Or maybe don't.

Because it's super private and we don't have to wear anything at all."

Don't look nervous...don't look nervous...

But clearly, she looked nervous, because Tanner completely backtracked.

"I mean...again, no pressure. Sorry. That was just... *ugh*...I got carried away. You don't have to do anything you don't want to. No worries," he assured her.

Reaching up, Chloe cupped his jaw. "Let's just see where the weekend takes us, okay?" Then, with another quick kiss, she stepped out of his embrace and began collecting her things. "How much time do I have before you want to pick me up?"

"Will an hour be enough? It's already almost 4:30, and by the time we get home and pack and I come pick you up, it will be almost 5:45. Our dinner reservation is at seven, so..."

"An hour is perfect," she told him. "Come on! This is going to be a great weekend!"

That's what she kept telling herself as they walked out of the school and she got in her car.

Then she panicked and immediately called Ash.

"Hey! Any chance you have time to come to the salon? I just had a cancelation and you're due for a trim."

"There is literally no time for that!" she said in a near hysterical tone. "I'm going away for the weekend with Tanner and it all sounded like a good idea, but...I've never gone on a sexy getaway before! Every time Evan suggested one, I chickened out!"

"Wait, so you're going on a sexy getaway? When did this happen?"

"Just now! Jeez, Ash, come on! Pay attention!" she huffed with annoyance. "We had dinner reservations up at the lodge and then Tanner suggested that maybe we get a suite for tonight. Then he called and because everyone there seems to know his name, they got us one of the VIP suites with a hot tub for the weekend! I don't even have sexy underwear! What am I supposed to do?"

"Well, first you have to breathe. Second, I'll meet you at your house in thirty minutes and..."

"Tanner's picking me up in an hour! There's no time!" And yeah, she was on the verge of hyperventilating.

"Okay, I'm already in my car. Just go home and start packing and stop freaking out. I'll be there as fast as I can!" Then the line went dead and Chloe knew her sister was right. She needed to stop freaking out and go home and get herself ready.

"Still doesn't make sexy underwear magically appear in my drawers," she mumbled, but drove home with a little more calmness than she had a few minutes ago.

Once at her house, she ran inside and took the world's fastest—and yet extremely thorough—shower. Then, with her hair in a towel and in nothing but her robe, she began rummaging through her closet for what she was going to pack. She'd already picked out the dress she was going to wear to dinner and it was hanging on the closet door; now, she just needed at least two casual outfits, another dress for dinner tomorrow night, and something to wear to bed.

Or do I?

"I'm here! I'm here!" Ashlynn called out as she slammed the front door. They always had keys to each other's places, and Chloe was glad to have her barging in right now. Running into the bedroom with an armload of stuff, she breathlessly dumped it all on the bed. "I bought stuff to quickly do your hair, and I had just ordered a bunch of sexy lingerie that I haven't worn and they still have the tags on them, but you can pick out whatever you like! *Whew...*" Bending over slightly, she nodded. "It's okay to call me a hero. Because I am."

"Good grief, Ash! Again, there's no time!" But as she moved closer to the bed, she began rummaging through the clothes. "Go plug in whatever hair stuff you need to while I see if there's anything here I'd be brave enough to wear."

"Already thought of it, and I think everything here will meet with your approval. Check out the teal blue bra and panties. The color is amazing and would look great on you." She walked into the bathroom. "Ugh, you have no real counter space in here! It's going to be a little hard to work my magic..."

She let her sister ramble on while she picked out a hot pink silk nightie, the teal set, a black matching set, and...

"You know what, Ash? I'm taking it all! I can't decide!"

"I know! That's only a portion of what I bought for myself. There's enough variety there to fit whatever you're feeling and Tanner's going to love it no matter what." She popped her head back into the room. "Now come in here and let's get your hair dried and styled."

Running in, she sat down and let her sister do her thing. "Am I crazy for agreeing to this? It's kind of soon, isn't it? Like...should I have said no or waited another week?"

"Do you want to wait another week?"

"No, but..."

"Then it's not too soon. You need to stop thinking so much and enjoy yourself. You seem to really be into this guy and you're not the impulsive one in the family. So if you said yes to him, then I'd have to say that it's something you really want."

And the thing is, she really wanted Tanner—probably more than she had ever wanted a man before, but...

"But...he's like...he's not the type of guy I thought I'd fall for. We have so much in common and I love just sitting and talking to him, but...he's kind of famous. He's lived a very different life than me, and he's probably been with, like... dozens of women. What if he loses interest because I'm not like one of those...you know...ski bunnies?"

Ashlynn snickered. "Sometimes the things that come out of your mouth are completely adorable. But you're wrong about this. It doesn't matter how many women he's been with before—and I'll bet you it's not nearly as many as you'd think. Remember that he wants to be with *you*. You didn't chase after him like a ski bunny, okay? He was the one who wanted to pursue you. So relax and don't get stuck in your own head, okay?"

Chloe nodded, but she wasn't there yet.

Still, Ash made her hair and her makeup look fabulous, and when they walked back into the bedroom, her sister even started putting her things in her weekender bag so she could get dressed.

"I don't know what I'd do without you," Chloe told her as she grabbed the black bra and panties and shimmied into them. "I planned on wearing the black dress hanging on the door to dinner, but should I wear it now or wear something else and change when we get to the hotel?"

"Change when you get there, but let's find you something fetching to wear now." In the closet, Ashlynn pulled out a pair of black skinny jeans, a copper-colored chunky sweater, and black ankle boots. "This way, it all works with the black undies. You know, in case you skip dinner and get right to the good stuff when you get to the suite." She pulled out a few more things and tossed them on the bed. "A hoodie, a flannel, I already packed you a couple of pairs of leggings, this hunter green wrap dress is perfect for another

145

dinner...these shoes are perfect..." And five minutes later, she was completely packed.

"Damn, Ash. That was impressive."

"I know, right?" her sister preened. "And just in time, because I think Tanner just pulled up."

"Oh my God! Already? How do I look?" she rambled as she finished getting dressed.

Ashlynn walked over and quickly fixed Chloe's hair. "Perfect. Now go and have fun. I'll lock up." She gave her a fierce hug. "Walk out there with confidence and rock his world tonight!"

"Oh God..."

"Or...simply cuddle with him and have a totally pleasant evening," Ash said as she hooked the strap of the weekender over Chloe's shoulder and ushered her out the door. "Take your purse and keys and have fun. I love you and you better call me when you get home on Sunday night! Or text me at some point this weekend!"

"I will, I will. Thank you for everything!" And then she was walking out the door and hoping she looked confident.

Because I certainly don't feel it...

But when Tanner climbed out of his SUV and smiled with appreciation, she suddenly felt it.

Confident.

Beautiful.

Desired.

And it was a heady feeling.

* * *

"Your room is on the tenth floor, concierge level," the desk clerk said as he handed over their key cards. "And on behalf of Summit Ridge, we hope you have a wonderful stay. Would you like help with your luggage?"

"Thank you," Tanner replied, "we would."

Someone was immediately at their side leading them to the bank of elevators. He took Chloe's hand in his and this all felt a little surreal. They had made small talk on the drive over, and he could tell she was a little nervous, but he hoped she wasn't regretting her decision.

"This place is amazing," she whispered as they got on the elevator. "I toured it when it opened over the summer, but we only got to see the common areas. I never saw any of the guest rooms. I can't even imagine what the VIP suite is going to be like."

He was going to say something blasé, but knew he'd end up sounding like he was bragging. "I'm sure it's going to be great. And hopefully the view will be spectacular." Then he realized it was dark out. "Something I guess we'll find out in the morning, right?"

"Mm-hmm..."

When the doors opened on their floor, the bellman led them to a room at the end of the hall. "You have one of the best rooms we have," he told them. "A corner suite with a view of the mountains and the lake." He opened the door and put their bags down before turning on the lights. "The concierge lounge is open nightly until eleven and you can get breakfast there until ten-thirty every morning, snacks from eleven to four, and then appetizers from five to seven, and dessert from eight to eleven. If there's anything you need, please don't hesitate to ask. Have a good night."

Once he was gone, Tanner looked around the room and had to admit he was impressed. There was a king-size bed and floor to ceiling windows where he knew there'd be a magnificent view tomorrow. The bathroom was deluxe spa quality, and there was a fireplace that dominated one wall. There was a small sitting area, a kitchenette, and overall, it was the perfect room.

"What do you think?" he asked her.

"I think this is the fanciest room I've ever been in," she said with a nervous laugh. "I almost feel like I don't belong here."

That's when he went over and put her mind at ease as he kissed her. It was just meant to be a little slow and sweet and something to relax her, but the moment she pressed up against him, things escalated quickly. In the blink of an eye, they were both a little needier. The kiss went deeper, and they were moving across the room in a less than coordinated manner.

When they were standing beside the bed, Tanner tore his mouth from hers and whispered her name. Swallowing hard, he took in her flushed skin, her glossy lips, and slumberous eyes. "That was..."

"Not enough," she told him, her hand smoothing over his chest. "I know we have dinner reservations in less than an hour, but...do you think they'd deliver it up here?"

"Sweetheart, if they don't, we'll find some other place that will." And then he dove in for another kiss, this one deeper and wetter than the one before. His hand anchored in her hair, holding her to him, and all he wanted to do was get them onto that massive bed, peel her sweater up and over her head, and kiss every inch of her.

"I need you, Tanner," she panted, her head slowly falling back as he rained kisses along her throat. "Please."

It was all the encouragement he needed.

Carefully, he maneuvered them both to the bed, and when he looked down at Chloe, with her dark hair fanned out against the white comforter, she looked like an angel.

He had really been looking forward to simply taking her out on a proper date tonight at a fancy restaurant where they could eat a fantastic dinner, maybe do a little dancing, and then come up to their room and do...well...exactly what they were doing right now.

And that's when he realized that's the night he wanted.

Even if it meant...stopping.

Reluctantly, he moved away from her and stood up.

"Tanner?" her voice was a little trembly as she pushed up on her elbows to look at him. "Is everything okay? Did... did I do something wrong?" Then she sat up, mumbling something about being afraid of this.

"Hey," he said softly. "What does that mean?"

"What?"

"You just said you were afraid of this happening. Afraid of what?"

She got to her feet and walked over to the wall of windows, wrapping her arms around herself. "It's nothing."

He didn't buy that for a second.

Walking up behind her, he said her name and then waited.

"Look, I get it," she said, and he could see her reflection in the glass. She was staring out and not really seeing him. "With your celebrity status in the sporting world, you've been with a lot of women who were more...I don't know... just...sexier and worldlier than me. I was mentally prepared for you to maybe be a little disappointed; I just didn't think it would happen in the first three minutes."

Grasping her shoulders, Tanner spun her around and didn't let those big blue eyes sway him. "Are you out of your mind?" he said with part offense and part amusement. "I didn't get up because I was disappointed in anything,

Chloe. I got up because I felt like I was cheating us out of the night I really wanted us to have!"

Releasing her, he took several steps away and huffed out a breath.

"Believe it or not, I genuinely wanted to have dinner with you downstairs and then dance and maybe just walk around the lodge and *then* come up here. I hated the thought of you thinking that sex was the only reason I wanted us to come here!" Raking his hands through his hair, he let out a growl of frustration. "I would have been fine if we just came back here and talked all night!"

She didn't look fully convinced. "But..."

"And as for my celebrity status? Believe it or not, that had nothing to do with my personal or sexual life. Yes, I competed, and yes, there were a lot of women who chased after me, but that doesn't mean I slept with all of them. Because I was going to school—high school and then college —and I was always either training or competing, I didn't really get a lot of time to date. So whatever number of women you have in your head, you need to seriously lower it. Like...really, really, *really* lower it."

"Oh."

Slowly, he sauntered back over to her. "You, Chloe Donovan, never have to worry about being enough." Reaching up, he cupped her face. "You're everything." And then he kissed her thoroughly before lifting his head. "But I would very much like to take you to dinner. What do you say?"

Her first response was a giggle, but she shook her head. "I'd like that very much. I would like to change, though."

"Why don't you take the bathroom to freshen up, and I'll change out here?"

The smile she gave him was radiant. "That sounds perfect. Thank you."

Fifteen minutes later, she stepped out of the bathroom looking like the girl next door with a hint of vixen to her, and it hit him—not for the first time—how deceiving first impressions could be. How had he ever thought her to be plain?

Holding out his hand to her, he smiled. "Shall we?"

"Is it too early for our reservation?"

"If it is, maybe we'll grab a drink at the bar or just stroll around and check out what else the lodge has to offer. What do you think?"

"I think that sounds lovely." Placing her hand in his, they walked out the door and to the elevators. "That bathroom is amazing. I'm not usually in awe of stuff like that, but I feel like I'm going to go home and make angry faces at my bathroom after this."

That made him laugh. "I have a feeling I'll be doing the same thing."

When they got down to the restaurant and checked in, they were told that their table was actually ready. Following the hostess, Tanner kept his hand on the small of Chloe's back and marveled at the atmosphere—the dark paneling, the massive stone fireplace, the soft music. It was exactly what he was hoping for.

Holding out Chloe's chair for her, he waited for her to sit before taking the seat beside her. "This is nice, isn't it?"

She nodded. "Maybe I'm being dramatic, but I feel a little like Cinderella tonight. I've been to nice restaurants before, but...just everything about tonight just seems special."

"And it's only just begun," he murmured before placing a kiss on her cheek.

After that, they looked at the menu, ordered a bottle of wine, and decided to share the chateaubriand for two. They talked about school—something they did a lot—and from there, the conversation flowed from one topic to another with seemingly no awkward pauses.

When they were done eating, Tanner led her across the room closer to the bar and held her close while they danced to the piano music. By the third song, Chloe grinned up at him, "I think I need to sit back down. It's been a while since I've worn heels."

"No worries." Leading her back to the table, he asked, "What about dessert?"

"What if...we asked them to pack it to go and we ate it up in the room?" And there was that hint of vixen in her again. It was fascinating to see that side of her come out, and he couldn't wait to see it more.

"That can definitely be arranged," he told her, and within minutes, they placed their orders for a slice of chocolate mousse cheesecake and an order of the crème brûlée while acting like they weren't anxious as hell to go upstairs.

Tanner paid the check; they accepted the bag with their desserts and thanked their server before he helped Chloe to her feet. Then, hand in hand, they casually strolled through the restaurant, commenting on the décor as they made their way toward the hotel lobby.

At the elevator, they each stared straight ahead. "Dinner was fabulous," she told him. "And the wine was perfectly paired."

He nodded and almost breathed a sigh of relief when the doors opened and no one was waiting to get in with them. As soon as the doors closed, he turned and pulled Chloe into his arms and kissed her. Neither said a word, but he could feel the tension building as they clung to each other—while keeping a precarious grasp on the dessert bag.

On the tenth floor, they broke apart and he took her hand and led her down to their room and cursed his impatience. They stumbled through the door with a laugh and he took a moment to carefully place the bag down before turning to Chloe and simply looking his fill. She kicked off her shoes and walked toward him.

"Thank you for a wonderful evening, Tanner. I'm glad we went down to dinner like we had originally planned."

"Me too," he said gruffly, reaching up to caress her cheek. "Why don't you get comfortable? I can go down to the lounge and grab us something to drink and..."

She silenced him with a kiss. "I don't want you to go anywhere. I want to pick up where we left off earlier and then do all the things we were both thinking of." Another kiss. "And then we're going to be totally decadent and eat dessert in bed." When she paused this time, she giggled. "And maybe order some room service for something to drink. But only if you think that's okay."

"Whatever you want, beautiful, I'll make it happen."

Her smile went from sweet to sexy in the blink of an eye. "Whatever I want?"

He nodded.

Turning her back to him, she asked, "Can you unzip my dress?"

Stepping in close, he placed a kiss on the side of her throat. "I can." He inhaled the sweet, floral perfume she wore and could feel her tremble. Carefully, he pulled the zipper down and then watched as the dress dropped to the floor, pooling at her feet. She had on tiny scraps of black satin and lace, and when she turned around to face him, he almost forgot how to breathe.

Her name came out as a breathless plea, and as he led her over to the bed, he knew he'd never forget how she looked right now. She sat down and shimmied to the middle of the mattress before holding out her hand to him, and just like that, they were back where they were earlier.

Only this time, she was even more glorious.

Tanner's hand shook slightly as he reached up and caressed her from her jaw to her throat, and down to her breasts. And when he looked up and met her gaze, she licked her lips and said, "Please."

And just like that, his body covered hers, and what had already been a perfect night got even better.

* * *

"This cheesecake is amazing," Chloe said sometime after midnight. "I'm not usually a cheesecake person, but I'm a sucker for chocolate mousse and figured I'd try it." She hummed as she licked the spoon. "Now I'm really glad I did."

"I have to agree. The crème brûlée was fine, but the cheesecake was the real winner in the dessert category." Leaning over to the bedside table, he poured them each a glass of wine from the bottle that was just delivered from room service. "I also got a couple of bottles of water too. Just in case you wanted something other than wine."

"Mmm...thank you." Taking the glass from him, she took a sip. "It's even good with cheesecake!"

Chuckling softly, Tanner took a moment before taking his own sip and had to agree. "Definitely." She handed him the plate and then curled up beside him, mindful of the glass in her other hand. "Are you done with the dessert? Should I put the rest in the mini fridge?"

"That would mean you'd have to get out of the bed, and you already did that to get the wine." Then she hugged him. "There's really only a little bit left. I think we can let it go, don't you?"

Placing a kiss on the top of her head, he nodded. "I do. Plus, there's always tomorrow. We can get another slice."

"I'm going to tell Billie about it. She doesn't really do a lot of cheesecake recipes, but I think this one would be something she'd enjoy. *Oops!*"

"What? What's the matter?"

"No family talk."

"Chloe..."

"So, what are we going to do tomorrow? Obviously it's too warm out for snow, but we can still do a lot. At the summer festival, there were so many great activities available." She paused to think for a moment. "Um...there's an Alpine slide, a mountain coaster, a rock-climbing wall, ziplining, scenic lift rides, and then there are ATV and hiking trails. Do any of them sound like fun?"

"Are you kidding? They all do! I guess I really didn't think about what else a ski resort offers in the offseason. When I came up here last month, I was more interested in the winter activities." He placed another kiss on her head. "What about you? What's your favorite?"

"Hmm...the line was too long for the coaster when I was here this summer, but the slide was amazing! I would love to do that one again, and I'm sure we wouldn't have any trouble getting on the coaster if it's open." She snuggled closer again. "The scenic lift could be fun too. I wonder if they do them at sunset because I bet that could be beautiful." Then she yawned. "What do you think?"

Carefully, he took the wine from her hand and placed the glass on the bedside table. "I think we should see how we feel in the morning and then see what we're in the mood for then."

A soft giggle was her first reaction, and he had a feeling he knew exactly what she was thinking.

Because he already knew what he was going to be in the mood for.

More of her.

But if they got to experience more of the things the lodge provided, that might be fun too.

Chapter Nine

"Did you see the project Mr. Westyn's class is doing? My son is having the best time!"

"My niece is in his class, and my sister can't stop gushing over the creative way he's teaching! That skiing theme is just fantastic!"

"I can't even imagine what he'll come up with once the winter really hits around here! Do you think we can convince the school to let him take the kids on a field trip up to the lodge for lessons?"

Chloe quietly sighed as she sat in the corner of Books & Beans and read over her lesson plan for the next day. It had been a week since she and Tanner had their weekend getaway, and while she was deliriously happy, hearing things like the conversation happening at the next table had her feeling a little...

Jealous.

And she was ashamed to even think like that.

"It's so wonderful to see these new teachers thriving! I'll admit I was a little worried about so many new classes starting this year and so many new teachers coming in, but Mr. Westyn is like a breath of fresh air! Such energy!"

Okay, that one hurt a little. Chloe knew she wasn't the most exciting person, but she loved teaching and adored her students. She felt like she created a very nurturing environment for them.

But obviously not as fresh and fun or as creative as Tanner's.

Ugh...

She should be happy for him and the students. Heck, she should be thrilled! But right now, it felt forced. Teaching was the one area she had stood out. After living in the shadow of her siblings, teaching at Sweetbriar Elementary had been a way that she made a name for herself. Winning the Teacher of the Year award two years in a row had filled her with pride and given her a confidence she'd lacked for most of her life.

And that was all over now.

Beside her, one of the women gently pushed her chair back and banged right into Chloe's.

"Oh! Miss Donovan, hey," she said sheepishly. "I didn't see you there. Sorry!"

Obviously...

The other two women gave her a sympathetic smile before they all got up to leave, making her feel like they were suddenly aware of how their conversation might have sounded insulting to her.

Or, at the very least, a little insensitive.

Once they were gone, she let out a long—and somewhat loud—sigh. Every day she and Tanner talked about what they did in their classes, and she had been rambling on for weeks sharing her ideas with him and...it seemed like he wasn't really doing any of the things she was suggesting.

Things he told her he was doing.

Wait...has he been lying to me?

Now that the idea was out there, it took hold—hard. There was only one thing she could do. Standing, she quickly packed up her stuff and ran out to her car. She needed some answers, and she needed them now before this whole thing festered and made her do something crazy.

Her driving may have been a little erratic, but fortunately, she didn't have to go far. And in no time, she was parked and storming up to the door, yanking it open, and...

"Welcome to Color Me Crazy! What's up, Chloe?" Heather, the front desk receptionist, said with a big smile.

"Is Ash here? I need to talk to her."

"Your timing's perfect; she just finished with a client and is back in her office."

"Thanks." Clutching the strap of her purse, she walked with purpose toward the back corner of the salon. Fortunately, Ash's door was open and when she looked up, she smiled.

"Hey! This is a surprise! You should have called and told me you were stopping by. I was really jonesing for a cake pop. Billie offered one to me earlier and I turned her down, and I've been cursing myself all day for it."

Stepping into the office, Chloe shut the door and leaned against it. "Tanner's been lying to me," she blurted out before she could even think about it.

"What?" her sister cried in disbelief, instantly on her feet. "The bastard! Where is he? Do you need me to go with you and kick his ass? Should I call Reid?"

Okay, this was the brief reality check she needed to calm down. "No, you don't have to call Reid, and you're not kicking his ass." Pausing for a moment, she asked, "Why is that always your immediate reaction? How many asses have you actually kicked? Because I don't remember you ever..."

"It's a figure of speech, Chlo. Sheesh. Now sit down and tell me what's going on. What did he do?"

Taking the only other chair in the office, she sat and sighed and then launched into the conversation she heard at the coffee shop.

"Um..."

"And it's not the only time it's happened. Sometimes when I walk the kids out for carpool, I hear the parents talking. People are seriously gushing over him. *Gushing*, Ashlynn!"

"I get that, but..."

"And in all the gushing, they're talking about projects and lessons that he's doing that he doesn't tell me about! So every day when we talk about lesson plans and...and..."

"Projects?"

"Yes! Projects! Every day when we talk, he never mentions the stuff he's doing. So I go on and on and on about things I think he can do or things I've done in the past and he's always so supportive and telling me it all sounds great, but then he doesn't do any of them! Why would he lie to me?"

Her sister blinked at her for several moments before she spoke. "Let me get this straight...you're upset because he's making his class his own and not doing what you tell him to do. Do I have that right?"

"Well, when you say it like that, I sound like I'm being petty and childish," Chloe murmured.

"Because you *are* being petty and childish," Ashlynn said with a frown. "That's not like you. What in the world, Chloe? So Tanner's doing his own thing and doing it well?

You should be happy for him! As your boyfriend, I would think you'd be all proud of him and stuff."

How was she supposed to explain this?

"I *am* proud of him," she argued, "but I just wish he'd be honest with me, so I don't feel like such a loser when I listen to people talk about him!"

"Wait...now you feel like a loser?" Leaning back in her chair, Ashlynn shook her head. "I think we need to back up here a bit. And maybe order some Chinese food and go to my place to talk. Reid's working the overnight shift, so he won't disturb us." She picked up her phone. "Should I call Billie and Jade? Maybe MacKenzie too?"

"What? No! *No!*" Groaning, she jumped up. "Why would I want even more people to know I'm acting like a crazy person? Just hearing you imply it is enough to make me want to cry!"

And then—dammit—her eyes stung and tears were streaming down her face.

"Oh, Chlo...come on. Don't do that!" Ashlynn immediately stood up and hugged her.

"Why am I being like this?" she murmured. "I shouldn't feel threatened, right? It's not like Sweetbriar is suddenly going to go backwards and only need one kindergarten teacher again and they'll pick Tanner over me."

Pulling back, she gasped.

"What if they choose Tanner over me?" And now she was crying in earnest.

"Okay, okay...hang on one minute. Sit down and let me just make sure my schedule's clear. I'll be right back." Then she dashed out of the office, shutting the door behind her.

"Probably making sure no one sees her crazy sister," Chloe mumbled, wiping away the tears. Her phone dinged with an incoming text and she stupidly reached for it.

> Tanner: Hey, Beautiful! I was just at the coffee shop and heard I just missed you.

> Tanner: I have to do a little shopping. What do you say to dinner at my place?

Groaning, she contemplated telling him exactly what she thought of his offer of dinner, but then realized she wasn't thinking clearly.

> Chloe: Thanks, but I ran into Ash and we're having dinner together.

> Chloe: I'll see you at school tomorrow.

There. No heart emojis or smiley faces, just words. *Right, like that's going to prove anything.*

> Tanner: Are you okay? Did I do something wrong?

Okay, maybe that did prove something.

> Chloe: Why would you even ask that?

Ugh...why did I pick up the phone?

> Tanner: Because you're being a little short with me and I can tell.

> Tanner: Can I call you so we can talk?

> Chloe: Everything's fine, Tanner.

Liar, liar, liar!

> Chloe: I'm sitting here with Ash and everything's good.

Chloe: I'll see you in the morning, okay?

Chloe: Have a good night.

Then she tossed her phone back in her purse as if it had burned her.

Just then, Ashlynn walked back in and shut the door behind her again. "Okay, my schedule is clear and you and I are going to my place for some Chinese food and ice cream sundaes for dessert. I already called in the dinner order, and my freezer is full of ice cream and the pantry is full of toppings." She paused and grinned. "And the toppings aren't always just for sundaes," she said with a dramatic wink. "Now come on. Follow me home."

Thirty minutes later, they were sitting in Ashlynn's dining room with way too much Chinese takeout in front of them, but it was perfect.

"You don't get it," she explained.

Again.

"Things always came easier for you with whatever you tried. Teaching is the first thing that I really excelled at. And now all everyone can talk about is how awesome Tanner is and I'm going to be forgotten. Just like I was the forgotten Donovan for most of my life."

Ash rolled her eyes. "Okay, no one ever forgot you."

"Mom left me at the mall that time..."

"Okay, one time!" her sister cried. "You were hiding in Santa's gingerbread house! And, in her defense, she left to find a police officer because she thought you'd been abducted!"

"This is getting us nowhere! This is how I feel, Ashlynn! You don't get to tell me how to feel or not feel! I'm sitting here telling you how I've felt invisible for most of my life! Being a teacher bolstered my confidence like nothing

163

else and you know what, I feel threatened by Tanner's showiness and success! There! Happy?"

Letting out a small huff, Ash tossed down her chopsticks. "Actually, yes. I love that you finally spoke up! I hate that you're feeling like this, but, like you said, I can't tell you how to feel. If you feel threatened, then that's how you feel. But what is it you want to happen here? Do you want Tanner to quit? To suddenly be a terrible teacher? I mean... think about it."

Rather than answer, she picked up a dumpling and bit it in half, thinking as she chewed.

What *did* she want to happen?

"It seems to me like you have two things going on here, and they both have to do with Tanner, and neither of them is good."

She nodded.

"You're upset that he's not being open with you about what he's doing in his classroom—and I think that's a really weird thing for him to keep to himself—and the fact that you're afraid of him taking away your place at the school."

Swallowing, she nodded again.

"We all like to be praised for the work we do. That was something that used to drive me crazy when I worked for Becky. But sometimes...we're not the best and that's okay. If we're trying our best and getting results, that's a win, Chlo. Your students love you. The parents love you. There are dozens of families in this town who have these great memories of the things you taught them. It's okay to share the spotlight."

"Maybe."

"Would you feel like this if that other woman had taken the position? The one who Tanner replaced? Would you

164

feel as threatened then, or is this because he's your boyfriend?"

She groaned. "I knew getting involved with a coworker was going to be a bad thing."

Reaching over, Ashlynn took her hands and gave them a squeeze. "It doesn't have to be. You need to talk to Tanner and..."

Chloe snatched her hands back. "And say what? Stop being awesome? Stop being charming and successful? That would be the worst!"

With a patient smile, Ash took a moment to take a bite of her dinner before replying. "Or...you could just tell him you wish he would be honest with you about what he's doing in his classroom. That it's okay if he doesn't do things your way or take your suggestions. Hell, Chloe, you had to figure it all out on your own and you were fine. It's not a bad thing that Tanner's just trying to do the same."

Sadly, everything her sister was saying was right.

It took her a few moments, but she reluctantly agreed. "How do I stop feeling what I'm feeling? I'm going to ruin this relationship before it even has a chance if I don't do something."

"I know you're not big on confrontation, but...you need to talk to him. It doesn't need to be an argument or anything dramatic, just a conversation where you tell him how you feel."

She snorted. "He'll think I'm a horrible person and break up with me."

"Then you know what? He's not the person you thought he was. Or...maybe he's the person you originally thought he was—the icky jerk." She laughed softly. "Either way, this is something that has the potential to strengthen your relationship."

"I don't see how..."

"True colors, Chlo. You're showing him your vulnerable side and hopefully he's going to show you he's...you know... not a jerk. Maybe he'll show you he's just as insecure as you are and maybe you need to take some of your...*ahem*... teaching advice, and keep it to yourself. Or at least wait for him to ask for it."

"*Ugh...*" she whined. "Why are you always right?"

Preening from the praise, Ashlynn hummed happily. "As much as I'd like to say it comes naturally, it doesn't. I've just had to do a bit of groveling and learning how to open myself up a lot with Reid. Sometimes it sucks and it's awkward and uncomfortable, but the results are worth it." She stood and took her plate to the sink. "Do you think you'll call him when you get home later or wait until after school tomorrow to talk about this?"

"Probably tomorrow so I can think about what I'm going to say that will make me sound a little less pathetic."

"Not pathetic," her sister corrected. "Human."

"Fine, human. Whatever."

Nodding, Ashlynn went to the freezer and pulled out a gallon of cookies and cream. "And to reward you for your bravery—though it's yet to be seen—we will celebrate with ice cream sundaes!"

It may have been a crappy afternoon, but it was turning into a really good night.

* * *

It wasn't like him to feel so out of sorts, but that's exactly how he felt.

Ever since Chloe hadn't responded to his last text, he'd been certain she was upset with him over something. But what? Last he checked, they were fine. When she left school for the day, she said she'd see him later. Sure, it was that generic kind of statement and they didn't make any plans, but...everything about her texts seemed off.

> Chloe: I'm sitting here with Ash and everything's good.
>
> Chloe: I'll see you in the morning, okay?
>
> Chloe: Have a good night.
>
> Tanner: Can I call you later?

But she'd never even responded or read that last text.

What the hell did I do?

At lunch, they'd talked about starting plans for the winter program and some potential holiday projects, and then she shared her selection of books she liked to read with the class this time of year. It was nothing out of the ordinary, and he'd appreciated her suggestions, but he didn't commit to any of them.

Was that it? Was that the problem? She felt like he wasn't contributing?

Hmm...

It was a little after nine and he wondered if she was home from dinner with her sister. He hated to let this wait until tomorrow because once they were at work, there really wasn't time to talk. And if there was one thing he hated, it was going to sleep when he was mad. He had a feeling she felt the same way. So if she was mad at him, he didn't want that to drag on until the morning.

With his mind made up, Tanner grabbed his keys before he could change his mind and walked out to his car. If she wasn't home, all he'd done was waste five minutes or less of driving.

But he seriously hoped she was home.

Her car was in the driveway and the lights were on, so he knew she was home and awake. He parked and walked up to her door and rang the bell, letting out a long breath as he did. His heart was racing and he couldn't believe he was nervous. When was the last time he'd ever felt this nervous?

"Tanner?" Chloe said, her confusion obvious as she opened the door. She was wearing a pair of flannel pajama pants, a t-shirt, a robe, and her hair was up in a ponytail. There wasn't even a hint of makeup on her face, and she looked utterly adorable.

Probably not the time to mention that...

"Hey," he said, sounding way too breathless for a guy standing still. "You never responded to my last text, and I can't shake the feeling that you're mad at me. There was no way I was going to sleep without trying to make things right." That was the fastest he'd ever spoken, and he felt mildly foolish, but this was just too important to wait.

Leaning against the front door, she bit her bottom lip. "I thought we would just talk tomorrow..."

"Then there is something wrong," he concluded, his shoulders sagging.

"I didn't say that."

"You didn't have to." Taking a step toward her, he fought the urge to reach out and touch her. "Chloe, we spend hours every day talking to each other, and I don't want that to stop now. If there's something I've done..."

"Tomorrow would really be..."

"I know that I come across as this confident guy with a colossal ego," he quickly interrupted. "You've told me that yourself. You gave me the chance to prove that I'm not really that guy and I'd like to think that I've showed you the true person I am. But that doesn't mean I'm perfect or won't screw up." Raking a hand through his hair, he let out his breath. "Sometimes I get so caught up in myself that I might not pay attention to things other people might find important, so if I did that, I'm sorry. Is this because I'm not contributing anything to the lesson plans? Because I have some ideas, but it seemed like you had everything down to a science and I didn't want to step on your toes."

That had her standing up a little straighter, and he knew he'd touched a nerve.

"Is it that you didn't want to step on my toes, or do you just have a secret plan that you don't want to share so you can be the superstar at Sweetbriar Elementary?" she demanded, stepping out onto the porch. "Because it seems to me like you've got all kinds of super cute, super fun projects and activities going on in your classroom that have all the parents going gaga over you, and you never once mentioned any of them to me!" Her eyes went wide and she went to turn and go back into the house. "Just...go home, Tanner. We'll talk tomorrow."

"Oh, hell no," he murmured, slapping his hand on the door before she could shut it in his face. "Are you seriously telling me you're upset because I didn't share my lesson plans with you?"

All she did was glare at him.

With his free hand, he pinched the bridge of his nose. "Chloe, can we please go inside and talk about this? I'm honestly confused as hell right now."

"Fine," she mumbled, stomping away from the door.

Tanner followed her to the kitchen, where she sat down with a mug that looked like it had hot tea in it, but she didn't offer him any.

Fine. Whatever.

Taking a seat, he asked, "Can you please explain this to me? I don't see what I did wrong."

"Figures."

And yeah, the sarcasm was a bit heavy before she seemed to just...deflate.

"Oh God, I'm sorry," she said, her voice trembling. "It's not you. It's me. All I've been hearing this week is about how awesome you are and all these great things you're doing with the students, and I don't understand why you don't tell me about any of it. All the times I go on about ideas for you, I realize now I was just making an idiot of myself!"

Ah...okay. *Now* he got it.

"Now I feel like I owe you an apology," he began carefully. "You've always offered to help and give me advice since the day we met and...it's kind of a weird thing for me. And not just with you. I was the same when I was skiing. It didn't matter how much more experience the other guys had; I didn't really listen." He shrugged and gave her a small smile. "Looking back, some of it I should have, but I was stubborn. Apparently, I still am."

"Oh."

He took a moment to think about what he was about to say. "When my brother died, my parents got a little...overbearing. With good reason," he quickly amended, "but there was a lot of comparing things my brother did with the things I was doing. After getting checked out by dozens of doctors and confirming that I was healthy, I resented the comparisons or the suggestions that were based on what my brother did or didn't do. That's where it all started and believe me, it makes me feel like a major jerk that I react that way."

Beside him, Chloe sighed softly. "One of the things I love about teaching is it's something my siblings have no part of. For once in my life, no one was comparing me to my confident and outgoing twin, or my super smart older sister, or athletic and popular older brother. This was my space, and I excelled at it. And it felt good."

Until he showed up.

Dammit.

"Okay, but...we all have our things, Chloe. And I'm sorry if my teaching style is upsetting to you, but...it's not fair of you to ask me to change it," he said carefully. "At the end of the day, this is my job and my reputation too, and I don't think I could teach the same way that you do, because it wouldn't feel natural. Just like you couldn't do it the way I am because that's not how you are."

She nodded. "I know, and believe me, I'm not proud of this. That's why I went to Ash's tonight. I needed to sit and talk this out because it was making me crazy." Then she glanced over at him. "And that's why I didn't want to talk until tomorrow, because I was still trying to work it all out."

Now it was his turn to nod. "So...what happens now?"

"It's my issue, Tanner, and I'm going to get over it. Teaching at Sweetbriar has been my only job, so I've never had to deal with this kind of situation before. And if it wasn't you in the room next door, it would be another teacher and potentially the same situation. I was living in a bubble, and you know...bubbles burst. I'm an adult and I'll deal with it." She stared down at her tea. "I just hope you can forgive me for being a brat."

Reaching over, he took one of her hands in his. "There's nothing to forgive. And I really didn't mean to hurt you by not talking about my lesson plans. It just didn't seem like that big of a deal to me. But if you want, we can compare binders moving forward and..."

"No," she interrupted. "That's unnecessary. There are

going to be things that we have to work on together, but... there's no reason for you to have to run anything by me. It's not my place."

"That's not what I'm saying. Maybe I need to stop being so secretive and keeping things to myself because I fear someone's going to find a weakness or...or...whatever. Skiing was an independent thing. I was a team of one. Perhaps it's time for me to stop thinking like that."

When her eyes met his, she smiled, and damn, did he love her smiles.

"Since I'm a twin, I've never been a team of one. I think that's what took me the longest to adjust to when I started teaching. I was completely independent, and it felt a little disconcerting. That's probably why I'm being so sensitive about this with you. With our...you know...relationship, I guess I felt like maybe we were a team. But then you were doing stuff that you didn't even mention to me and..."

"And you felt alone."

Another nod. "Exactly."

Tanner breathed a sigh of relief because this was all great information for them to share with each other. He was really falling hard for Chloe and as much as he thought he knew a lot about her, it was fascinating to delve a little deeper.

Plus, knowing more about her meant that maybe he wouldn't screw this up.

He gave her hand another squeeze before pushing away from the table and standing. "Thank you for being willing to talk to me about this. I'm not usually the kind of person who just shows up unannounced on someone's doorstep late at night..."

"It wasn't that late," she gently corrected.

"Still, you asked for time and I didn't give it to you. But

in my defense, I was genuinely worried, and now I'm glad I took the chance and came over."

She stood. "Me too." Glancing around for a moment, she asked, "Would you like something to drink? I know I should have asked when you first sat down, but..."

"But you were mad," he said with a grin. "And rightfully so."

"It didn't give me the right to be rude."

"Chloe?"

"Hmm?"

"I don't need anything to drink." He moved closer and slowly wrapped his arms around her waist before placing a soft kiss on her forehead. "It's a school night, so I'm going to go home because I know you prefer to be in bed by ten." Another kiss. But when he went to release her, she held on tight. Resting his head on top of hers, he decided to simply enjoy holding her for a little longer.

"Tanner?"

"Hmm?"

"Do you have to go home?" she quietly asked, and he felt himself smiling.

"No, I do not," he told her. "Everything's locked up and I don't believe there's anything there that I need." And yet another kiss. "I have everything I want and need right here."

When he lifted his head, Chloe looked up at him and he saw the play of emotions on her face—the want, the need, the relief...

"Ask me to stay," he said gruffly.

"Stay."

Without a word, he scooped her up in his arms, strode out of the kitchen, and went straight to her bedroom. It wasn't until he placed her on the bed that he smiled and said, "I like your jammies."

She groaned even as she softly laughed. "They are the least sexy things ever. I should be mortified."

But Tanner shook his head. "Whatever you're wearing is sexy. You looked like an absolute fantasy when we stayed at the lodge. All that silk and lace made me forget how to breathe a time or two. But there is also something incredibly arousing about all this flannel that has me dying to know what you have on underneath."

The impish grin she gave him said she couldn't wait for him to find out.

With one knee on the bed, he slowly moved over her. "Are you going to tell me, or do I get to find out for myself?" Then he was kissing his way up her throat and along her jaw before settling in on her lips.

After that, it didn't matter how he found out. All he knew was that he was exactly where he wanted to be and with the woman that was becoming everything to him.

Life was pretty damn good.

Chapter Ten

For a week, everything was a bit idyllic. As much as she hated that they had to have that talk, it made her feel stronger and more confident in their relationship. Heck, she felt stronger and more confident than she ever had in any romantic relationship, and it was a great feeling.

Outside of school, life for the Donovans was chaotic. Her mom was doing okay in rehab, but she was very vocal about going home. The key problem was finding someone who could realistically stay with her all day and all night because they couldn't afford twenty-four-hour nursing care for her.

So on Saturday afternoon, they all met up at Jade and Levi's house to discuss the possibilities and to work out a schedule where everyone took a night staying at Marie's house. It wasn't ideal, but it made the most sense. When she'd mentioned it to Tanner, he asked if she wanted him to go with her, and while it hadn't been something she'd initially thought about, she had agreed.

Now, walking up to the door with Tanner's hand in

hers, she felt like a peer to her siblings—like she could walk in there and not be the baby of the family, but an equal.

Which was silly because having Tanner with her really didn't change anything, but he bolstered her confidence. And when dealing with the Donovan family and the craziness that went with them, she definitely needed it.

"Chloe! Tanner! Hey!" Levi said as he opened the door. "Come on in! Everyone's in the kitchen right now."

They followed and it was crazy how loud such a small group of people could be. They were greeted with a round of hellos and Chloe put the bowl of guacamole and the bag of chips she'd brought with her down on the kitchen island. Levi poured them each a drink, and everyone helped themselves to some snacks before they all went and sat down at the dining room table.

"I'm so glad everyone could make time for this today," he began. "I know the last several weeks have been trying for all of us, but Mom's going to be coming home soon and I think we really need to all be on the same page for it."

"I think we're being a little overdramatic," Ashlynn said. "By the time she comes home, she's going to be in much better shape than she was in the hospital. I don't think she's going to need round-the-clock supervision like you're all thinking."

"That very well may be," Billie commented. "But it still doesn't hurt to be prepared just in case. Obviously, we all work during the day, so we can't be there for her."

"Well, I kind of can," Levi volunteered. "Not every day, but I do work from home a lot. So if I needed to, I could just as easily work from Mom's house."

"Let's call that Plan B," Jade said, patting his hand. "The things your mom is going to need help with, she might not want her son doing for her."

It took Levi a minute, but then he realized what she was saying. "Ah. Gotcha. Okay."

"I don't think it's a bad thing for us to each take a turn sleeping over," Chloe said, wanting to contribute to the conversation. "But I know that I have to leave early in the morning, and Billie would have to leave even earlier unless you changed your baking schedule."

"Which I could do if I had to," Billie agreed.

"My schedule's a bit more flexible," Ashlynn begrudgingly chimed in, "but we all know that Mom and I still aren't on great terms. I don't want to be the one to hinder anything because we're arguing."

"Well, I think you can be mature enough to have a little self-control," Levi said. "And things have gotten better between the two of you, but we all know that Mom can be a little...you know...um...you guys know what I'm saying."

"She's a pain in the ass," Ash finished for him. "Sheesh! Just say it, Levi. She's not here. She can't hear you."

Before he could respond, the doorbell rang and he jumped up to answer it.

"My mom has offered to help a day or two during the week," Jade offered. "She and Marie have become friends, and I have to agree with Ashlynn. I don't think this is going to go on for as long as we all first thought."

"Has anyone reached out to her friends?" Tanner asked, and then kind of seemed to regret saying anything.

"It's fine," Chloe assured him. "That was a great question." Then she looked around. "Have we?"

"I know I haven't," Billie said. "But I could easily make some calls and see if anyone's available to help. It might make her feel better if she's surrounded by friends instead of more nurses. You know how they've been making her cranky."

"Everything makes her cranky," Ash mumbled.

Voices came from the entryway and Chloe glanced in that direction, wondering who else could be here. "Did Levi invite Patrick and Marissa?"

Jade shook her head. "They're not planning on coming back to town until after the new year. Marissa said it's too hard to travel back and forth so much with the baby. Plus, there isn't anything they're really needed for here that they can't do over a video call."

"I wonder who..."

"There are my girls!"

"Dad!" They all called out, and Chloe instantly got to her feet and ran over to hug him. "What are you doing here?"

Ronan hugged her tight and then did the same to Ashlynn before giving a more reserved hug to Billie and then straightening. "Well now, I've been keeping in touch with all of you about your mom and I've come to help!"

You could have heard a pin drop.

"Um...what?" Billie asked as she slowly made her way back to her seat.

Nodding, Ronan smiled when Levi handed him something to drink. "I've had to cut back on my hours at the pub. Kate and Shane keep nagging me about taking it easy, but they're just worriers. Plus, with Jamie essentially running the pub, I'm feeling like a bit of a dinosaur there." He let out a happy sigh. "So it was the perfect time to come up here and see where I can lend a hand!"

"But...uh, Dad?" Chloe asked hesitantly. "I'm not sure you're exactly the...right person?"

"Bah! Your mother and I have had some time to talk through some things since I've been coming up to visit all of you some more. And while I'm never going to be her favorite person, I'm probably the most qualified to step in and help her."

Ashlynn's maniacal laughter brought everyone up short. "This is perfect!" she laughed. "Perfect!"

"Ash, come on," Chloe murmured, nudging her sister. "That's not funny."

"But it is! Can you see the two of them together with Mom on crutches and unable to do anything for herself? It's poetic justice!"

"Ashlynn Jane!" Ronan boomed. "You will respect your mother! She's injured and you should not be mocking her or taking delight in her trauma. Shame on you!"

At least her sister had the good sense to look remorseful. "Sorry."

"Believe it or not, I've spoken to Marie several times since she got to that rehab place and she knows I'm coming. And again, I'm not her first choice and she openly admitted that I was the last person she ever thought would come through and help her, but...there was a time when we loved each other. I don't wish her any ill will. Plus, I know how hard all of you work and how little free time you have. She doesn't want to be a burden on any of you..."

There were several snorts that no one seemed to want to own up to.

Ronan paused and his attention turned to Tanner. "You're new," he said with a big smile. "Ronan Donovan. And you are...?"

Beside her, Tanner gently cleared his throat. "I'm Tanner Westyn, Mr. Donovan. Chloe and I are...uh...we're dating."

"Really?" Ronan sang. "Well, it's very nice to meet you! How did the two of you meet?"

"We work together," Tanner explained. "I just started teaching at Sweetbriar Elementary."

"Fabulous! What grade?"

"Kindergarten."

Ronan's eyes went wide. "Oh, my! What a wonderful coincidence! Like fate!"

Oh God...

All she wanted to do was slink down in her seat and slide under the table out of embarrassment.

Tanner laughed softly as he nodded, but all her siblings were giving her sympathetic smiles.

"Are you from around here, Tanner?"

"Um, no, Sir. I grew up in upstate New York."

"Tanner used to ski professionally," Levi said cheerily, winking at Chloe.

Why? Why wink, you doofus? She wanted to yell!

Her father's eyes went wide as he looked back at Tanner. "You don't say! That is fascinating. I don't think I've ever met a professional skier." He shifted slightly in his chair before leaning a little closer. "So tell me, what exactly does that mean? Did you compete in the Olympics? Do you have any gold medals?"

Folding his hands on the table, Tanner shook his head. "I competed in two Olympics, but never placed. I do, however, hold several national titles, and I've competed in several Alpine World Cups. And while an Olympic medal would have been great, I'm very happy with everything I've accomplished."

"As well you should!" Ronan said. "Good for you! Your parents must be very proud of you!"

He nodded. "They are."

"And now you're teaching kindergarten? That seems like a complete one-eighty for someone like you. I would think you would have gone on to coach or be a spokesperson."

"Oh, I am a spokesperson for a major company, but it's not something that I could make a career out of. Besides, I've always wanted to be a teacher. Skiing was just something that went from being a hobby to a little something more for several years. Now I'm exactly where I was always meant to be."

Chloe listened to him and couldn't help but notice how passionate he sounded.

And instantly wondered if she'd ever sounded that way when she talked about her job.

Of course you have...everyone always says how much you light up when you talk about teaching. Stop comparing yourself, dang it!

"Good for you," her father said, sounding like he was proud of Tanner, even though they just met. "And you're dating the best teacher this little town has ever seen! You could learn a lot from my Chloe."

"Dad..." she whined.

"What? Can't a father brag about his daughter? Especially when she's won awards, too?"

"It's not a competition," she murmured.

"Okay," Ashlynn said loudly. "Back to you being here to take care of Mom. Now that I think of it, I really don't think this is a good idea."

To his credit, their father didn't look the least bit offended. He took a slow sip of his drink before he addressed them all. "I know every one of you has ideas about how you're going to juggle your jobs and your busy lives while taking turns to help Marie. And while it's all very commendable, it's not practical." He paused for a moment. "The last thing she wants is to be a burden."

There was a collective round of snorts and murmurs of disbelief.

"Dad, I don't think you're familiar with the current version of who Mom is," Billie said diplomatically. "She kind of...thrives on being a martyr. I think I speak for all of us when I say it's going to be worse if we don't all inconvenience ourselves a bit to help her when she gets home."

Frowning, Ronan shook his head. "Then it's an even better thing that I'm here. I know staying out of your lives for all those years was a mistake, and this sort of thing just confirms it. Now, I can't tell any of you not to make time to help your mother, but I am telling you not to disrupt your entire lives to do it."

"Dad," Levi began, but his father stopped him.

"Son, you've got a company to run. Almost every business in town relies on you for their advertising needs." Then he looked over at Jade. "And you run a very successful coffee shop every single day while being a great mom to Silas." Then he looked at Billie. "I don't even know when you sleep, Wilhelmina."

"Dad!" she cried in mortification. "No one calls me that! Ever!"

"Bah," he said, waving her off. "It's a fine name!"

"Oh my God..."

"Fine, I don't even know when you sleep, *Billie*. Happy?"

She nodded.

"You're already overextended between all the baking you do and helping both Jade and Ashlynn with their businesses. When's the last time you did anything that was just for you? Heck, when's the last time you went away for a few days and just had some fun with your friends? Or a boyfriend?"

Groaning loudly, Billie gently banged her head on the table. "Make it stop."

"We get what you're saying, Dad," Levi countered, "but..."

"Ashlynn, your salon is always busy! Your customers are willing to wait weeks to get in to see you. The first year of business is critical. You can't just take time away or go to work grouchy because you spent too many nights with your mother and she made you crazy."

That made them all snicker a bit.

"And you, my sweet Chloe," he went on. "You are preparing our greatest treasures for so many things. You are the foundation of everything they're going to learn in school. Your mother is so proud of you and everything you're doing, and no matter how big a martyr she may think she is, she isn't the kind that would feel good about taking you away from your students."

Honestly, Chloe wasn't so sure about that, but she kept it to herself.

"Dad, we all really appreciate what you're saying and what you're doing, but...we're skeptical, okay?" Billie said.

Finally, he nodded. "And I understand that. I'm not suggesting tough love or anything, just...have a little faith that things are going to work out." He paused before nodding again. "And maybe...have a little faith in me." The last words were a mere whisper, but they packed a punch.

No one spoke for a few moments, but Reid broke the silence. "Between Ronan, her friends, her physical therapist, occupational therapist, and the visiting nurses that are going to be coming in to check on Marie, she might actually prefer having some time to herself. I'm not saying it's wrong to have a plan in place for an emergency, but maybe we need to wait a bit and take our cues from her once she's home."

"It just feels a little wrong not to be prepared and ready to step in," Billie admitted. "I feel like we're being bad kids."

"But we're not," Chloe argued, surprising herself. "We all took turns at the hospital. We slept in chairs or chairs that turned into beds and brought meals up to her. And when she moved to the rehab facility, we all went up to see her almost daily. They didn't allow us to sleep there, but we've been showing up and loving on her. How could that make us bad kids?"

"Chloe's got a point," Jade said. "Everyone that's come into Books & Beans and asked about Marie has marveled at how much time all of you have been spending with her. And you know your mom has loved all the support and care and love you've given her."

"I know I think it's been enough," Ashlynn commented dryly. "Some days she's just not in the mood to even be social, but I still sit there and chat away with her. I think she's going to love coming home and having some time to herself without people hovering all the damn time."

"Maybe," Bille said.

"I think we've beaten this topic practically to death," Ronan said. "How about we change the subject for a little while so we can relax?"

"That sounds good," Levi agreed. "How about we move all the snacks in here and just eat and talk and catch up?"

Everyone got up and helped move all the food to the dining room table before refilling their plates. Levi refreshed all the drinks, and Silas ran in to say hello to everyone and give Ronan a hug before running back to his room to play video games.

When everyone was settled and there were multiple

conversations going around, Chloe leaned back and felt Tanner's arm go around her. "Sorry about all the craziness. I knew we were going to talk about my mom's situation a little, but I hate that you had to sit through all of that."

He placed a soft kiss on her cheek. "It really wasn't a big deal. Plus, it's been kind of cool listening to your father. You've never really mentioned him before, so..."

"Yeah. Long story," she murmured. And it wasn't one she particularly liked to talk about, so hopefully he'd be willing to leave it at that and not want to bring it up ever again.

As if reading her mind, he reached over and picked up a tortilla chip and scooped a bit of guacamole on it. "As usual, the guac is delicious."

She felt herself blush. "Thank you."

"So Tanner!" Ronan called out. "Tell me about this Alpine skiing. Do you think I'm too old to try it, or is it a younger man's game?"

Chuckling, Chloe got comfortable and simply enjoyed listening to her boyfriend diplomatically explain all the reasons why her father should not take up skiing.

* * *

It was after nine when he and Chloe left Jade and Levi's, and Tanner had to admit that he had a great time. Watching the family dynamic had been riveting.

His brother passed away so long ago that he kind of forgot what it was like to be in that kind of setting. For years, it was simply him and his parents so he'd never had the opportunity to witness a gathering like this. It was intimate and emotional one minute, loud and boisterous the next, and then, when you least expected it, things got heated and almost instantly resolved.

Yeah, riveting.

Everyone was very welcoming to him and there wasn't ever a time where he felt like an outsider. However, he had been wildly curious about Ronan Donovan. He could tell that it wasn't something Chloe wanted to talk about. The whole, "Yeah. Long story," spoke volumes. Fortunately, he and Reid had stepped out into the yard at one point, and that's when he got the scoop.

"About a year ago, it sort of all came out that Marie had kind of pushed Ronan out," Reid explained. "She wasn't having an affair, exactly—at least not sexually. It was more of an emotional affair at that point. But once Ronan was gone..."

"Then it turned...?"

"Exactly. Unfortunately, she couldn't explain that to her kids, but she really painted Ronan as the bad guy. And to be honest? He was in a small way. Just not motivated to take care of his family. He loved them, just not enough to buckle down and actually work hard at supporting them. For years, they all accepted that he was a deadbeat and the fact that he never came around just made it all plausible."

"So he just took off?"

"Basically. It finally came out that he stayed away because Marie told him it would be best for the kids and he listened. It's all fairly recent that they're working on repairing their relationships."

"And now he wants to come and help take care of Marie?" he asked incredulously. "Am I the only one that doesn't think that's normal? Are we sure he's not going to torture her or something?"

He was only partially kidding.

"Nah. Ronan couldn't hurt a fly," Reid explained. "But you should know that this is all kind of new to them—having him in their lives like this. Honestly, I think Chloe and Levi were the most forgiving and have really welcomed him back with open arms. Ashlynn put up a good fight for a little while, but then she got furious with Marie. They all were upset with her, but my girl can really hold a grudge."

"Wow."

"And Billie's been the most forgiving of Marie, not so much with Ronan, but I can tell she's warming up to him. She's the oldest, so I think his leaving hit her the hardest."

All he could do was nod. It was a lot of information to take in.

"Ash and Chloe blamed themselves for Ronan leaving."

"Seriously? Why?"

"Because they felt like they were the reason their father left. Both of them have some abandonment issues. Ashlynn was a bit hard to pin down when we started dating. She was defensive and standoffish one minute and then the next...?" He shrugged. "And I think Chloe tends to hold on to people that she shouldn't because she doesn't want them to leave."

Tanner stiffened. "Are you trying to say...?"

"What?" Reid asked and then laughed softly. "No. Sorry. I wasn't talking about you at all. It's something Ash has shared with me and I've noticed that sometimes she takes the scraps of attention friends or colleagues may give her because she doesn't want to do anything to push them away." He paused and grinned at Tanner. "Honestly, seeing the two of you together has been a really good thing. She looks happy and seems a little more confident in herself. A few months ago, she never would have chimed into that conversation with anything more than a plea to do more to help. It was cool to see her have an opinion of her own."

"Oh, well then...that's definitely a good thing."

"Just know this," Reid said, some of the friendliness gone from his tone. "The Donovans are tight now, but some of that is fresh. However, they are fiercely protective of each other. And Ash has been known to threaten more than a few people who have hurt Chloe. So just a bit of advice, don't cross her. Ashlynn, I mean. Because she can be a little scary when she wants to be, and since she and Chloe are twins—and she's the older by like three minutes—she's especially protective of her."

He nodded. "Good to know. And for what it's worth, I have no intention of crossing Ashlynn or hurting Chloe."

And because he didn't have anyone else to talk to about this, he figured he might as well confide in Reid.

"I'm crazy about Chloe," he said. "I didn't see this coming, and we had a really shitty first meeting, but that was solely on me. I came here with the intention of beating her at the Teacher of the Year award. And the fact that it was Chloe didn't faze me in the beginning. Then I got to know her."

Raking a hand through his hair, he wasn't sure how much he should share, but his mouth wasn't waiting for permission.

"We had a...a thing last week because she felt like I was outshining her. I didn't share with her the things I was doing with my class because they were very different from what she was doing, but that's more because of my teaching style than anything else. I needed to make this position my own. I've been waiting a long time to get started, so..."

"There's nothing wrong with being your own teacher, Tanner. She can't fault you for that."

"But...she did. And I have some guilt because of...you know...the way I was when I first got here. Ever since we talked it through, I've had to keep asking myself if I'm doing this because it's my teaching style or if it's the competitive part of me still looking to be the Teacher of the Year. Even when the person I'd be beating is the woman I'm involved with."

"Damn."

"I know."

"And what conclusion have you come to?"

"Honestly? I don't know. The thing is, this is who I am. I'm competitive! It's something I'm working on to try to curb it a bit, but I don't want to hurt Chloe. You have to believe me."

"I do," Reid told him. "But it sounds like if this relationship is going to go anywhere, she has to accept that part of you—the competitive guy—and you need to accept that maybe that guy already had his days of glory."

"Yeah, but...not in this field."

"You don't need to be the best in every field. You know what, I'm a great firefighter. I've received a ton of commendations and I have the respect of my peers. It's awesome. On the side, I work in construction and I'm not so great at it. I'm the guy who goes in and does the demo—you know, tearing down walls and ripping out cabinets. And you know what? I love both jobs! I'm not looking to be the best; I'm just happy to be there doing the work to help the rest of the contractors."

"O-kay..."

"Look, you can be great at your job and still not be... well...Teacher of the Year. It doesn't mean you did anything wrong. And you have no idea how much that title means to Chloe."

But...he did.

Dammit.

"What if I can't repress the competitive guy?"

"Then you're probably going to have Ashlynn threatening to punch you in the throat."

He groaned.

After that, Levi called them in for dessert, but the conversation was still heavy on his mind.

Even on the short drive back to Chloe's.

He parked in her driveway and followed her to the door. They had already agreed that he was staying over tonight—something he'd been looking forward to all day—and yet they both seemed a little quiet. He knew why he was; he just wasn't sure what was on her mind.

"Everything okay?" he asked once they were inside.

"Hmm? Oh, I think so. Sometimes it takes a lot of energy to get through a day with my family. It's a little like sensory overload, and I need some time to decompress."

"I get that." He glanced around and got the perfect idea. "How about you draw yourself a hot bath with some of those bath bombs you have stockpiled next to the tub? And I'll pour us some wine, and when you're done soaking and relaxing, I'll give you a massage. What do you say?"

She blinked at him for a moment. "You want to give me a massage? Really?"

He nodded. "Absolutely." Then he moved in close, wrapping his arms around her waist. "You already know how much I love running my hands all over your body." He placed a kiss on her cheek. "So really, it will be good for both of us." He placed another kiss along the shell of her ear. "And then when you're like putty in my hands, I'm going to make love to you until you're breathless and boneless and barely know your own name." The kiss he placed on her lips was deep and possessive and full of promise.

When they broke apart, Chloe was breathless. "Or maybe I can skip the bath and..."

But Tanner was already shaking his head. "Nuh-uh. I think you need that time to really make the rest of it even more enjoyable." Placing a soft kiss on the tip of her nose, he gently turned her toward her bedroom. "Go and do your thing while I get everything else set up. I left my duffel bag out in my car, but as soon as I grab it, I'm going to work my magic around here."

She giggled. "You're amazing, you know that?"

"Only for you," he whispered, giving her a soft nudge. "Go. We've got all night, but I'm eager to get started."

And as she turned to walk away, his conversation with Reid started playing in his head again.

"Honestly, seeing the two of you together has been a really good thing. She looks happy and seems a little more confident in herself."

He was genuinely happy that this relationship was making her happy.

"I'm crazy about Chloe. I didn't see this coming."

And he hadn't. A relationship was the last thing on his mind when he accepted the position at Sweetbriar Elementary. Picking up and moving his life on such short notice had been his top priority. But now that they'd found each other, it made him realize that this was possibly the first time in his life that he felt like he had...everything. He'd accomplished what he wanted as an athlete, he had the job he'd been working toward—almost—and he had a woman who he could easily see himself falling in love with and having a future with.

He just had to hope that he didn't do anything stupid and ruin it.

Chapter Eleven

The unit on fall was finished.

Winter units were being planned separately.

And her parents were living together.

"Ugh...how is this my life?" Chloe murmured for at least the tenth time that day.

Her father had been back for almost two weeks, and her mother came home from rehab a week ago.

They'd been shacking up together ever since, and it was weird and awkward every time she went over to visit.

The last of her students had just left and she was sitting at her desk contemplating whether she should just fake a teaching emergency and avoid going over there. Slowly, she lowered her head to her desk and let out a long sigh.

"Well that doesn't sound good."

Tanner.

Honestly, he was the only thing keeping her sane right now.

Crouching down beside her, he asked, "You doing okay?"

"No."

"Want to talk about it?"

"No."

"Chloe, come on. It can't be that bad."

Another sigh.

But...she knew she couldn't sit here like this forever. "I don't want to go and see my mom today," she mumbled.

"O-kay..."

"It's weird with my dad there. Like...I don't even really remember what it was like to live with the two of them; all I know is how my mom used to talk bad about him. Now he's like the only one willing to be there for her and they're all cheery and happy and having a great time!"

Placing a hand on her knee, he said, "But that should be a good thing. They're getting along and trying to finally move forward."

Now she raised her head. "They should have done that while we were kids when it was actually important." And yes, she was pouting, but she felt fully entitled to this. "I would have loved to sit and hang around doing puzzles with the two of them when I was younger! Now it's just awkward."

"They're doing puzzles?"

She nodded. "Oh, yeah. A big 1,000-piece Thomas Kincaid Disney one. It's sickening!"

"Don't you think you're being just a little..."

"Crazy?" she interrupted. "Because I do. I think I'm totally behaving like I'm crazy, but I can't help it." With a huff, she twisted to fully face him. "You know what? The last couple of years have been great. And do you know why?"

He shook his head.

"Because things were steady and predictable. I was settled into teaching my class, my siblings all had some drama, but for the most part, my life was nice and boring and it really worked for me. But now? Now...the town's changing, school's changing, I just moved into a house, my parents are living together, and...and then there's you!"

"Me?"

Another nod. "And you're seriously the only thing keeping me sane throughout most of this, but there's still an element of me not knowing what's around the corner and it scares me!"

God...why? Why are you blabbering on about this stuff?

When she really looked at him, he was frowning. And Tanner rarely frowned.

"Wait," he began as he stood and straightened. "I'm not sure what just happened here. One minute you were upset about doing a puzzle with your parents and then it went to your life being out of control. I'm kind of at a loss for words."

"Well that's shocking," she murmured.

"Excuse me?"

"Tanner, you always have something to say. All the time. In every situation. You're like a PR dream because you always seem to do and say the right thing. Can't you just... do that now?"

He blinked at her for a moment. "I honestly don't even know what we're talking about," he said with a mirthless laugh. "You're uncomfortable with your parents? So don't go there today. No one's forcing you. As for the town and school growth? There's nothing I can do about that. Things change and not all change is bad. And honestly, none of that has anything to do with you. You're still this awesome teacher who everybody loves. Maybe stop focusing on all the things you think are bad and focus on...you know...all the things that are good." He took a hesitant step toward her. "Like us."

Her shoulders sagged because she truly was acting out of character. It felt like she was on an emotional roller coaster and she really wanted to get off, but didn't know how.

"We really are good," she quietly agreed, reaching out and taking one of his hands in hers. "And I appreciate you so much. I feel like I've been a little selfish in this relationship and I'm sorry about that. It's been a lot about my family and me and my feelings."

He considered her for a moment. "Well then, this might just be your lucky day."

"Oh?"

Nodding, he explained, "The pro shop up at Summit Ridge just called and asked if I could come up there and meet with some of their management people. They want to do an interview with me for their company newsletter and take some pictures and I thought maybe you'd like to come with me. You know, see a bit of my world."

Chloe felt her smile grow. "That sounds amazing! When do we need to be there? I'd love to run home and change first, if that's okay."

"I told them I'd be up there at six and that I was bringing my girlfriend," he told her with a lopsided grin. "They want to take us to dinner and I think it's going to be a fun night. Are you sure you want to go? It doesn't give us a lot of time to get ready."

She was already collecting her things. "Then we better get going now!" Leaning in, she kissed him. "Text me when you're on your way to pick me up!"

"You got it!"

Already feeling lighter after her mini breakdown, she

was beyond thankful to have a legitimate reason for not stopping by and seeing her mother.

"Note to self: send her a text when you get home so she doesn't worry."

When she got to the house, she ran in and took a quick shower before rummaging through her closet for something to wear. Was she supposed to dress up? Go casual? Something in between?

And now I need to text Tanner too.

Wrapped in a towel, she ran out to the living room and fished her phone out of her purse.

> Chloe: Hey, Mom! Hope you're feeling good today. Tanner is taking me up to Summit Ridge for a PR event with the pro shop. Sorry for the short notice. I'll see you tomorrow! Love you!!

Okay, that's done.

Next, she reached out to Tanner.

> Chloe: How dressy or casual do I need to dress?

> Tanner: I don't think you need to really dress up. Wear whatever you're comfortable with.

That was the least helpful thing he could have said.

> Chloe: What are you wearing?

> Tanner: Black jeans and a sweater. Nothing fancy.

> Tanner: And stop worrying, you're going to look beautiful no matter what you wear.

> Tanner: I'll be there in 30 minutes.

> Chloe: Okay! Thank you!

Running back to her closet, she also chose a pair of black jeans, an ivory sweater, and her black boots—simple, yet elegant.

Her makeup needed to be completely reapplied, and she blew out her hair. By the time she got dressed and added some jewelry, it was almost time for Tanner to pull up.

Walking around the house, she turned on a few lights since it was definitely going to be dark when they got home, and then looked at her phone and saw she had a text from her mother.

> Mom: Feeling good today and no worries about not coming over. It sounds like you're going to have an exciting evening!

> Mom: Your father made a fantastic pot roast for us for dinner. It's your Aunt Kate's recipe, but it smells amazing. Would you like me to save you some?

> Chloe: Thanks, but you enjoy it. I'll stop by tomorrow after school. Would you like me to pick up anything for you?

> Mom: I think your father's going grocery shopping tomorrow, so we're good.

> Mom: But I'd really like it if you would bring your boyfriend with you. Everyone's been talking about him, but you haven't brought him to meet me.

The groan was out before she could stop it.

> Chloe: I was trying to be respectful. I didn't think you'd want to meet anyone new until you were fully healed.

> Mom: You're so sweet, and with any other person, you'd be right. I was so worried when you told me that you and Evan had broken up. But I hear Tanner is quite an amazing man. I really would love to meet him.

> Chloe: I'll see what I can do.

Just then, her doorbell rang.

Saved by the bell.

> Chloe: I've got to go. Tanner's here to pick me up. I'll see you tomorrow. Love you!

> Mom: Love you too!

Tossing her phone into her purse, she walked over and opened the door. "Hey! Just let me grab my coat and I'll be all set."

"You look beautiful," he told her, and she felt herself blush.

Locking up, they walked out to his car and it wasn't until they were pulling out of the driveway that she asked, "Is it unusual for something like this to come up on short notice? You know, with a pro shop asking you to come in for an event?"

He shrugged. "This is the first time something like this has ever happened, but considering it's fairly local, I didn't mind. Any publicity is good publicity, right?"

She didn't honestly know, but if he was okay with it, who was she to argue?

"What kind of things do you think they'll talk about?"

For the rest of the drive, he explained what it was like to be a spokesperson. All she could do was sit back and listen, because it was a lot to take in.

"Basically," he went on, "celebrity branding or celebrity endorsement is a form of advertising campaign and marketing strategy that uses a person's fame or social status to promote a brand or product. Since my name is widely known in the skiing world, it makes sense that they'd want someone with my reputation and skill to promote a certain brand of gear. In the interview, I'll be sure to brag about how great their company is, and hopefully it will garner a lot of sales for them."

"And do you really use their products? Like exclusively?"

He shrugged. "Not exclusively, but I have used them."

"Oh."

"It's not like I have to only use their gear," he went on. "But I get to test new products and they get pictures of me using it, so it lends some authenticity to the campaign. Once it snows here, I'm sure I'll go up and they'll want pictures of me using some of the gear out on the slopes."

She nodded and within minutes they were pulling up to the lodge and the valet was helping them out. "Thank you," Chloe said softly as she climbed out of the car. Tanner was right there to take her hand and lead her inside. There was a team of people waiting for them and it was a little like an out-of-body experience.

"Tanner! So good to see you!"

"Tanner! Thank you so much for coming!"

"Tanner! We have some great idea for photos up in the shop if you're ready!"

And before she knew it, Tanner was being whisked away and she was left to simply follow the crowd.

* * *

This felt great, he thought. It had been a long time since he'd felt so valued and appreciated, and he was beyond grateful that he could take advantage of this opportunity. They had taken a ton of photos up in the pro shop—there was a new clothing line that they wanted to get pictures of him in—and all the while, they asked him about how much he was looking forward to skiing here once the first snow hit.

Naturally, he had gushed over all of it—the clothes and how much he couldn't wait to get his gear on and be the first one down the mountain—and the management and PR team were eating it up. Now they were all sitting around a massive table down in the same restaurant he and Chloe had dined at a few weeks ago, and they were conducting the interview while they ate. It wasn't his favorite way to be interviewed, but the food and wine were fantastic, and everyone was having a great time.

Except Chloe.

One look at her and he could tell she was miserable. She was eating silently, only making eye contact with her plate, and he didn't want to say anything to call attention to it and risk embarrassing her.

"Tanner, if you could pack up and compete again for a season, where would you go?" Margaret, the journalist, asked.

Grinning, he replied, "Why would I pack up and go anywhere when Summit Ridge has so much to offer?"

Yeah, everyone got a kick out of that response, but he heard a very faint snort from Chloe.

"But if you *had* to pick one?" Margaret prompted.

"Without a doubt, the Aosta Valley in Italy," he said.

"Between Mont Blanc, the Matterhorn, and the Monte Rosa, there's something almost magical about the area. Those towering mountains offer high-altitude skiing, snow-sure slopes and a view that can't be beat." Pausing, he took a sip of his wine. "And the food is phenomenal!"

"That's for sure," someone agreed, and then the conversation moved on for a bit to some of the places in the world he'd skied and was the food as good as the snow. It was a silly conversation, but he was enjoying it.

He just wished Chloe was too.

"You went out at the top of your game," Margaret interjected a few minutes later. "And now you're a teacher. It's a commendable profession to be sure, but don't you miss the excitement of competing?"

"I retired when I did because I had accomplished everything that I wanted to. My end game was always going to be in education," he explained.

"Why not open a school to train future athletes? Or even give lessons here at Summit Ridge?"

"I'd be open to giving lessons, but only as something on the side. I love what I'm doing now. Teaching kids is incredibly rewarding." He paused and nodded. "And the fact that I was lucky enough to be offered a position in a school that was so close to a ski resort? What are the odds?"

"It seems like this was meant to be," Margaret went on. "So, what have you been doing in your spare time while you wait for the snow to start falling?"

"Well..." This time he reached over and took Chloe's hand in his and gave it a squeeze to get her attention. "Chloe is also a teacher. That's how we met. We've been spending a lot of our spare time together working on lesson plans and school projects. She's shown me around Sweetbriar Ridge and I'm actually loving small town life."

"Chloe," Margaret began, zeroing in on her. Tanner felt her tense a bit and hoped Margaret wasn't going to say anything offensive. "How does it feel to be dating someone as famous and talented as Tanner Westyn? Were you a fan of his before he came to teach at your school?"

"Oh, um...I actually didn't know anything about him," Chloe admitted. "I don't follow any sports, but Tanner's been teaching me about skiing since we met. I'm looking forward to seeing him in action when the season starts."

"Any chance you'll let him teach you how to ski?"

Beside him, she laughed softly. "I'm not particularly athletic, but I'm more than happy to be a spectator and cheer him on."

"And who couldn't use their own personal cheerleader, right, Tanner?" Margaret asked with a laugh. "In the past, you've always been involved with women who either competed just like you or who at least could ski. Do you think not having this aspect of your lives in common will cause any conflicts?"

For a moment, he was too stunned to respond. Chloe had gone completely still, and Tanner had no idea if he should call out Margaret for being so tactless or comfort his girlfriend.

He went the diplomatic route instead.

"I don't think couples have to have everything in common," he said stiffly. "And I love all the things Chloe and I *do* have in common. This is the best relationship I've ever been in, and I feel lucky that she's been so willing to put up with me talking incessantly about the glory days of my skiing career."

Everyone was silent and he hoped he made his point.

"Anyone ready for dessert?" their server asked with perfect timing.

It appeared that the interview portion of the evening ended, and for the rest of the meal, the conversation was still focused on the sport, but things were a little more neutral and less focused on him and Chloe.

"I'm so sorry," he whispered for only her ears. "That was a little catty and I will reach out to my rep to let them know."

"It's fine," she said. "I don't blame her. You're...you know...you. This big, famous athlete, and I'm just...me." She shrugged. "Trust me, I'm used to it."

And he hated that more than anything—the fact that she put herself down.

Suddenly, he couldn't wait for this night to be over, to take Chloe home and show her how amazing she was and how much he truly adored her.

Loved her.

Because...yeah. He did.

It took another hour before they could leave, and he was mentally exhausted by the time the valet brought their car around. Neither said a lot on the drive back to her house, and he was okay with that. Right now, he needed a little peace and quiet to think about what he was going to say. Was tonight the right night to profess his love for her? Should it be something he did on a romantic night out? Would she freak out when he told her?

Or worse, would she tell him she didn't feel the same way?

And then, because he was an overthinker, would she think he was throwing the L word out there to make up for the awkward evening? Would it appear trite or a bit like he was trying to mollify her?

Pushing that particular thought aside, he let out a long,

low breath. Beside him, Chloe was staring out the window into the darkness.

"Penny for your thoughts," he said before he could stop himself.

Without looking his way, she said, "They're not even worth that."

Shit.

"Chloe, look, I know this night didn't go quite the way I had hoped, but..."

Now she turned her head to glance at him. "Don't, okay? You're not responsible for the things that Margaret person said. I know that."

"But I'm definitely going to make sure my publicist knows how rude she was. That was totally not cool. I probably should have said more, but..."

"But you have an image to uphold and a professional relationship with these people that you need to maintain. I get it. It's not a big deal." Then she returned her attention to the passing scenery and his heart sank.

This was her go-to reaction. He'd learned enough about her to know it. She retreated and got quiet when she was hurt or overwhelmed because she wasn't confrontational. And as much as he didn't want to argue with her, he certainly was going to fight *for* her.

Just...not here in the confines of the car.

By this point, they were literally only five minutes from her house, so Tanner was fine with finishing the drive quietly. Once they pulled into her driveway, however, what Chloe said kind of shocked him.

"I don't think you should come in tonight." Her words were spoken softly but firmly.

"Chloe..."

Even in the darkness, he could see her close her eyes as

if to fortify herself. When she looked at him, however, he saw a world of weariness.

"Please," he said gruffly. "I don't want to just go home. We need to talk about this. You know we do. I won't stay long, just...just enough so that we both feel good about what we say."

She agreed, but he already knew he was losing her.

Following her into the house, Tanner mentally scrambled to find the right words—the words that would make everything okay again. Or maybe find some sort of magical time machine that would take them back to after school today and he could simply opt to go to the lodge by himself and leave Chloe out of the whole thing.

Only...he didn't want to leave her out. He wanted her to be part of his world.

But he also just wanted his world to be kinder to her.

She tossed her coat onto the one oversized chair in her living room before sitting on the sofa and looking at him expectantly.

Okay, so...he was going to have to start the conversation. Awesome.

Carefully, he began. "I know tonight didn't go the way we were expecting. In my defense, I've never done a meeting or event like what happened tonight. This was all so random and even I wasn't sure what exactly was going to happen." Pausing, he sat down on the opposite end of the couch. "But it didn't give anyone the right to speak to you— or about us—the way that journalist did. I'm going to ask to have the interview pulled. It's only fair."

For a moment, she looked a little confused, but then... she sighed. "Tanner, it wasn't just the interview, it was...it was everything. From the moment we walked into the lodge, I disappeared. No one saw me. You got swept up in the excitement and I ended up following the group like some sort of reject."

"No," he argued, but then took a moment to think and...

Oh.

Shit.

"Chloe, I..."

"When we got to the pro shop and the manager tried to tell me this was a private event and I'd have to come back tomorrow, that was when you finally acknowledged me and introduced me. Then I was relegated to a spot in the corner for almost two hours! No one offered me anything to drink or even a place to sit! It was incredibly uncomfortable!"

"Okay, but..."

"All I wanted to do was leave," she went on. "I contemplated texting Ash and asking her to come and get me, but I didn't want to embarrass you."

"I had no idea. I'm so sorry!" But he realized that might be too little, too late.

"Here's the thing, the last guy I dated was a big-time corporate lawyer."

"Wait...seriously?"

She nodded. "He worked with the billionaire guy responsible for all the growth here in Sweetbriar. Anyway, we had nothing in common—not really—but ultimately we figured that out. I didn't fit in his world. I enjoy my life here. It's simple and uncomplicated, and I'm really beginning to see how much I need that for my happiness." Another sigh. "I don't fit in your world, Tanner."

"But you do!" he countered. "What happened tonight is beyond rare! Hell, I can make sure it never happens again!"

She shook her head. "That's not what I want, and if you're being totally honest, it's not what you want either." Pausing, she gave him a sad smile. "I watched you tonight and you were...you looked happier than I've ever seen you. You were eating all that attention up and there's nothing wrong with that. You are a big deal and you deserve to have people praising you. It's just not something I enjoy being around and I didn't appreciate being treated like I was invisible."

"Chloe, that will never happen again. I promise. I'll make sure that you are front and center at every event moving forward! That you get treated like a VIP! I can totally work that into any contract for any promotional event I do!"

Her shoulders sagged. "You're not hearing me, Tanner. I'm not asking you to change anything for me. I'm not a VIP and I don't *want* to be a VIP. I hate the spotlight. It makes me incredibly uncomfortable. I...I just want my life back. The one where there are no surprises, and my family is just all happy and healthy and...that's it."

"Chloe, sweetheart, that's not a life. That's not living," he told her. "That's asking to live in a bubble. Life is messy sometimes. People screw up and make mistakes, but then they make things right. And surprises don't only have to be bad. Just like changes. You know the saying that change is the only constant in life? If you refuse to handle the changes..."

"I don't expect you to understand," she clarified. "But tonight just...it made things clear for me. We already know I'm not handling the stuff with my parents very well, and we talked about my feelings about all the other changes earlier today. And with the upcoming ski season, it sounds like your time is going to be pretty full with that."

"I'll back out of all of it," he said, willing to beg.

But she shook her head again. "It's not you, Tanner. It's me. I think it's best if we just...cooled things off for a while.

It seems like we both have outside distractions and obligations, and they'd be better handled...separately. I'm sorry."

For a moment, he couldn't quite comprehend what he was hearing.

"I understand what you're saying and that you think it's what you want, but...I've seen this...this...change in you since we met. I've seen you step out of your comfort zone and simply turn into this even more amazing version of yourself. I know things are scary and a bit unsettling for you right now, but I don't think reverting back into your shell is going to make you happy, and it certainly isn't going to stop all the things from happening."

"Tanner..."

And it was something in her tone that stopped him.

"It won't matter, will it?" he murmured. "I could sit here all night and tell you all the ways you inspire me or how incredible you are, and you won't believe it. You don't want to. I can list a thousand ways that you're amazing and you won't see it."

Her eyes shone bright with unshed tears, but she looked away before any of them fell.

"Do you want me to beg?" he asked, his voice raw. "Because I will. I think we're worth fighting for. I think we have something good here, Chloe. Something that has the promise of an incredible future."

"Sometimes you have to know when it's not going to work out. Even if it hurts more than you ever thought possible," she said quietly, letting out a shaky breath. "Sometimes wanting someone isn't enough."

"It's not just wanting you. What we have is so much more than that, and I think you know it."

She looked up at him. "I need to feel good about myself, and I don't right now. I'm sorry."

They sat in silence for several long moments, and he had to admit the truth—there wasn't anything he could say to fix this. He could schmooze with pretty much anyone in the world and win them over, but for the first time in his life, he didn't have the words.

He didn't have the charm or anything to win over the one person in the world he wanted most of all.

And it crushed him.

"Okay, then," he whispered. "I guess I should go."

A nod was her only response.

Slowly, Tanner got to his feet, but instead of walking to the door, he walked over to her and gently kissed the top of her head. "I'm willing to give you the space that you need, but I'm not giving up on us." He straightened and waited to see if she'd look up at him, but she didn't. "I'll always be there if you need me. For anything."

And when she still didn't look up, he turned and walked out the door.

Out of her life.

The cold air hit him like a slap in the face and yet...he was numb.

How had this night gone so wrong? Six hours ago, he couldn't wait to introduce Chloe to the athlete part of his life. Now he wished he'd never done it.

Hindsight and all...

With nothing left to do, he trudged over to his SUV and climbed in. He wished he lived farther away so he could let the drive clear his head. Two blocks simply wasn't far enough, but he also wasn't interested in driving just for the sake of driving.

So he went home and walked into his quiet house.

Normally it didn't bother him, but tonight it felt like a weight on him.

An awful, heavy weight.

"Better get used to it," he mumbled as he hung up his coat. "This is going to be your life for the next long while."

Having Chloe come over had been like a breath of fresh air. He'd lived alone before and was fine with it, but there was something to be said for having a person in your home who meant something to you and who cared for you in return. Before moving to Sweetbriar Ridge, he'd spent so much time traveling that the apartments he'd rented and townhomes were merely places to sleep. It wasn't until he moved here that he realized what it was like to have a home.

And now he'd lost it.

Kicking off his shoes, he made his way through the house, shutting off the lights on his way to the bedroom. Tomorrow was a school day and he had to be up early.

He just had no idea how he was going to handle working so closely with Chloe and knowing they were over.

"And I don't want to know," he whispered as he undressed and crawled into bed.

But sadly, he was going to find out.

Sooner rather than later.

Chapter Twelve

The following weekend, she walked into Books & Beans to meet Ashlynn for coffee and ended up facing her entire family.

"Um...what's going on?"

Ashlynn stepped forward first. "We've all given you space because we didn't want to upset you, but it's obvious that that was a mistake. You've had excuses for not going over to Mom's, you blew off our last two coffee dates..."

"I'm here now, aren't I?" she interrupted.

"And this is a small town and news travels fast whether you like it or not," her sister said. "You and Tanner broke up and we're all worried about you, okay? If you didn't show up here today, we were all going to your house." Then she leaned in close and whispered, "Be very glad it didn't come to that. We'll all have to behave here in the coffee shop."

That made her chuckle a bit. "Okay, fine. Let's get this over with."

And while she wasn't really in the mood to have such a public intervention—for lack of a better word—she was also seriously impressed that they had given her this much time to herself.

Ashlynn took her hand and led her to a cluster of tables that were already set up with food and pointed her to the corner chair.

Harder to get up and escape that way, she assumed.

Chloe took her seat and then looked up. They were all there—Ash, Billie, Reid, Levi, Jade, and...her parents. Inwardly, she shuddered and just forced herself not to focus on them being there together.

Her shoulders sagged as she asked, "Okay, now what?"

"How are you doing?" Billie asked carefully.

She shrugged. "I'm sad, I can't deny that, but...it's for the best." Then something occurred to her. "I guess I'm confused about why this is such a big deal. People break up all the time—heck, when Evan and I broke up a few months ago, no one staged an intervention about it. I said I was fine and that was that. Why are you all making such a fuss about this?"

"Because there was a huge difference in the way you were with Evan and the way you were with Tanner," Jade replied. "I think you were fond of Evan, but it never seemed like a relationship you were particularly invested in."

That was...surprising.

"Really?" She glanced around at her family. "Why didn't anyone ever say anything to me about that?"

"What was the point?" Ash asked. "You were happy and we just thought it was a casual relationship and no big deal. And apparently, we were right. But you were different with Tanner. It looked serious. Like...really serious." She gave Chloe a sad smile. "Chlo, you are my other half and whenever you would talk about things with Tanner, I just...I knew. I knew he meant something to you. What happened?"

"Ash, come on," Levi murmured. "Some things are personal and don't need to be aired in public like this. As much as you might think this is helping, Chloe deserves some privacy." He looked at Chloe. "There is literally zero pressure for you to share anything that you don't want to. We all just want to make sure you're okay."

And for some reason, that was exactly the right thing to say, because the next thing she knew, she was telling them everything. From all her doubts and insecurities over teaching and competing with him to the awful PR dinner at Summit Ridge. She'd kept the entire thing bottled up and had said none of this out loud for over a week, and it felt fantastic to just say it.

Seven pairs of eyes simply blinked at her for several moments and she feared that maybe she had overshared. But then...

"What a dick!" Ashlynn declared. "I mean...seriously, what a *dick*. What was the point in even bringing you along if he was just going to star in his own damn parade?"

"Okay, to be fair," Reid interjected, "I doubt he knew how that night was going to go. Chloe said that he'd never done anything like that before."

But her sister wasn't buying it. "He didn't have to know exactly how it was going to go. He behaved like a total egomaniac! When everyone greeted him, he should have been holding Chloe's hand and not letting go! According to her, he let them sweep him up and left her standing there to follow along! I would seriously kick your ass if you ever did anything like that to me!"

"Again with the ass kicking," Chloe mumbled, but no

one was listening. Apparently, they all had something to say.

"It was completely rude of him..."

"Inexcusable!"

"But he apologized..."

"Some people just can't live if they're not in the spotlight..."

That last one came from Billie, and Chloe looked over at her and nodded. "That's the one that was the breaking point for me. It gave me a glimpse into his world and...that's not me. I'm not a spotlight person, but I'm also not a...shove-me-out-of-the-way-so-*you*-can-be-in-the-spotlight person either. Does that make sense?"

"Absolutely," Billie assured her. "I'm so sorry you had to feel that way. Just know that it's not you. There is nothing wrong with you. Sometimes it doesn't matter how much you care about someone; some things are just...not compatible."

"Bullshit." This came from their father, and everyone turned to look at him. Ronan was sitting at the opposite end of the table, his arms folded, his expression stony.

"Dad," Billie hissed. "What the hell?"

He leaned forward, bracing his hands on the table. "I am tired of that attitude," he said firmly. "Yes, sometimes people aren't compatible. I believe that. What I don't believe in is throwing someone away because things get tough." Then he looked directly at Chloe. "Do you care about Tanner?"

"Dad..." she whined.

"Do you? Did you see yourself having a future with him or was it something casual like that Evan person?"

Ugh...

"I don't know," she said weakly. "I guess I didn't let

myself think about the future because the present was such a mess."

He looked at her oddly. "What in the world are you talking about? What was messy?"

"This!" she cried, pointing to everything around her. "Mom's accident! New teachers at school! Moving into a new house and hating the fact that I was trying to do it all on my own! Having to prove myself as a teacher all over again while everyone praised everything Tanner was doing! You showing up and moving back in with Mom! I mean... how can the two of you get along now when you couldn't do it when it was really important, huh? Why are we all supposed to be happy about you showing up to help now when we all needed you years ago?"

You could have heard a pin drop. The entire coffee house went silent, and Chloe wished a hole would open up in the floor and put her out of her misery.

"Maybe we should move this to our place," Levi said diplomatically, but she wasn't having any of it.

"Oh, no. You all wanted to talk, so let's talk," she argued as her heart hammered like thunder in her chest. "It didn't seem to be a big deal to ambush me when I walked in here, but when I'm the one asking a tough question, we need to hush up and move the discussion someplace safe." Then she glared at the group defiantly. "And to that, *I* call bullshit!"

Ashlynn burst out laughing even as she started to clap. "Yes! Preach! It's about time this side of you came out!"

"Hush," she snapped. "Now is not the time for that."

"Oh, I think it's the perfect time. I think you've been bottling up so many things for so damn long, and you're right. We're all used to just keeping our own stuff private, but trying to make everyone else deal with their shit publicly." Then she looked around the table. "Anyone have anything to add?"

"I can't help that I was in an accident," her mother said stiffly. "Believe me, this wasn't something I'd wish on anyone."

Rolling her eyes, Chloe said, "I didn't say I blamed you for being in an accident. What I'm saying is that it contributed to me feeling overwhelmed."

"Okay, but you're easily overwhelmed," Billie reasoned. "We all know that about you and we still love you. But..." Pausing, she huffed. "Sometimes it's kind of annoying to coddle you when you're upset over things that you shouldn't be! The town's growing, and it's been great for everyone, and yet it overwhelms you. The school had to hire more teachers, but you still have a job. You moved into a house that you can totally afford to buy on your own—something so many people can't, and you don't see that as a good thing. I mean...come on! Do you not see what a downer you are? Everything to you is like the glass is half empty!"

"That's not true! I am everyone's cheerleader! I always try to help people to look on the bright side of things!" she countered.

"Yeah, you do that for everyone else, but not yourself," her mother said. "You're the hardest on yourself, Chloe. You don't have faith in the person you are. You don't see what we see."

"Apparently you all see me as being a whiny crybaby," she murmured.

"Sometimes you are," Ash said, and when Chloe gasped with disbelief, she said, "Sorry, Chlo, but it's true. Sometimes, that's exactly what you are. Hell, sometimes that's what we all are, but not all the time. If there was something really horrible going on—like when Levi lost his job and had to move back home or when I was accused of burning the salon to the ground—yeah, it was okay to be a whiny crybaby. But your life is freaking amazing and yet it's like you just keep looking for a reason for it not to be. Why?"

"I...I..."

"Because I left," her father said miserably. "I wasn't there to lift you up and encourage you. I wasn't there to wipe away your tears and tell you that everything was going to be okay." He sighed. "I failed you. A child deserved to know they are loved and special and have people around to guide them when they're scared, and...I wasn't."

"I was there," Marie said primly, but everyone just sort of groaned and waved her off.

"So not the time to go down that rabbit hole," Ashlynn said wearily.

"Chloe, we've all experienced self-doubt, but there has to come a point where you embrace all that's good in your life and realize all the possibilities," Levi said. "When I came back to Sweetbriar, I thought my life was over. And for a good reason. But it turned out to be the greatest thing to ever happen to me." He smiled over at his wife. "The people we were when we met shouldn't have made sense. We were opposites in every way, but when you love someone, you find a way to make it work."

"I struggled so much with letting Levi in," Jade explained. "My life was structured just the way I liked it and I didn't want anyone changing that. But once I realized how much I missed him and needed and wanted him, we made it work." Then she laughed softly. "That's not to say that every day is perfect, but at the end of the day, I get to be with the greatest guy in the world."

"It sounds a lot like you and Tanner," Levi went on. "You have this structured world and he disrupted the balance that you feel you need to be happy. But...are you happy now that he's not in your life? Did ending the relationship make everything better?"

"Um..."

"The town's going to continue to grow," he said, not letting her say anything. "At some point, they're going to have to build another elementary school because they're going to need that many more classrooms. You're an amazing teacher, but you can't expect to be the only amazing teacher. That's just not reasonable."

"People are going to get hurt," her mother interjected. "You can't control that. Life—and relationships—get messy. And just because a relationship didn't work out at one point in your life doesn't mean that you can't forgive and try to make things right."

"I swear, if you are telling me that you and Dad are back together, I'll..."

"What? No!" Marie cried and then laughed a bit. "What I'm saying is your father and I have been working on communicating with each other and forgiving each other. We both made mistakes—mistakes that hurt all of you. But we are always going to be in each other's lives because we have the four of you. It's time to stop being bitter and try to move forward in a healthier relationship."

It was crazy how much of a relief that was.

"All I'm trying to say," her mother continued, "is that life is going to pass you by if you are determined to stay in one place, in your own little bubble. I don't want that for you. It's okay to love living in a small town and being a teacher, but it's not okay if anything outside of that frightens you to the point of hiding out in your house alone."

Letting out a long breath, Chloe looked over at her twin. "Why didn't you come and talk to me? Like...you never had a problem just showing up at my place and demanding that we talk. What made this different?"

"Honestly? I felt like you needed to work some of this out yourself. I thought you'd eventually call or show up at the salon or text, but...you didn't. It wasn't that I didn't want to be there for you; I just felt like maybe you needed some time to yourself first."

Nodding, she said, "I thought I did."

"And now?"

Looking up, she smiled sadly. "Now I don't know. I don't know anything anymore." She paused. "No, that's not true. I know that I miss Tanner. So damn much."

"Have you spoken to him at all?" Jade asked.

"No. Obviously, I've seen him at school, but he sort of stays out of my way—so much it's almost painful. And I didn't want to bring any of...you know...this...to school. When I'm there, my students are all I'm focused on."

"Okay, but it's not like you couldn't call him or text him or just go to his house," Ashlynn said. "He only lives like two minutes away."

"And what was I supposed to say, huh? Until a few minutes ago, I was perfectly fine living in my own pity party!"

"That's fair," Billie said. "But what about now? Do you think you could call him and talk to him?"

"I want to say yes, but...I'm not ready. I'm not sure what I'd even say. That night was a big deal to him and even though he was partly to blame, I wasn't exactly under-standing and I certainly didn't even try to be a part of what was going on. I just shrank into a corner and let it happen. So really..."

"The whole thing was an unpleasant experience and you need to chalk it up to a one-time thing," Levi said.

"Now that he knows how you feel, I doubt he'd allow that to happen again."

Tanner's words came back to her.

"That will never happen again. I promise. I'll make sure that you are front and center at every event moving forward! That you get treated like a VIP! I can totally work that into any contract for any promotional event I do!"

Now she realized he meant it.

Just like some other things he said to her that night.

"Do you want me to beg?" Because I will. I think we're worth fighting for. I think we have something good here, Chloe. Something that has the promise of an incredible future."

"I'm willing to give you the space that you need, but I'm not giving up on us. I'll always be there if you need me. For anything."

And she did need him.

For everything.

She just had no idea how to ask.

* * *

"Mr. Westyn! Mr. Westyn! My mom signed me up for skiing lessons and I saw your picture in the ski store!" Alex Maynor told him on Monday morning. "I told everyone you were my teacher and they said that maybe you would teach my ski lessons! Will you?"

He smiled patiently. It seemed a bit early for ski lesson sign ups since it would be at least another month before the snow started, and even then, the prime skiing time wasn't until January. "I didn't think they were doing sign ups yet since we don't know when it's going to snow," he said.

"I'm going to the kiddie ski camp," Alex explained. "It's inside with a little hill, and my mom said it's gonna be fun!"

For a moment, Tanner racked his brain to remember if he saw that facility or if anyone had even mentioned it. It wasn't something he'd be interested in participating in to teach, but it could be a fun field trip option. Perhaps he should call them and see about it.

"I'm sure it will, Alex. And I promise to let you know if I'm going to be one of the instructors!"

"Yay!" And as the boy ran back to his seat, Tanner looked around the room and couldn't help but smile. All his ski-themed stuff was on the walls, his shelves were now almost completely full of books, and the room looked great. He'd been doing this for almost two months, and this was the kind of classroom that would make any teacher proud.

But it especially did that for him.

This wasn't the grade he wanted, and it certainly wasn't the situation he had always envisioned for himself, but it was better—so much better. The only thing that would make it perfect was if he and Chloe were still together.

Eleven days.

The longest eleven days of his life. She was literally so close and yet so far away. He could see her every damn day, but he didn't want to do anything to upset her, so he kept his distance.

And it was killing him.

Unfortunately, now wasn't the time to be thinking about that—again. It was time to take his class down to lunch. "Okay, everyone!" he said cheerily. "Let's put our pencils down and grab our lunches. Line up by the door and let's see who's going to be the best listener today!"

They all silently scrambled over to their cubbies and grabbed their things while wiggling their way into a straight line. It was so damn adorable that it made his heart feel lighter than it had in days. As soon as they were all ready, he led them down to the cafeteria and left them with the aide.

Quietly, he walked back to his classroom and decided to call Summit Ridge and inquire about a field trip and what it would involve. Once he had some information, he could go to Principal Kincaid and see if it was something they could make happen. It wasn't like he wanted to take the entire elementary school there, just his class. That was allowed, wasn't it?

Back at his desk, Tanner took out his own lunch and set it out before grabbing his phone. Between bites of his sandwich, he spoke to several people who explained that the indoor ski and snowboard facility was indeed open to field trips, and they were emailing him all the forms he would need. And he had shamelessly used his name and connection to the pro shop to negotiate a lower price per student and was already planning to reach out to his publicist to see if she could put a spin on it for PR for both the lodge and the school district. And the best part? They could realistically have a date as early as next week if he wanted.

Which he did.

"No time like the present," he said, popping the last bite of his lunch in his mouth. He still had fifteen minutes before he had to get his students, so he headed down to the office to see what he had to do next.

On the walk down the hall, he spotted Chloe walking his way, but there was no way he could just dive into a closet without looking like an idiot, so he simply nodded and kept on walking. Actually, all she did was nod too, so... clearly this was how they were going to be now.

"This sucks," he murmured before opening the door to the front office.

"Hey, Tanner," Susan said with a smile. "What can I do for you?"

"How do I go about scheduling a field trip?" he asked.

"Well, you can tell me where you want to go and when you want to go, and I'll help you with the permission slips and scheduling transportation."

His eyes went wide. "Really? You do all that?"

She laughed softly. "We're a small school and there's not a lot going on. I like to help where I can." She laughed again. "So, what are you thinking?"

"There's an indoor ski school up Summit Ridge," he told her. "They actually do ski and snowboard lessons, but they also do special events like field trips and they have equipment and instructions geared for the kindergarten age group. We'd obviously need a bus and several parent volunteers, but I'm just looking to take my class—not the entire school."

"Hmm...what about Chloe's class? It would be great if it were a kindergarten field trip."

Crap. He hadn't thought about that.

"Um...I'm not sure it fits in with her lesson plans," he said carefully. "You know how my room is all about skiing and I just thought..."

She held up a hand to stop him. "I totally get it. Let me make some calls and see what I can find out and I'll talk to you at the end of the day. I'll have to see about the cost per student..."

"Already done," he told her before breaking down the financing he'd secured.

"Oh...well, that's amazing! I'm sure they have some forms we'll need..."

"Already have them," he said confidently. "They just

emailed them over. I can forward them to you. And I'm sure they'll include the cost per student we discussed."

"Perfect! Okay, I'll get things together and talk to Principal Kincaid, and you should be all set." Another pause. "Wait, when did you want to do this?"

"Um...next week?" he hesitantly replied.

"Ooh...that's ambitious. I'll call the transportation department and see if I can work some magic. See me before you leave for the day."

"I can make some calls too..."

"Tanner?"

"Hmm?"

"We're a team here at Sweetbriar," she told him with a serene smile. "You've come a long way from the guy who steamrolled his way into a faculty meeting with a frittata and cookies, but there are things that literally take a village to pull together. Go and teach your class and let me handle what I handle, okay?"

And for the first time, he didn't argue. He simply nodded and thanked her. "I really appreciate the help, Susan. Thank you."

Her smile was radiant. "I think this sounds like a very cool field trip and I can't wait to help make it happen!"

The alarm sounded on his phone to remind him it was time to head back to the cafeteria. He thanked Susan one more time before heading out of the office with a bit of a spring in his step.

How cool would it be if he actually pulled this off? It would be the perfect way to tie in all the work he put into his classroom while doing something he knew his students would enjoy. As he approached the cafeteria, he spotted Chloe again out of the corner of his eye and felt a twinge of guilt. It would have made for a great kindergarten field trip, but he was fairly certain she wouldn't want anything to do with it. So, he'd keep it to himself. And when she found out —because he knew she would—he'd just chalk it up as another reason for her to be mad at him. He hated it, but that was how things were going to be, and he had to accept that.

And maybe someday he would. Right now, it hurt just to look at her and know that he was the last person she wanted to see.

At least...he thought he was, but she seemed to be heading straight for him. Did this mean...?

"Hey," she said a bit stiffly when she was close enough. "I just wanted to give you a heads-up about the firefighter assembly this afternoon."

"O-kay..."

"Reid's leading it and he might have mentioned wanting to...um...have a few words with you."

It took a moment for that to make sense. "Ah. Got it." Nodding, he did his best to put her mind at ease. "I'm sure he's not going to start a fight with me in front of all the students, but I appreciate the warning."

"I told him to just leave you alone, but..."

"But he's going to be your brother-in-law and he's protective of you. I'd do the same thing in his position."

That seemed to give her pause. "Well, I think it's ridiculous. This doesn't have anything to do with anyone else, and if we're fine, then they should all be."

Sliding his hands into his pockets, he asked, "Are we? Fine, I mean?"

Chloe let a shuddery breath that told him that maybe she wasn't. It was wrong for that to give him hope, but...it did.

"I...I think so," she said quietly. "This isn't an ideal situation, but we're both adults and we're handling it, right?"

With no other choice, he nodded. "Right." There was more he wanted to say, but the aide was lining up their students and now just wasn't the time. "Thanks again for the heads-up. Reid's a reasonable guy. I'm sure he's going to just do what he feels he has to do. Although I really thought Ashlynn would have been the one to come at me first."

She let out a mirthless laugh. "Yeah, she likes to throw around the threat of kicking people's...you know...um..."

Now it was his turn to laugh because she was trying not to say anything offensive that little ears could overhear. "I know what you're saying and I was already warned about that where she's concerned."

"You were? Really?"

"The day we were all at Levi and Jade's. Reid and I had gone outside and were talking, and he mentioned it. Your sister is definitely a bit scary and intimidating, and I'm not gonna lie, I've looked over my shoulder a time or two since you and I...um...since we..."

"Broke up," she said miserably, and again, the way she said it gave him a little hope.

How twisted am I that her misery looks positive?

Well, maybe not her misery, per se, but the fact that she seemed as miserable as he was. That was better, wasn't it?

"Miss Donovan, my belly hurts," one of her students whined pitifully. "I don't feel good."

"Oh, Kimmy..."

"Listen," Tanner said, "why don't you take her down to the nurse and I'll take both our classes back? Your students can come into my room for a few minutes until you're back."

"I don't know, Tanner..."

"You'll only be a few minutes," he reasoned. "It will be fine."

"Miss Donovan..." Kimmy whined again.

"I'll only be five minutes," Chloe assured him before whisking the little girl off toward the nurse's office.

"Okay, everyone!" he called out with a big smile. "Miss Donovan's students, you're all going to come with me and my students to our room. Miss Donovan will come and get you in a few minutes. Now let's all walk quietly in a super straight line, okay?"

It was crazy how that worked, but he had forty kindergarteners following him without a peep.

Well, maybe one or two peeps, but nothing he couldn't handle.

In his room, he instructed his students to take their seats and Chloe's students to line up by the cubbies. Then he talked to them all about the firefighter assembly they were going to attend soon.

"We're going to learn about fire safety, and see how a fire truck works," he told them. "What is something you want to learn about the truck?"

A flurry of little hands went up while shouting out questions.

"How does the ladder work?"

"How much water can the truck hold?"

"Do they have a dog?"

"Can we go for a ride in the fire truck?"

"These are some great questions," he said enthusiastically. "And I'll bet all the firefighters are super excited to answer them! Has anyone here visited the fire station before?"

Everyone seemed to say no to that one, so he supposed this was really going to be a great assembly for them all.

"Does anyone know a firefighter?" he asked.

They all shook their heads, and that's when Chloe breathlessly came into his room. "Sorry about that," she said, and then smiled at her students. "Did everyone behave for Mr. Westyn?"

"Yes!" they told her.

"Very good! Now let's go next door and finish up our coloring sheets before the assembly, okay?" Looking over at Tanner, she smiled. "Thank you for the help. Kimmy made it to the nurse just in time. We had to call her mom to come and get her."

"Poor kid," he said as he walked closer. "I guess we'll see you at the assembly in a little while."

She nodded. "Yes, we will. And...really. Thanks again." With a small smile, she led her class out of the room and back to hers, and it felt like a big step for them. Sure, they could be coworkers and it would be okay.

But that didn't stop him from still hoping for more.

Chapter Thirteen

Friday afternoon, all of Chloe's students were quietly reading.

Except one.

James Emme kept looking over at her, and she knew he had something on his mind. So, she smiled and quietly waved him over. "Is everything okay, James?" she asked.

"Miss Donovan, how come we aren't going on the field trip?" he asked quietly.

"Field trip? What field trip?"

"My best friend Tommy is in Mr. Westyn's class and they're going skiing next week," he explained with a pout. "How come we can't go?"

She looked at him oddly. "I...I didn't know about the field trip," she told him, doing her best to smile again. "But I'll tell you what, I promise to go down and talk to Principal Kincaid while you're all in art class and see what I can find out, okay?"

He smiled and looked like he wanted to jump for joy, but then he looked over at everyone reading and reconsidered. "Thanks, Miss Donovan," he whispered and went back to his seat.

She had ten minutes before she took her class down to art, and her mind was racing. Tanner was taking his class skiing? What in the world? How was that even possible? Or practical? Or safe? Was he using this as a publicity stunt?

The snort was out before she could stop it.

Just when she thought she was ready to test the waters with them again, he goes and pulls a stunt like this. Unbelievable. For over a week, she'd been struggling with keeping her distance. She missed him so damn much and then something like this was like a giant bucket of ice water being thrown at her.

By the time she made it to the front office, she was fuming.

"Hey, Chloe!" Susan said. "What can I do for you?"

"How on earth is Tanner taking his kids on a ski trip?" she demanded. "And why wasn't I told about it?"

Susan looked incredibly offended by Chloe's tone as she shifted primly in her seat. "Well, if you must know, Tanner organized a trip to the indoor ski school up at Summit Ridge. It was something he said felt went along with the theme of his room this year. And as for why you weren't told, no one thought you'd be interested," she said stiffly. "You're very regimented, and it didn't seem like something you'd want to do. Your classes aren't joined, Chloe, and if you want to know what Tanner's doing with his class, then the two of you should discuss that."

Crap.

"Oh God, Susan. I'm so sorry. That was incredibly rude of me."

"Mm-hmm..."

"I just...one of my students just told me about it and it caught me off guard. Maybe it's not something I would have thought of, but it doesn't seem fair for one kindergarten class to go and not the other."

"I agree. But it was something Tanner worked out with Summit Ridge and..."

"Is it a publicity thing? Is this something his...his PR team asked him to do to drum up business for their newest line of ski apparel?"

The look on Susan's face this time was almost comical. "Um...no. That's not it at all. He specifically asked that his name not be used at all. This is to be a school field trip. Although, he asked for me to reach out to the local paper and possibly the news to draw attention to the first ski season up at Summit Ridge and how it's a family-friendly place. And last I heard, he's even made it into a fundraiser for school supplies. Again, without once putting his name on any of it for publicity's sake." She smiled smugly. "So if you have any concerns, you need to talk to him. We're supposed to give them a final head count on Monday. If you'd like your class to go..."

"I'll talk to Tanner," she murmured while silently cursing herself. "Thanks, Susan. And again, I'm so sorry for being so awful."

Susan studied her for a long moment. "You haven't been quite like yourself for the last several weeks. Is everything okay? I know your mom had the accident and all, but..."

"She's doing much better, but there's been a lot of... personal issues that I'm trying to deal with."

"Like breaking up with Tanner?" she quipped before her hands flew to her mouth. "Oh! Now I'm sorry! That sounded very catty."

But Chloe just waved her off. "Not at all, and yes. Breaking up with Tanner was a huge part of it."

"I honestly think that's why he didn't reach out to you about the field trip. He didn't want to make it awkward. I know the students should come first, but it's not worth it if the two of you are going to be that uncomfortable."

"It shouldn't be this hard," she said miserably. "And I hate that it is. We work together and should be able to put those personal feelings aside. I know my students would love to go up to Summit Ridge and learn to ski."

"I looked up Tanner online and saw a lot of videos of him when he used to compete. He's really impressive."

"Yeah, I have too. Especially lately."

"The man looks good in a ski suit," Susan said with a wink. "I'll bet a lot of women wouldn't mind getting a skiing lesson from him."

And that's when inspiration hit.

"Susan, I'm not going to talk to Tanner about this. I mean...I will, but not to ask his permission. Can you print me out permission slips and email me everything I need? I'd like to send out an email to all the parents this afternoon and send reminders home in everyone's book bags today. Just tell me what I need to do, and the date and time of the field trip and count us in!"

Susan's smile grew. "Going to fight for your man, aren't you?"

It wasn't a question.

"I'm certainly going to try."

"I'm emailing everything right now, and good luck!"

"Thanks! I think I'm going to need it." With a quick wave, she rushed out of the office and back down to her classroom. As much as she would have loved to talk to Tanner right now, she didn't want to interrupt his class.

Plus, it would be better for her to look over everything about the field trip and take it from there.

At her desk, she pulled her laptop out of her bag and quickly logged into her email. And what she read was... amazing.

Tanner had managed to pull together an incredible opportunity for not only the students but to benefit the school as well. For every family that used the ski school between now and the end of the year, Summit Ridge would donate a percentage of the sales for school supplies. It was the most selfless thing he ever could have done.

And she loved him for it.

The gasp was out before she could stop it.

Love? Did she love Tanner?

"Oh my God...I do!" she whispered. "I really, really do!"

That was immediately followed by a wave of self-loathing because she had made a serious mess of everything where they were concerned. In the past, if an obstacle seemed too hard to overcome, Chloe's go-to was to just give up.

And...sometimes hide.

"Not this time," she murmured. This time, she was going to do exactly what Susan suggested. She was going to fight for her man.

Just...in her own way.

Feeling energized, she quickly put together an email that included all the pertinent information about the field trip, attached the permission slip, and sent it out to all the parents in her class. Then she emailed Susan to thank her and ask if she could print out copies of everything for her so she could send physical copies home as well. By that time, she needed to pick up her students. Her plan was to speak to Tanner after school.

She just hoped she'd be able to wait that long.

Of course, the rest of the day dragged on and by the time her last student was picked up, Chloe quickly gathered her things and ran next door to Tanner's room and...

It was dark.

He was gone already.

Drats.

Okay, all hope was not lost. She could call him. And as she walked out to her car, she pulled out her phone and did just that.

It went directly to voicemail.

"O-kay..." She didn't leave a message because she decided to go to his house on her way home. The urge to stop at Books & Beans and grab some snacks was tempting, but she was a little too eager to talk to him.

But, because she seemingly had crappy luck, he wasn't home when she got there. It was possible that he stopped somewhere on his way home, but she wasn't desperate enough to sit in his driveway and wait.

Now what do I do?

Her mind was filled with questions about the field trip. Were all the students going to get one-on-one attention? Were the parents going to be able to take part or just watch? Would she have to get on skis or a snowboard?

And while that last one filled her with a bit of dread, it also filled her with a great idea to pass the time.

After driving the two blocks to her house, she ran inside and changed her clothes. Wearing a pair of leggings, a bulky hoodie, and a pair of UGG boots, she grabbed her coat, purse, and keys and was back out the door. It was possible that she should have called Summit Ridge to see if it was too late in the day for a lesson, but she'd rather talk to someone in person. And if they couldn't help her today, then she'd reserve a spot for either tomorrow or Sunday.

Excited, she turned on the radio and sang her way all the way up the mountain. At the lodge, she parked and practically jogged inside. She had no idea where the indoor facility was, but figured anyone at the front desk could point her in the right direction.

"May I help you?" a young man with a bright smile called out as she walked toward him.

"Hey," she said breathlessly when she approached the desk. "My name is Chloe Donovan and my class is coming up here next week for a field trip with the indoor ski school." She paused for a moment. "And here's the thing, I can't ski. It actually terrifies me a little, and I thought if I could come up here and maybe get a lesson or two, I'd feel better about helping my kids next week. I don't want to look like a baby in front of them."

He gave her a sympathetic smile. "I think that is awesome, and you are in luck. We have an instructor who has availability right now!"

She frowned. "But...how do you know that off the top of your head? Don't you have to look it up or something?"

Now he laughed softly. "Oh, he was just up here at the desk. He's new to the Summit Ridge family and the school, and we were all encouraging him that it wouldn't be long until he had a student! And here you are! It's like you were sent here just for him!"

"Um..."

"I'll tell you what, I'll walk with you to the indoor summit. There are a lot of twists and turns when you come in from the main entrance here."

"Thanks," she said, relieved.

"I'm Ted, by the way." Stepping out from behind the

desk, he came up beside her. "And I think you're a great teacher to be doing this for your students."

"Thanks, Ted. I'm hoping there's a tiny hill for me to start with." They began to walk. "And I obviously don't have any equipment. Will that be a problem?"

He shook his head. "Not at all. We'll provide everything for you, and I promise it won't be scary at all."

Yeah, she wasn't sure she believed him, but there was no way she was going to back out now.

They went down a flight of stairs, down a long hallway, turned and went down another glass-encased hallway, up a flight of stairs, and then stepped outside and walked under a covered, paved path that led to what she assumed was the ski school, talking the entire time about what it was like to be a teacher. Ted opened the door for her and stood back.

"Here you go, Chloe! Good luck!"

"Ted, wait!" she said nervously. "Who am I supposed to talk to? Who's my instructor?"

He laughed softly again. "Oh, right! Forgot about that." He stepped inside and looked around before waving to someone. "He's heading this way now."

Chloe turned and looked in the same direction as Ted and froze.

"Chloe Donovan, let me introduce you to your instructor, Tanner Westyn," Ted said cheerily.

"Chloe?" Tanner said in wide-eyed shock. "What are you doing here?"

"Um..."

"Do you two know each other?" Ted asked.

"Um..."

"I need to get back to the front desk, but Chloe's your first student, Tanner! And go easy on her. She wants to make a good impression on her students." And then he

236

turned and walked away, completely oblivious to just how awkward everything was.

The door closing sounded incredibly loud, echoing throughout the area.

"I don't understand what's going on," Tanner said slowly.

And rather than stand there second-guessing herself, she embraced the awkwardness. "I hear we're taking our students on a field trip next week," she said confidently. "And I'm going to need you to show me how to ski."

* * *

For a moment, Tanner looked around as if this was some sort of prank, because there was no way this was happening. It wasn't possible for Chloe to be standing here in front of him for any reason, let alone to learn how to ski. It didn't make sense. It wasn't...

"Wait, what do you mean *we're* taking our students," he said, now even more confused. "It was just supposed to be my class."

She nodded. "It was, but my students heard about it and were very upset about being left out. You're not looking to shun my class, are you? Because if this is your way of one-upping me in your quest to be a better teacher, then let me tell you something, Tanner Westyn! I won't allow it!" Poking her finger into his chest, she kept getting closer. "We were supposed to be the kindergarten *team* and you have done everything possible to keep us separate and I'm putting an end to it!"

There wasn't anything funny about what she was saying, and yet she was kind of adorable when she was riled up.

And it was a bit of a turn-on too.

So not the time, dude...

"Oh, you are, are you?" he asked, deciding to play along. "So you're just going to tag along on my field trip?"

Crossing her arms, she nodded. "Yes, I am, and there's nothing you can do about it. I already emailed all the parents and sent home the permission slips in everyone's backpacks. And since it's so spur of the moment, I plan on following up with all of them over the weekend to make sure no one misses out."

He nodded thoughtfully. "I would have thought you'd be completely against this. After all, it's not part of any lesson plan or curriculum and it's all about skiing. Something you hate."

The eye roll was a given. "I don't hate skiing, Tanner. I never said that. I just can't ski. There's a difference."

"That part I knew, but where me and skiing are involved..."

"Still never said I hated it," she interrupted firmly. "I didn't like a situation that I was put in. What you do and the career you had were amazing. I'm not looking to be a part of that—not as a VIP or mindless cheerleader who's supposed to just stand in a corner while everyone fusses over you. And that doesn't make me a bad person," she went on. "I was completely honest with you about how I felt."

"Okay, I get that, but...I still don't get why you'd want to be here with me. I get that your students would have been disappointed, but you could have come at another time without me."

"Absolutely not." She stomped her foot. "We are the kindergarten team, Tanner. All this separation is over, do you hear me? Over!" Another stomp. "My class and I are coming on this field trip and since you're the instructor here, I'm going to need you to teach me how to ski right now!"

Glancing around nervously, he wondered how rude it would be for him to ask one of his new coworkers if they would take Chloe on. There was no way he could do this with her, no matter how much he wanted to. It was entirely possible that he would end up groveling and begging her for another chance, and he wasn't sure he could handle the rejection again.

"Maybe I can ask one of the other instructors..."

"No," she said defiantly. "I want you to teach me. You're the ski pro, Tanner."

"Yeah, um..."

"Are you afraid to work with me? Do you think I'm unteachable or that you're not up to the challenge?"

Now he looked at her weirdly. "What's going on with you? Why are you trying to pick a fight with me? I've been respectful, Chloe. I've stayed out of your way because I didn't want to do anything to make you uncomfortable. Now you show up here and you're kind of not doing the same for me."

For a moment she didn't say anything and he figured he'd made his point. But then she surprised him.

"We're adults, Tanner. We work together. There's only so much avoiding we can do. And you know what, it didn't help anything." Her shoulders sagged. "I've missed you. A lot. So many times I thought about picking up the phone or just going over and talking to you, but...I always chickened out. It's what I'm good at."

"Chloe..."

"But I'm trying, okay? I want to try again."

Wait...was she saying what he thought she was saying?

Taking a tentative step toward her, he asked, "You mean...you want to give us a try? Like...get back together?"

She nodded even as she bit her bottom lip. "I behaved so poorly, Tanner. And bratty. When I heard about this field trip, I was convinced it was a publicity stunt. I got into it with Susan about it, and..."

"I went to extremes to make sure no one took this as a PR thing. At least, not PR for me," he quickly interrupted. "That's not why I did it, I swear."

"I know."

He explained about how he found out about the ski school and his thought process on why it would make for a fun field trip. "I wasn't doing it to outshine you or win any popularity contest—real or imagined. This is just a huge part of my life and the thought of being able to combine it with teaching my class..."

"I'm sure your students are going to have even more of an appreciation for all the work you put into decorating your classroom after coming here next week. And when they see you demonstrate everything, they're going to think you're the coolest teacher ever." There was no condescension in her tone. If anything, she sounded genuinely happy.

Like she was proud of him.

"And what about you?" he asked gruffly. "I like the thought of us doing this trip together, but...why come here for lessons? No one was going to make you get up and ski in front of the kids. I would have never let that happen because I know how you feel about it."

She laughed softly. "I'm not trying to compete, so please don't think that. I'm doing it because I know some of the kids are going to be scared and I want to be an example. I want to be able to say that I understand and then share how I got up and did it too." Pausing, she laughed again. "I just didn't want to have to do it for the first time with an audience in case I failed and fell and made a complete fool of myself."

Closing the distance between them, he carefully wrapped his arms around her waist. "I promise to catch you if you fall." Resting his forehead against hers, he added, "And not just while we're skiing. We can take things as slowly as you want, and I'll still be there to catch you. Always."

Smiling, she moved her arms around him as well. "You may regret saying that. My athletic skills are seriously awful."

"Doesn't matter. And for the record, I would thoroughly enjoy holding you up as well. It's not just the catching."

He leaned in to kiss her, but she pulled back. "I think if we do that, the lesson is never going to happen," she told him with a grin. "And it took a lot for me to come up here and do this, so before I chicken out..."

"Ah. Got it." Taking her hand, he led her over to the area where they had all the equipment. "Come on. Let's get you fitted with boots and skis."

She nodded, but didn't say anything and he could tell her nerves were starting to get to her.

"There's nothing to fear." Gently, he turned her toward the ski area. "There are several hill levels. We're only going to go on the smallest one and that's only after I get you used to having the skis on. We'll go over how to walk and move in them and then how to get up off the floor in them."

"Already planning on me falling?" she asked with a nervous laugh.

Unable to help himself, he hugged her. "Everyone falls. And for the record, everyone gets that part of the lesson. It's actually one of the first things we teach everyone."

"Oh. Okay."

They got her a pair of boots, and Tanner picked a pair of skis for her before taking her over to a bench to sit down. Together, they got her into the boots before he showed her how to get them attached to the skis. "Always listen for the click and check to make sure the skis are on right. I know it sounds silly, but to really be sure, you can jump up and down a few times. Not big jumps, just enough to test that they're attached." He helped her to her feet and made her do it.

And she almost fell.

"Dammit," she mumbled, frantically reaching for him.

"It's okay. You got this." Slowly he let her go and explained how to waddle walk in the skis and the best ways to keep her balance with and without poles. Next, he explained some of the positions she'll be using at the top of the hill.

Glancing over toward the hill, she bit her lip before looking back at him. "Do I have to walk all the way over there from here with the skis on?"

"No," he assured her. "This is just a little practice area to get you comfortable with the equipment. When you're ready, we'll take the skis off and I'll show you the proper way to carry them. Then, when we get over there, I'll let you get the skis back on to make sure you're comfortable doing it on your own."

It took another twenty minutes before they made the move to the hill. He wanted to make sure she felt confident in not only walking in the skis, but in the poses, positions, and how she'd be starting, stopping, and picking herself up if she fell. When they walked up to the hill, she seemed way more at ease than he would have predicted.

Then he stood back and watched as she clicked her

boots into place, stood up straight with her poles, and got into position. She looked serious but determined.

He talked her through everything they had just learned and didn't want to rush her. "Just take your time. You have this entire hill to yourself. Remember when you want to slow down, all you have to do is..."

She was gliding away before he ever got to finish.

With a bit of a squeal of delight, she made her way down the hill without waiting for him. He jogged after her —because as her instructor, that was what he was supposed to do—and caught up with her near the bottom. She stopped just like he had taught her, and when he came up beside her, her smile was positively radiant.

"I did it!" she cried. "I seriously did it!" Then she dropped her poles and launched herself at him, knocking them both off their feet in a fit of laughter.

Tanner held her tight as they rolled away in an awkward tangle of limbs. She twisted her body a bit to keep the skis from breaking off or from hurting herself, and it was a great moment.

"I know that was just a kiddie hill, but can I try the next one? Please? Please? That was amazing!"

Hugging her tight before helping her to her feet, he said, "How about we try this hill a few more times first? Then we'll move on to the next one."

The pout she gave him was adorable. "Fine. But I think I could totally do it now."

"Trust me. You don't want to get too cocky about this. Just humor me and then we'll move on. I promise."

"Fine."

"Now let's see if you can get up to the top of this hill just doing side steps." It wasn't steep at all and it was a good exercise for her to learn. She did it and as soon as she got to the top, she got into position and took off again.

They did that another three times before he told her to remove the skis so they could move over to the next hill.

"Yay!"

And for another hour, he stood back and watched as she mastered this new skill. It was longer than he was supposed to do an average lesson, but there was no one else waiting for his assistance, so he didn't think it was a big deal. Together they walked back down to return to boots and skis, and as they sat down on the bench, he reached for her hand and smiled.

"I'm proud of you. You did a great job."

The smile she gave him was beautiful. "Thank you. I feel really great about bringing the kids here now. Like…I know what to expect and I can fully help any of them who might struggle or be afraid." She squeezed his hand. "Thank you for this. And for everything. For bringing me out of my comfort zone without pushing." She paused. "Most people around here know me and just sort of…well…they treat me the way they've always treated me. And while it's comforting, it's not always what's best. That night at my house, you gave me a lot to think about. It just took me a while to do anything about it."

"You did the same for me," he admitted. "I'd been walking around for a lot of years thinking everything I did was great and how everyone should want to be like me. It never occurred to me that it wasn't like that." He let out a long breath. "I can't say that I'll never be that guy whose big mouth or colossal ego won't be an issue again, but…I'm working on it."

"The colossal ego might not be a great thing," she teased, playfully nudging his shoulder with hers, "but I genuinely like the person you are, Tanner. I fell for that guy —huge ego and all. You don't have to change for me. I think who we are and all our differences make us a great team."

He ached to kiss her, but he wanted to put everything he felt out there. "I want to be there beside you, Chloe—to be a team with you not only as a teacher, but...in life. I want you to lean on me and be confident in knowing that I'll always be there for you. You are what's important to me. I can walk away from being a spokesperson. That's a part of my life that was never going to be permanent. But you? I think you could be. When I think of the future, I'm not seeing what products I can promote, but I see you. And me. And...a life. If you'll give me another chance..."

He never got to finish. Chloe turned, pressed her lips to his, and it was the perfect interruption. Her hands cupped his jaw as he took the kiss deeper. If they were anyplace else, he'd have her in his arms, in his lap, and making this something wildly erotic.

And later, he would.

Slowly, he broke the kiss, but then dove back in for one more taste before pulling back. "I'm in love with you, Chloe Donovan," he said gruffly. "I love the way you're passionate about teaching and your town and your family. Every day without you was miserable."

"I felt the same way," she told him, still caressing his jaw. "But it gave me time to take a good look at my life and all the ways I wasn't handling things well. My family had an intervention with me and I sort of...well, let's just say that I went off on everyone. I'd never done that before. And you know what happened?"

He shook his head. "No, what?"

"The sky didn't fall. I was able to express how I felt and no one freaked out. The only thing that happened was that

I felt better. It was wild!" She laughed. "Although, I felt a little bad afterwards because some of the stuff I freaked out about really wasn't such a bad thing."

"But to you they were. There's nothing wrong with that. You're entitled to your feelings, and if people can't handle it, that's on them." He paused. "Believe me, I know from personal experience. I didn't want to accept the things you were telling me that night because it wasn't convenient for me. And that was wrong. We don't have to feel the same things, but we have to respect each other's feelings."

She nodded. "I think that's something everyone struggles with. I don't think it's exclusive to us, but thank you for saying that." Now she let out a long breath. "Either way, it's kind of nice to not internalize so many things. It changed nothing. All it did was make me feel sad and alone."

Holding her close, he placed a kiss on her forehead. "And that's something you had to come to on your own." Then he paused. "Why did your family have an intervention?"

"After you and I broke up, I didn't tell anyone. I just sort of stopped doing things with them for like a week. It wasn't a big deal and I think they completely overreacted, but it was sweet that they cared."

"Definitely," he agreed, realizing he didn't share their breakup with his parents either. Any time they talked in the last two weeks, he'd focused on school and how teaching was going. They'd asked about Chloe and he'd said she was fine and then changed the subject. "I should probably call my parents tomorrow."

"Oh?"

"I haven't exactly been honest with them either. It just seemed easier because they worry over every little thing—

and not in a bad way, but I just didn't want to upset them. Does that make sense?"

"It does. And I know that my family worries, but I realized I'd never talked to them about my relationship stuff. I mean, I talk to Ash about it, but not the rest of them. This time I didn't even talk to Ash."

Pulling back, he looked at her. "How come?"

"Um..."

He realized immediately that she might not want to talk about it and quickly backpedaled. "You don't have to tell me. It's not a big deal. You're entitled to your privacy."

Chloe instantly groaned. "Please don't do that. Don't feel you have to walk on eggshells with me, Tanner. The reason I didn't talk to Ashlynn about our breakup is because deep down, I knew I was being unreasonable. I was overwhelmed in a way I'd never been before and was lashing out like a brat. And if anyone was going to call me out on it, she was." She shrugged. "So it was safer to just keep canceling plans and seeing how long I could get away with it." Then she chuckled. "It actually lasted longer than I thought it would."

"Is that a good thing or a bad thing?"

"Definitely a good thing because it forced me to work it out for myself before I had anyone trying to tell me I was wrong or why I needed to look at it their way. It felt good to know I could do it on my own. That I'm not as weak as I always thought I was."

Again, he hated that she saw herself that way, but it sounded like things were changing. "Then I'll agree and say it was a good thing."

They sat in companionable silence for several moments. "So what happens now?" she asked. "Should I come back here tomorrow for another lesson and again on Sunday? Are you working all weekend or would you just come here with me to cheer me on?"

He laughed as he shook his head. "I think we may have created a monster. Tonight you did great and I don't think you need any more lessons before the field trip."

"I'm not worried about the field trip. I guess I wanted to keep learning so I could be ready when the actual season starts. It's going to be fun for us to come up here on the weekends and ski! Obviously, I can't possibly ski on the trails that you're going to use, but it will be great if we could come up here together and I can watch you do your thing, you can watch me, and then we can come inside and have cocoa..."

"That sounds like a perfect weekend," he said before leaning in and kissing her. "And while we can totally come back here over the weekend—I'm on the schedule for Sunday afternoon and it's only to see if this is something I want to do—what I'd really like is to spend some time alone with you. I've missed you."

"I've missed you too," she said softly. Sighing, she rested her head on his shoulder. "What time are you done here? Maybe you can come over when you're done?"

"I'm here until eight and..." He glanced at his watch. "It's already 7:30. We can grab dinner here and then go to your house if you'd like."

"Or...I can leave now and pick something up for us to have and we'll eat at my place. I think I'd rather have you all to myself sooner rather than later."

"I love the way you think." Getting to his feet, Tanner held out his hand to her, helping her up. "Can I pick up anything?"

She thought about it for a minute before giving him a sexy grin. "Maybe just your overnight bag."

Hauling her in close, he kissed her again. "Like I said, I love the way you think." He gave her one last kiss. "I should be at your place by nine. Is that too late?"

"Not at all. I'll see you then!"

Watching her leave, Tanner's heart felt ready to burst. He had his girl back.

Life was good.

Chapter Fourteen

Chloe: Tanner and I made up!

Ash: YAY!! Finally!!

Chloe: And I skied!

Ash: Wait...what? How? When?

Ash: I'm looking out the window and there's no snow

Chloe: Indoor ski school dummy

Chloe: And it was awesome!

Ash: Good for you!

Ash: Is that how you wooed him? With your skiing skills? Lol!

Chloe: Nope. I wooed him with my words and then dazzled him with my skiing skills.

Chloe: I was very impressive and persuasive

Chloe: You should be proud

Ash: I am! And you're back together!

An almost obscene amount of heart emojis followed.

Ash: Where are you now? Still up at the lodge?

Chloe: I'm home now and waiting for Tanner to get here.

Chloe: I picked up some Chinese food so we're having a late dinner.

Ash: I'm really happy for you, Chlo. I know that had to be hard for you to go and see him.

Chloe: It was, but I had some great motivation to do it. The timing was perfect.

Ash: Ooh...I'm intrigued. What happened?

Chloe: How about we talk tomorrow? I've got a few more things to do before Tanner gets here.

Ash: Wear the sexy underwear! Promise you'll wear the sexy underwear! Trust me, you can never go wrong with sexy underwear!

Chloe: It's incredibly weird that you keep saying that, so stop it.

Ash: I'm simply speaking the truth.

Chloe: Yeah, well...the sexy underwear was the first thing I put on when I got home, so...

Ash: LOL!

Ash: Good girl!

Ash: Go and have some great makeup sex and we'll talk tomorrow.

Ash: But not about the sex.

Ash: I seriously don't want to know.

Chloe: Oh, but the underwear was okay to talk about?

Ash: Yes. That's allowed. Now go have fun.

Ash: I love you!

Chloe: Love you too!

As soon as she put her phone down, she heard a car door slam and knew it was Tanner. She quickly ran into the bathroom and fluffed her hair and put on another quick coat of lip gloss and hoped she looked as sexy as she thought she did.

By the time she stepped out into the living room, Tanner was knocking on the door. And when she opened it, his eyes went wide.

Just like she hoped they would.

She had on a navy blue silk robe and only the sexy underwear under it. The robe gaped slightly so the lace of her bra was showing and, from Tanner's reaction, it made an impression.

A sexy impression.

I kind of like my inner vixen...

"Hey," she said, her voice a bit husky. "I picked up Chinese food. I hope that's okay." Stepping aside, she motioned for him to come in.

Once inside, he shut the door, his eyes never leaving her. "You can think about food right now?"

A small smile tugged at her lips. "Well...I didn't want to just pounce as soon as you walked in the door..."

In the blink of an eye, Tanner scooped her up in his arms and strode right for her bedroom. "Pounce any time you want," he said, placing her down on the bed. "And while I appreciate you picking up dinner, we can definitely reheat it."

And then he was kissing her and they were tugging at his clothes and it was wonderful madness. He was crawling over her on the bed as his shoes fell to the floor. His sweater got stuck for a moment and they laughed before he sent it flying.

"I'll work on my jeans while you lose the robe," he told her with a hint of a growl of frustration. It took less than thirty seconds for him to be down to just his boxer briefs and her to her underwear, and that first touch of skin on skin was practically orgasmic.

Moaning, Chloe pressed herself against him. "I love this. You're so warm and hard and wonderful. I missed this."

Tanner was kissing his way along her jaw, her shoulder, her breasts...his hands doing their own wicked things as they moved over her. She writhed beneath him, torn between slowing things down so they could savor it or simply staying at this pace and going wild so they could take the edge off.

Going wild won out and nearly wore her out.

Minutes later, they were a breathless tangle of limbs, and she'd never felt better. Humming softly, she kissed his shoulder. "That was a much better way to start off the night than just having dinner."

Beside her, he chuckled. "Absolutely. But now I've

worked up an appetite." Then he glanced at her. "And I'll be the first to make the joke that it was too short to work up an appetite, but I still did."

Chloe laughed with him before sitting up. "It might have been short, but I think we were extremely enthusiastic. Our appetites are well deserved." Sliding off the bed, she picked up her robe and slid it on. "I have everything warming in the oven, so..."

He was pulling his briefs back on. "I'm going to grab a pair of sweats from my bag, and I'll meet you in the kitchen."

Walking over to him, she kissed him softly on the lips. "Deal."

Strolling into the kitchen, she smiled at the already set table before picking up the oven mitts and pulling the covered dishes from the oven. She'd gone with a small variety of stuff she knew they both enjoyed and set them on the table before pouring them each a glass of wine.

"Wow," he said as he walked in, looking shirtless and yummy. "I didn't expect you to go to so much trouble. I would have been fine just putting plates in the microwave." He accepted the glass she handed him. "Actually, I would have been fine with some peanut butter and jelly sandwiches."

"Not me," she countered as she sat down. "I was starving when I left the lodge. I grabbed a bag of pretzels and a bottle of water from the gift shop on my way out just to tide me over."

"I had a ham and cheese sandwich on my way there this afternoon. My plan had been to grab a burger and fries to go from the restaurant and eat it when I got home. This is so much better."

It was crazy how a simple conversation made her feel so happy.

Pulling the lids off of everything, she said, "Help yourself."

As he began putting food on his plate, he asked, "How's your mom doing? I'll bet her recovery sped up once she got home."

"It did, but only because she couldn't wait for my dad to leave," she said with a laugh. "He was the one staying with her and I really thought some sort of weird reconciliation was happening there, but it turns out they know they aren't right for each other. Now they're just friends and...I'm getting used to it."

"That's great! And if your dad being there motivated her to get up and around faster, then...even better!"

She agreed. "Apparently it didn't take long for Dad to remember what a handful Mom could be, and for Mom to remember how Dad never did things the way she liked them. Still, his heart was in the right place and it helped me, Ash, Billie, and Levi a lot. We all struggled with finding the time to be there for her, and for a few weeks, we didn't have to worry as much."

"Is your dad still here or did he go back home?"

"He's back home now. As much as he says he'd like to move back here full time, his heart is back in Laurel Bay. My Uncle Shane has a pub there—it's really a Donovan family pub, but he's the one who inherited it—and my dad's worked there with him for a long time. I think this trip here was more to test the waters and see if he could handle being back here and if we'd really accept him back into the family on a more permanent basis."

"And? Would you?"

"I think so. His relationship with my mom was so

strained for so long that I think that was the last thing holding him back. Now that Levi's married and he and Jade are planning to start a family any day now, Dad's motivated to come back more often. Once Ash and Reid get married, I'm sure he'll be here more than back in Laurel Bay."

"And when you and I get married, he'll definitely want to be here."

"Exactly." Gasping, she stared at him. "I mean...what? Did you just say...?"

Reaching across the table, Tanner took her hand in his. "I'm not asking you to marry me right this minute, Chloe, but someday I will. I love you. This is where I'm meant to be, and you're the woman I'm meant to be with."

Tears stung her eyes. "Oh my goodness...I love you too." Then she was gently tugged out of her seat and found herself in Tanner's lap while he kissed her senseless. It took several moments before they broke apart with goofy grins on their faces. "This is turning out to be quite the spectacular day."

"Mm-hmm..." He kissed her throat and then groaned before giving her a tiny shove to go back to her seat. "Food. We need to eat before it gets cold."

"Fine, but..."

"No, buts," he interrupted with amusement. "Let's talk about something completely neutral so we can eat and then go back inside and work up our appetites again."

"Good thing I picked up dessert too," she said with a wink.

"You're killing me. But I love it."

Even though she felt herself blushing, it wasn't out of embarrassment. "So...neutral topics. Why did you want to teach at the ski school?"

He took a bite of his meal before responding. "It's not

really appealing to me like I thought it would be. When my student Alex mentioned it to me, it sounded like it could be a great way to ski before the season started, but I think I'd rather have my weekends and evenings free and then just ski when I want to during the actual season." Another bite. "Although teaching you tonight was great, it was more because it was you."

"Aww...you're sweet. And I don't think I would have felt as comfortable with another instructor. Being with you made me want to succeed even more."

"See? A great team."

"Definitely." She took a bite of her shrimp and broccoli. "It might not be a bad thing to do once in a while. It's good to have a hobby or even something for a small secondary income. I have an Etsy shop where I sell some stuff and it feeds my artistic and creative side while giving me some extra money. It's not anything I'd like to do full time, but sometimes it's just fun to do something a little out of my regular routine."

"I don't think you ever mentioned that before. What do you sell?"

The funniest part of this conversation was that it was something she never discussed. "I call it my secret side-hustle. Art is something I've always enjoyed and I know I'm good at."

"Your classroom seriously blew me away the first time I saw it. I enjoy drawing too, but I rarely found an outlet for it."

"That's how I felt. I always had a sketch pad lying around in case inspiration struck, but about two years ago, I decided to get serious about it. I took up painting, but I also do a lot with pen and ink, and I do pictures of all kinds—landscapes and seascapes, but also a lot of character-driven stuff, especially superhero and sci-fi stuff. I'm also a seamstress and have a shop for custom costumes for cosplay. My goal was to build up my online inventory so I could generate enough income so I could buy a house sooner rather than later."

"Chloe, that's freaking amazing! Can I see your stuff?" Then he glanced around. "And are you still set on buying this place or are you maybe open to waiting and buying something else? Maybe something bigger that would be perfect for us and a family?"

"Tanner, I..."

"I know, I know...I'm getting way ahead of ourselves, but...I'm just excited about all the possibilities! Like... between the two of us, there is no end to what we can accomplish!" He popped half of a dumpling into his mouth. "Can we look at some of your stuff now? Is it here, or can we grab your laptop and look at it?"

She knew he wasn't going to let up until she showed him something. "One of the guest rooms is set up as my studio," she explained as she stood. "Come on. We'll finish eating after we look."

"Awesome!"

At the door to the guest room, she let out a long breath and opened it.

It was one thing for random people online to look at her stuff, but it was another when it was someone you knew and loved.

Leaning against the door, she turned on the light and then...stood back and watched. Tanner slowly walked around the room looking at the canvases hanging on the walls, the costumes on the dress forms lining one wall. There was stuff everywhere and honestly, this was only a small portion of her portfolio.

"Chloe...I...holy crap. This stuff is amazing!" He went back over to the wall of canvases. "Do you think you could do stuff like this on snowboards?"

"Um...what?"

He nodded. "Some of these characters would look amazing on boards. If you're interested, I'd love to work with you on something like this and maybe create our own line of snowboards. You could sell them in your shop or we can find other outlets—even the pro shop up at Summit Ridge! We could even..." Muttering a curse, he stopped. "Sorry. I do this sort of thing. I get an idea and then I run with it without thinking. This is your stuff and I'm already trying to horn in on it. I...damn." Raking a hand through his hair, he walked out of the room.

Of course, he didn't go far; she found him in the kitchen sitting back down.

"You weren't horning in, Tanner. I kind of love how your mind works. I'm a little of a think-inside-the-box person. But you? To you, the sky's the limit! I've never dreamed that big. And listening to you talk made me feel like...I could do this!" Sitting down, she laughed. "Then I thought, why didn't I think of that? It's a vicious cycle. But again, this is what makes us..."

"A great team," he said, looking visibly relieved. "Thank you for being so gracious. I had a total flashback to that first teacher meeting and..."

"Yes, you horned in there like a big fat steamroller," she teased. "But this is different. This is you wanting to work *together*, not take over and show off." And with a wink, she added, "I like this guy so much better."

Fortunately, he laughed. "Yeah. Me too."

* * *

The weekend passed in a flurry of making love and making art.

And damn if it wasn't the most satisfying time of his life.

By Sunday night, they had gone through Chloe's portfolio and picked a dozen designs they wanted to try on boards. The brand that Tanner was a spokesperson for had a line of snowboards and he was ready to pitch his idea of a line with her artwork on them. They just needed to come up with a name for them so they each got credit. At first, she said she didn't need her name on them—didn't want that kind of attention on herself—but the more they talked, the more he could tell that it was something she was afraid to ask for.

So...he was going to make damn sure it was going to happen for her.

The week at school had been great, and their field trip was an incredible success. The students all had an amazing time and he had watched Chloe put more than a handful of kids' minds at ease when they were scared to go down that tiny hill.

When the weekend rolled around again, they made plans to have dinner with her family on Saturday. While he wasn't someone who was normally intimidated, he had to admit that being back with the Donovans made him feel a little self-conscious. Reid had never really given him any grief that day at school, but considering her family had had an intervention with Chloe because of him, he figured he was going to get the stink eye from at least one or two of them before everyone just accepted him back.

That had him a little on the defensive even as he walked into Jade and Levi's house with a smile.

"Tanner! It's good to see you again!" Jade said,

accepting the platter of fresh veggies and guacamole Chloe had made. She shut the door and motioned for Chloe to head into the kitchen and then stepped in Tanner's path to stop him. "I can see that you're a little tense, and I want to put your mind at ease. No one's going to say anything out of line because of the temporary breakup. It's none of their business. So please go inside and relax."

He almost sagged to the ground. "Thank you, Jade. I was kind of afraid I was going to get the third-degree from at least one member of the family. I wasn't sure who, but..."

"That was never going to be Levi, I promise," she assured him. "Chloe put everyone in their place a few weeks ago. We all thought we were helping her, but it turns out she helped all of us to see that we need to respect each other a little more."

"I really wish I would have been able to see that," he said. "I'm so proud of her for standing up for herself like that."

"We all are." She smiled. "Maybe hitting pause on your relationship wasn't a bad thing. But we're all really glad you're back together."

"Believe me, no one's happier about that than I am."

Her smile grew. "Come on. Everyone's in the kitchen. Including my parents. I don't think you've met them yet. We're just waiting for Ronan. He was driving up this morning, but we haven't heard from him yet."

"I hope he's okay..."

"You hope who's okay?" Chloe asked when he joined her in the kitchen.

"Oh, um...Jade said your dad's on his way here, but no one's heard from him yet," he said and hoped he wasn't speaking out of place.

"He just texted me a few minutes ago," Marie said as

she walked over and hugged him. "He stopped for gas and should be here in ten minutes. And apparently he's bringing a bunch of food from the pub." She rolled her eyes. "We have food here. Why he felt the need to bring food like that on a five-hour drive is beyond me."

"Mom," Levi said wearily. "How about we just be thankful that he wanted to bring anything?"

"Fine. Whatever. But we can all cook just as good as Kate can," she murmured.

"I can't!" Ashlynn said proudly. "And I will never turn down anything Aunt Kate makes. I wish some of her food traveled better. Or that we lived closer so I could go there and eat more often."

Marie mumbled something under her breath before walking out of the room.

"Mom is not a fan of Aunt Kate's," Ashlynn told him with a sly grin. "And sometimes it's just fun to poke the bear."

"Maybe a little less poking," Billie said as she put a bowl of chips on the table. "We're supposed to be having fun today, remember?"

"We're having fun! And for me, sometimes having fun is poking at Mom." She shrugged. "You can't control how people enjoy themselves, Bill."

Now it was Billie's turn to mumble something and walk away.

"I'm not sure how fun this is," Chloe said, glaring at her sister. "Can't you just play nice? Why the poking?"

"Because after everything Dad did for her, she still picks on him. That makes me want to pick on her to prove a point."

"I don't think she's getting that point."

"Maybe." Then she looked at Tanner. "So, I hear you taught my sister how to ski! I'm seriously impressed."

Wrapping his arm around Chloe's waist, he held her close. "She did a great job all on her own. I was just there to talk her through it. With a few more lessons, she'll be ready to hit the slopes with the first snow."

"I really can't wait," Chloe said happily. "I hope we can do a family ski day. How fun would that be?"

Ashlynn grinned from ear to ear. "I still can't believe I'm hearing you say that! Heck, I never thought I'd hear you say it!"

"Me either, and yet...I am!" She snuggled closer to him. "I mean, none of us will be able to do what Tanner does, but we can all have fun and then sit around the fire and drink cocoa. It will be great!"

In the distance, the doorbell rang. "I got it!" Levi called out.

"I'm surprised Dad came back so soon," Chloe said. "I figured we wouldn't see him until Thanksgiving at least."

"Yeah, I thought so too, but Levi said he wanted everyone here for dinner today. Like we don't get together enough?" Ashlynn mused. "But maybe they want to discuss the holidays? You know, to make sure we're all on the same page since there's more of us?" Again, she looked at Tanner. "Are you going up to New York for the holidays or will you be here?"

"Um...the plan is to be here. My parents are coming down. At least, they are for Christmas. I think they're staying home for Thanksgiving."

"I wish I could meet them before Christmas," Chloe said with a soft sigh. "With the pressure of the holidays, it's hard to really have any quiet time to sit and talk."

"Maybe I'll see if they can come down a few days before so we can sort of ease into Christmas. What do you think?"

"Wait...so are you spending Christmas with Tanner's family or ours?" Ashlynn asked.

"I just thought we'd all spend it together," Chloe replied. "At least Christmas Day." Then she waved her off. "This is all the stuff we need to discuss with everyone over dinner. Thank God Levi thought to get us all here for it."

After that, everyone ate and drank while spreading out and talking about how their week went. Tanner spent part of the time simply observing but wondered about how he and his family were going to fit into the Donovan family Christmas. When he invited his parents, he just assumed he and Chloe would be together both days. Now he realized how unrealistic that was.

However, he needed to have at least part of Christmas Eve alone with her with neither family around. If everything went as planned, he'd have some first-run snowboards to give her as gifts. He couldn't wait to see the look on her face when...

"Tanner!" Ronan said jovially, breaking him out of his reverie. "It's good to see you again!"

Shaking his hand, Tanner said, "It's good to see you too. How was the drive?"

"Long! My God, every time it feels like it takes a wee bit longer and I'm getting too old for it." He sighed loudly. "I know it's only a matter of time before I move back, but I just wish it didn't take so much out of me to make the trip."

"That's understandable. My folks drove down here when I moved, and they both said the drive home felt like it took forever. They were originally going to fly home but changed their minds."

Nodding, Ronan studied him. "Are we going to get to meet your family anytime soon?"

"That's the plan. They'll be here for Christmas, so I'm sure we'll all be together at some point."

"That's good. Hopefully you'll be with us for all of it. No need to stay at home with just your parents. The holidays are meant to be spent together. The more the merrier!"

"Well..."

"Look around this house. It's huge! I'm sure Jade and Levi are going to open their doors to everyone for Christmas. Trust me."

Tanner wasn't going to argue; he'd simply prefer to wait and see and not make any assumptions.

Reid walked over and joined them and for several minutes they talked about skiing and how Chloe had learned and how there was now talk of a family ski day.

"Everyone? Can you join us in the living room?" Levi called out.

Tanner followed Reid and Ronan before sitting down beside Chloe. Jade and Levi were standing in front of the fireplace, along with Silas.

"We're so glad you could all join us today," Jade said sweetly. "I know we get together a lot and we see each other throughout the week, but there's something extra wonderful about getting together just for fun."

They all nodded.

"We wanted to talk about Thanksgiving and Christmas," Levi said. "I believe Mom has offered to host Thanksgiving at her house as long as we all help with the meal, right?"

Marie nodded. "I have enough space and I love having everyone over. I just don't think I can do the entire meal. So, if we can divide and conquer, we'll be fine."

More nods.

Billie raised her hand. "I had planned on hosting Christmas Eve. We can do a buffet since my dining room isn't big enough for all of us to sit down and eat, but it will still be great." She looked over at Jade's parents. "You're both invited, of course." Then she looked at Tanner. "And you and your family too. The more the merrier!"

"I told you!" Ronan said, raising his glass.

"And we'd love everyone to be here for Christmas Day," Levi went on. "We have the most room and we're planning on handling dinner if everyone will contribute to appetizers and desserts like we usually do."

Everyone nodded again.

"Aren't we gonna tell them about the baby yet?" Silas said with a huff. "Why are we talking about food all the time?"

"Baby?"

"Baby? What baby?"

"Oh my God! Jade, are you pregnant?" The questions seemed to come from every corner of the room, and then suddenly everyone was on their feet congratulating Jade and Levi. Tanner stood back and let the family celebrate, feeling oddly left out.

For now.

There wasn't a doubt in his mind that he and Chloe were going to be celebrating these milestones in the future—maybe even this time next year.

And honestly, he couldn't wait.

Just then, she was back at his side, her eyes shining with unshed tears. "This is amazing," she said. "The first Donovan baby."

Tanner pulled her into his arms.

"I'm so happy for them. I mean...look at them. Silas is so

266

excited, my brother has that sappy smile, and Jade looks positively radiant." She sighed happily. "This is the best news. The absolute best."

Nodding, he continued to hold her. "It's a definite cause for celebration," he said.

As if on cue, Levi called out, "We have champagne chilling inside! And sparkling grape juice for Jade and Silas! Let's move this into the kitchen!"

And for the rest of the day, every conversation was about the future and the good things to come. Tanner was in total agreement. The next year promised to be the best one yet.

Having Chloe with him and knowing all the good that was to come involved her—and was because of her—made him feel even luckier. His life had changed in so many ways in such a few short months, but it was all for the better.

He just couldn't wait until they were all raising their glasses to them.

To her.

His Chloe.

And maybe to them being Couple of the Year.

That was a thing, right?

Epilogue

Christmas Eve...

It was late—almost midnight. Tanner's parents were at his house and Chloe felt a little guilty that he was here with her instead of home with them. They'd gotten home from dinner at Billie's a little while ago and it had been so much fun. It was loud and chaotic, and her family had just totally embraced the Westyns—not that she expected anything less. Her family was awesome and so were the Westyns. But she had to admit that she had a moment or two where she feared they wouldn't hit it off.

After dropping his parents off, Tanner brought her home and now they were curled up on her sofa, watching the fire in the fireplace, and enjoying the peace and quiet after such a boisterous evening.

"I feel bad that your parents are home alone," she told him.

"Are you kidding? They both said they were exhausted and were going to bed. Then they said that they'd see me in the morning, so..."

"So...you're going to stay tonight?"

"If that's okay."

Turning, she smiled at him. "Of course it is!" Glancing at the tree, she sighed. "Growing up, we had a tradition where we got to open one gift on Christmas Eve. It was always pajamas, but I loved it."

"We did the same. As a matter of fact, my parents gave me a new pair of pajamas earlier, before we left for Billie's," he said with a laugh.

"Obviously you saw us all open pajamas tonight too." Straightening, she nodded toward the tree. "I have something I wanted to give you tonight, but it is most definitely not pajamas."

He laughed. "That's good, because I think we both know I don't really wear them. At least, not when I'm with you."

Blushing, she stood and walked over to the tree, picking up a tall box from the back. "There are more for you under the tree that we'll open tomorrow, but...this one I wanted you to open tonight." Standing in front of him, she held it out. "Merry Christmas, Tanner."

"Chloe..." He glanced around. "I have something for you too. Let me get it and we can open them together."

"Absolutely not. I can wait. Please." Then she sat down beside him, eager to see the look on his face.

"O-kay..." Carefully, he tore the wrapping and pulled it off before studying the nondescript box.

Her heart was racing because this was a first for her and she hoped he loved it.

"Holy...Chloe, this is...this is amazing!" he said, his voice filled with wonder. "Is this hand-painted?"

She nodded. "You won't be able to use it out on the slopes, but it's something that I hope you'll want to display. It was a labor of love."

"This is the most thoughtful thing I've ever received. I can't believe you did this."

It was a snowboard that she had painted herself with a picture of him when he won his final competition. She'd found the picture online and thought it captured him so perfectly. Painting on a snowboard was a fresh experience—and not one she particularly enjoyed—but for this gift, she made it work.

When he turned his head and looked at her, his eyes shone brightly. "You are the most amazing woman in the world," he said gruffly. "Thank you for this." Leaning in, he kissed her softly. And just when she thought he was going to take the kiss deeper, he pulled back. Placing his gift carefully to the side, he smiled at her. "My turn."

"Yay!"

He stood and walked over to her front closet, and she watched in confusion as he opened the door and pulled out a huge box.

"Um...when did you put that there?" she asked with amusement. "I can't believe I missed that!"

"When my folks and I picked you up earlier. Remember when my mom asked you about your paintings and you showed her the guest room?"

She nodded.

"That's when." Grinning, he walked over and placed the box in front of her. It looked big enough for a giant flat-screen TV, but she hoped that wasn't what it was. She wasn't big on sitting in front of a television.

Be thankful, no matter what it is.

"Well? Aren't you going to open it?" he asked, still standing beside the box.

Nodding again, she tore at the paper and on the front of

the box was the logo of the snowboard company they were working with on their designs.

"Oh my goodness! Is this what I think it is?" she asked excitedly.

"You're going to have to open the box and see!"

He helped her lay the box down on the floor before opening it. Inside there were several wrapped boxes. She glanced up at him. "Um..."

"They're numbered," he told her.

"O-kay..."

Picking up the first one, she opened it and found a three-foot snowboard with the very first design she and Tanner had decided on—a wintery fairy castle. For a minute, all she could do was marvel at it. It was so much more than she ever dreamed it would be. Tears stung her eyes and she was about to thank him, when he gently took it from her hands.

"Open the next one."

The second one had one of her original superhero characters. There were gorgeous shades of blue and green, and it was absolutely stunning. "Tanner, these are..."

"Shh...there's more," he urged, handing her the third one.

Laughing, she took it from him, and it had a group of popular superheroes on them. They were working on getting the licensing rights to them, but she figured these boards were just for them and not for sale. Before she could comment on it, he was handing her the last board.

"These are so much better than I thought they'd be," she said, tearing open the wrapping. "Ooh...the space one! And the stars actually sparkle! I love it!" But when she looked up, Tanner was holding another box. "Shouldn't we leave some for tomorrow?" she joked.

"Oh, there will be more tomorrow. And honestly, these aren't gifts that I bought. They just happened to arrive in time for Christmas and I wanted to give them to you when we were alone."

"That's very sweet of you. Thank you. I love them all! I never even considered seeing my art in this way."

"Everyone loves your work." Then he sat down beside her. "And I love you."

Smiling, Chloe leaned in and kissed him. "I love you too." Then she looked at the boards. "I was feeling like you were trying to outdo me again... I mean, I only got you one board and you got me four!"

"Five," he said, handing her the other box.

"Tanner..."

"This one I did do myself. Well...I ordered it. I didn't paint it myself. I leave that level of artistry to you."

He was so damn precious and she couldn't believe he did all of this. "As long as you don't expect me to actually use this...because even though I mastered skiing..."

"You mastered the indoor bunny hill..."

"I don't think I'm ready for snowboarding." Grinning, she tore off the wrapping. "Maybe next year I'll give it a try." Pulling the board from the box, she stared at it, mildly confused. "Um..."

It was a plain white board with the words "Team K" on it.

"What am I missing?" she asked.

"That's us," he said. "Team K. Team kindergarten. And I thought maybe that could be our...our company name for the boards and gear we're going to do artwork for."

Her heart simply melted. "Tanner! I love that! It's perfect!" She launched herself into his arms, kissing him with everything she had. "I love you so much."

"I love you too, beautiful. Merry Christmas."

"Merry Christmas." Resting her head on his shoulder, Chloe didn't think she'd ever feel this happy, didn't think she'd ever find what everyone else around her was finding. She'd never been so happy to be wrong. "I want to stand them all up over by the tree," she said. "Then we can come back here and snuggle."

"Sounds like a plan. I'll get rid of all the wrapping paper, but the box will have to wait until tomorrow to go out."

She agreed and began moving the boards so she could enjoy looking at her tree and seeing all of them at the same time. It took a few minutes to get them all standing just right, but when she stepped back, it was exactly what she had envisioned. "I think I need to get a picture of this because it looks great! Can you...?" But when she glanced over her shoulder, Tanner wasn't sitting on the couch; he was down on one knee. "What...what's happening right now?"

Holding up a ring, he said, "I had one more gift for you tonight that I didn't want anyone else around for."

He said all the right words—everything she could ever possibly dream of. And for the first time in her entire life, Chloe felt like she was the luckiest Donovan of them all.

Looking for your next small town read?? Go back to where it all began!!

Meet
THE DONOVANS
In

Dare Me

One

It sucked sleeping on a bouncy house.

Technically it was just the crappy mattress in her brother's guest room, but to Arianna Donovan, that's what it felt like.

"Ugh..."

She tossed and turned and bounced, all the while cursing the fact that she now had to sleep in the guest room after a year of having the main bedroom to herself. But Liam was finally coming home for good—his contract with the US Marine Corps was over—and that meant he was going to want to sleep in his own bed. And really, she couldn't blame him. It was glorious—king sized, memory foam with cooling gel. Seriously, it was perfect.

This coiled twenty-year-old nightmare of a mattress? Not so much.

With a huff, she flipped onto her back and stared up at the ceiling. Liam wouldn't be home for another few days, so...technically...she *could* still sleep in the main bedroom. She had thought transitioning to the guest room would be a good thing and had hoped if she was settled in there, that her brother wouldn't be too eager for her to move out. But if the choice came down to having to move back in with their parents and sleeping on their couch or sleeping on this thing, she would almost rather move back in with her folks.

Liar.

Okay, yeah, it was the last thing she wanted to do.

When she'd come home from her internship in San Francisco a year ago, she had figured she'd be sleeping in her old room and it would be a temporary thing.

But they'd turned it into a home gym.

After that, she'd crashed on her sister Ryleigh's couch, but that would not work long-term, and her other two brothers never offered her a place to sleep, so...she'd decided to crash at Liam's. It was sitting there empty. Well...not right away. Her brother had let a friend of his stay there after his time in the Marines was up, but as soon as he moved out, Arianna had moved in.

And when Liam got home, she'd be sure to thank him.

Technically, he had no idea she was staying there, but she knew he wouldn't mind. After all, she was his favorite. There were five Donovan children—Liam, Patrick, Ryleigh, Jamie, and Arianna—but she knew Liam loved her the most. As the baby of the family, how could he not?

Rolling onto her side, she punched the pillow with a loud sigh and was almost comfortable when her phone chimed with an incoming text. Groaning, she snatched it off the bedside table and tapped the screen.

Mark: Had a really great time tonight. Hope we can get together next weekend.

She contemplated replying, but...didn't.

Mark was a really nice guy, but there were no sparks

there. Just like there weren't any with John, Paul, Matt, and Greg. They were all great guys and they were perfectly fine to go out with. Once. Arianna knew exactly what she was looking for in a man. Hell, she'd even found the perfect man.

Sadly, he'd completely ghosted her a year ago and she'd been in a dating funk ever since.

And, because she was clearly a glutton for punishment and her phone was in her hands, she tapped on her photos app and scrolled to her San Francisco album. Dozens of photos of her and Will popped up. She looked at his handsome face, his incredible smile, and wondered how he couldn't have felt the same way she did.

Although, to be fair, they'd only had one day together.

One glorious day.

Sighing, she slowly scrolled through the pictures. There was a time when looking at them made her cry, but...she'd gotten past that stage.

Almost.

Her friends had dared her to introduce herself to him after their last brunch together. She was flying home the next day and they encouraged her to have a fling before coming back to Laurel Bay. So, being the sassy, confident woman she was, Arianna had walked right over to Will as he was eating alone, introduced herself, and joined him. Brunch had turned to walking all over San Francisco together, going on a sunset cruise around the Bay, dinner in Chinatown, and then staying up all night up on Twin Peaks and watching the sunrise. They had kissed until they were breathless, but Will had been a total gentleman and told her he wouldn't sleep with her, knowing that was their only night together.

Plus, they were in the middle of a public park, so...

She'd been devastated when he'd dropped her off at her apartment the next morning, but then she thought fate had lent them a hand when they ended up on the same flight to Atlanta.

Even *that* had been perfect. They'd talked and kissed and napped together and she was certain they were going to try their hands at a long-distance relationship. After exchanging phone numbers, Will had left to catch his flight to D.C. and Arianna had gone to her gate for her flight to Wilmington, North Carolina. He'd promised he'd text her when he got on the plane.

But he didn't.

He'd promised to keep in touch.

But he hadn't.

For weeks she'd tried reaching out to him, but never got a response and there had been no listing for a Will Jameson in Washington D.C.

Or anywhere.

At least, not her Will.

Chasing after a guy who clearly didn't want her wasn't her thing, but every now and again, she wondered just what had gone wrong. How could someone fake that kind of connection?

Why didn't he want me?

Yeah, that one had been messing with her the most. If it weren't for her family—minus Liam—Arianna didn't know how she would have gotten through the last year.

True, no one knew about Will—except her sister—and there was no way she was going to share with anyone how she'd met this great guy who just disappeared off the face of the planet after spending twenty-four hours with her.

Being part of a large Irish-Catholic family meant that you were supposed to find someone to love and marry and have a bunch of kids. For most of her life, Arianna had gotten around anyone focusing that theory on her. She'd gone away to college and then took an internship on the other side of the country and thoroughly enjoyed having her privacy and independence. But ever since she'd come home to Laurel Bay? The hints and not-so-gentle nudges for her to find a nice guy to settle down with had been a constant.

The only plus side to it? It meant her parents were leaving her sister Ryleigh alone for a little while. Apparently, she had been their prime target for the last four years, and poor Ryleigh was at her wit's end. So for now, Arianna was willing to take one for the team and go out on some dates to make her parents happy. They didn't need to know that she was still harboring a bit of a broken heart. She'd get over it eventually.

Maybe.

And now that she was an adult, no one was scaring guys away like they used to. Just thinking about all the boys her brothers had harassed and threatened back in the day was enough to make her roll her eyes. They never truly succeeded in making anyone run or break up with her, but it was cute how they tried.

Now, no one was getting chased away. If anything, whenever she was down at their family pub, Donovan's, Patrick and Jamie were practically sending eligible guys her way! It had actually become a bit of a fun family game and maybe it wouldn't be so bad if even one guy had given her even a hint of the feels, but...they hadn't.

Damn you, Will Jameson!

Flopping back against the pillows, she tossed her phone aside with disgust. She couldn't keep doing this to herself. The smart thing to do would be to delete all those pictures and just forget about the whole thing. Maybe she'd be able to focus on meeting a nice guy if she didn't keep pulling up Will's picture and making comparisons.

Maybe.

Her phone chimed again. "Dammit, Mark, I said I'd let you know," she murmured before grabbing it. Her sister's name popped up and it made her smile.

Ryleigh: So? How was your night?

Rather than texting her back, Arianna simply hit the call button.

"I wasn't expecting you to call," Ryleigh said with amusement.

"Well, I know why I'm home and in bed by eleven, what's your excuse?"

"The date went that well, huh?"

"Mark was really nice, but..."

"Ugh...not again, Ari. They can't all be nice guys that you have zero interest in. It's just not possible!"

"Sadly, it is," she said wearily. "We had a great dinner and then he wanted to take me to some bar where a friend of his was playing in a band."

"Say no more. I hate when they have a friend in a band," Ryleigh replied. "It never goes well."

"Exactly." The sigh was out before she could stop it. "Look, I'm more than happy to keep going out with these guys if it takes some of the pressure off of you. I know mom and dad have been pressuring you to find Mr. Right..."

"And Gram and Pop," Ryleigh interrupted. "They joined the campaign too."

"Oh, no..."

"So did Nana and Grandpa. And Uncle Ronan. I'm telling you, it's been brutal. I appreciate you stepping in and giving them a new focus, but they haven't forgotten about me. I'm going out with Gram's hairdresser's nephew tomorrow." She groaned.

"And you couldn't get out of it?"

"Nope. I said I had planned on working at the pub that night since Saturdays are so busy, and dad said not to worry, that he'd get someone else to cover the shift."

"Damn."

"I know." Now it was Ryleigh's turn to sigh. "Is it wrong that I just want them to back off a bit? I mean...I'd like to meet a great guy too! Most of my friends are married already and here I am getting old and running out of prospects!"

"Ry, you're only twenty-six. That's not old."

"Tell that to mom and dad. If you listen to them, I'm practically ancient and potentially becoming an old maid."

"Oh, stop. They did not say that!" she said with a laugh.

"Wait...keep passing up these nice guys and they'll start labeling you just like they're labeling me."

"Doubtful. I'm only twenty-three. I've got a few good years in me yet."

"That's what I thought too and yet...here I am." She paused for a moment. "Other than the friend in the band thing, what was wrong with this guy?"

"I don't know..."

"He wasn't Will," Ryleigh stated, because...well...she was the only person Arianna had confided in.

"I didn't say that."

"You didn't have to. Look, I'm not trying to be mean, but...it's been a year. It's time to move on. You have to accept the fact that he just used you."

"But he didn't!" she countered. "How did he use me? We didn't have sex; we walked around San Francisco and ate dim sum and went on a sunset cruise! Where was the using?"

"Okay, okay...calm down. Don't go getting all pissy."

"It's not fair, Ry. How could the universe find me this perfect guy like that and he just disappears?"

"Something could have happened to him, Ari. Have you thought about that?"

"Why would you even say that?" she cried.

"Um..."

Tears stung her eyes. "I've tried not to think like that, but...oh, God! What if it did?" Honestly, she had thought that exact thing far too many times and would immediately tell herself not to think like that.

"This isn't helping anything," Ryleigh reasoned. "The important thing here is that you stop thinking about this guy because he didn't care enough about you to keep in touch. Let's just say that he was a major jerk and move on."

They'd had this conversation at least a dozen times in the last year and, as much as it pained her, Arianna knew this needed to be the last time. Swallowing hard, she nodded. "You're right. It's been a year and...and I just need to pretend like that day never happened."

"I'm so sorry..."

"Don't be. I'm the idiot who fell in love on a single date. I mean...knowing me, I'm probably over-romanticizing the entire thing."

"Yes! Yes, that's it! You made it seem like so much more in your head when, in reality, he wasn't all that."

Nodding, she forced herself to agree. "Okay, no more talking about this or any other dating topics. Let's talk about Liam. Has anyone gotten a definitive date out of him yet for when he'll be home?"

"All I know is it's next week sometime," Ryleigh told

her. "Have you thought about where you're going to go? Have you even looked at apartments for yourself?"

"Um..."

"Ari! Come on! You make great money, how is it that you can't find an apartment? Have you talked to Patrick? He's always got property available."

"I haven't really talked to him about it in a while. Most of the places he manages are out of my budget. Plus, I guess a part of me wasn't sure this was where I wanted to stay."

"You mean at Liam's?"

"No. Laurel Bay. I've been looking at jobs...elsewhere."

Her sister was silent for several long moments. "Like how far elsewhere?"

"Like...back in Chapel Hill, where I went to school. There are a lot of opportunities there, and..."

"Stop. Just stop." She let out a long breath. "Why are you just now telling me this?"

"Because I don't know if it's something I'm going to do. I know everyone will freak out if I move away again."

"You can't live your life for everyone else. Trust me. I'm doing it and it sucks."

"Then maybe you need to stop doing it," she challenged.

"Please, one crazy Donovan daughter at a time." She paused. "So...you really think you'll move away?"

"I'm not sure. I keep looking at positions in bigger cities and...there's nothing keeping me here in Laurel Bay. Once Liam gets home, you know he'll only tolerate me staying here for so long. He's going to want the place to himself and probably resent having his baby sister in the next room when he wants to bring a woman home."

"Ugh...I don't need that image in my head."

"You know what I'm saying. I didn't want to sign a lease

on someplace here if I wasn't going to stay. Maybe Liam's coming home is the push I need to make that decision."

"Damn. I'd really hate it if you moved, Ari. I feel like you just got back. I missed you."

"I'm only a few hours away," she said softly. "And you can come and stay with me anytime. Like when you need to run away from all the matchmaking." Then she laughed.

"Sure, laugh it up, but I'm telling you, soon it will be your turn and then it won't seem so funny."

"All the more reason for me to leave town. And who knows? Maybe I'll meet a nice guy and fall in love in Chapel Hill."

They didn't stay on the phone much longer and when they did hang up, Arianna studied her phone and pulled up her photos one last time.

It would be easy to delete all the photos of her and Will right now, but as she scrolled through them again, she just couldn't do it.

"Tomorrow," she whispered before putting the phone face down and doing her best to fall asleep.

* * *

"It's decided, you're coming home with me."

Will Jameson looked over at his friend and was seriously at a loss for words. Not that he didn't appreciate the offer—because he did—but...it was complicated.

More complicated that he cared to explain.

"Do you want to go back to California?" Liam Donovan asked him.

"No."

"Have you made any plans or even thought about where you're going to go?"

"Not exactly."

"Will, we're out of here in two days! How could you not know where you're going to go?"

With a shrug, he replied, "I'll figure it out once I drive out the gates of the base."

Which was a huge lie because he'd done nothing *but* think about it for the last year. In a perfect world, he could very easily agree with his buddy and go with him to Laurel Bay—to Arianna—and have a pretty spectacular life.

But he'd totally screwed that up.

At the time, it seemed like the perfect thing to do—to just never talk to her again once he realized she was related to Liam. He just never told her that he knew. And now, a year later, he wondered why he didn't just say screw it and let things just play out the way they should.

With his buddy beating the shit out of him for touching his little sister.

Beside him, Liam was scowling as he looked down at his phone.

"Problem?"

"Let's just say it's a good thing I'm heading home."

"Why?"

"I think my whole family's gone mad," he murmured. "Honestly, I don't know what's gotten into them."

"Yeah, you're going to have to elaborate, because I don't know what you're talking about."

"My sisters," Liam said. "It sounds like my parents practically have a "Come date our daughters" campaign going on at the pub! It's insanity! I mean...are they even checking these guys out?"

Will didn't know what to say, but the thought of Arianna going out with a bunch of guys did not sit well with him either.

If anything, he was probably more pissed off than Liam.

"How...um...how do you know this?" he casually asked as he scrolled the local news on his own phone.

"Jamie's texting me and telling me how he's going to set Arianna—she's the youngest out of all of us—with some guy he used to play lacrosse with! *Lacrosse!*" he added with a snort of disgust. "I bet he's a total douche."

Will had to agree.

Liam began to furiously type out something to his brother, but Will needed to know more. "So...what's the big deal? She's obviously a grown woman, right?"

Shooting him an angry glare, he said, "She's only twenty-three and my dufus brother should *not* be setting her up with any of his friends! They're all older than her and...and...just no. Brothers are supposed to protect and look out for their sisters, not set them up with their friends."

"Um...sure, but...how much older? Aren't the two of them close in age?"

"Dude, whose side are you even on? She's young and doesn't need my brother or anyone fixing her up. She doesn't need to be dating. Period."

"That sounds a little unrealistic," Will countered. "You know she's probably dated plenty of guys while she was in college."

The look his buddy gave him told Will that was the wrong thing to say.

And this is why I had to say goodbye to Arianna...

Yeah, he knew Liam well enough to know how protective he was of his sisters and the fact that Will was nine years older than her would not have gone over well.

"Why is your brother even texting you if he knows this is a sensitive topic?"

"Because my brother's an ass sometimes." Tossing his

phone down, Liam leaned back in his chair and raked both hands through his hair. "I swear, sometimes it's like he's baiting me and thinks it would be funny to watch me come home and go off on everyone. It's so stupid."

"And yet you're taking the bait."

"No," Liam quickly replied. "Well, yes. Maybe." He growled in frustration. "I'm not going to go home and create a scene, but it's good to know what I'm walking into."

"I don't see how you're walking *into* anything. It's not really any of your concern." Will knew he was now the one baiting Liam, and yet he couldn't seem to help himself.

"Will, just...trust me. You don't get it. You're an only child. You have no idea what it's like to have sisters." He growled again. "All your friends hit on them and it's just... it's wrong."

Well, there was the definite confirmation that he'd made the right decision, but it didn't make him feel any better.

"You know what? I don't want to talk about this anymore," Liam said as he got to his feet. They were hanging out in the barracks while most of their squad was out celebrating the weekend. "I want to know if you're in on my business plan."

Liam's plan for when he returned to Laurel Bay was to form a construction company and his first project was going to be a tiny house community that would either be some kind of fishing resort or perhaps a fifty-five and over one. Either way, it sounded fascinating. Will had an architectural engineering degree and he knew the two of them together could really do something amazing, but the thought of being that close to Arianna and not being with her was really holding him back.

"Before we switch gears," Will began, "let me ask you something."

"Sure."

"What if...say...your sister..."

"Which one?"

"Either one."

"Okay..."

"Let's say your sister meets a guy on her own and he's older than her," Will said cautiously. "What if he's a genuinely good guy and you scare him off because you've got it in your mind that he can't be good for her because of his age? Have you thought of that?"

"No."

His eyes went wide. "That's it? Just no? Liam, come on. You can't be so closed-minded."

"Look, I get what you're trying to say, but...I don't know. Maybe it wouldn't be such a big deal for Ryleigh, but any guy older than Arianna? It would just feel a little creepy. I've beaten the crap out of several good friends just for looking at her."

Awesome.

"O-kay, so..."

"Why are we still talking about my sisters when we have a serious business opportunity ahead of us?" Liam asked as he took the seat across from Will. "I really think you and I have a chance to make this great. Why aren't you as excited about this as I am?"

There was no way he could answer honestly, so he had to go with some of his other concerns.

"For starters, I think this is going to take a lot of time and capital to get this project off the ground, Liam. Neither of us has sat down with a bank or lawyers or whoever else we need to, so...I'm just hesitant to make a decision to move someplace where things might not work out."

Nodding, Liam considered him. "That's fair. And I

realize Laurel Bay isn't a big city, but you've always said how you hoped you could settle down in a small town. And trust me, Laurel Bay is as small as they get." He grinned. "Personally, I think it's exactly what you need."

"I can't imagine there's a lot of real estate there..."

"You can crash with me. I've got a two-bedroom apartment that I plan on keeping only for a short time, but then you're more than welcome to it."

"Why? Where are you planning to go?"

"Not only have I been looking at real estate for our project..."

"Your project," Will corrected.

"Our project," Liam stated firmly, "but I've also been looking at houses for myself. I've spent so many years here in the service either living in barracks or tiny apartments. Before that, I grew up in a small house with four siblings. I'm really looking forward to buying a place of my own and having a yard and not sharing walls or rooms with anyone." His smile grew. "And I think I've found a few places that could work. My brother Patrick dabbles in real estate and property management and he's going to help me out."

"Oh, well...good for you."

"What about you? Are you interested in a house? Condo? Do you want to rent or own...?"

"Hard to decide until I know where I'm going to land. I joined the Marines right out of high school, and I guess back then I always thought I'd go back to Oakland." He shrugged. "With my mom gone, there's no reason for me to go to the west coast, but..."

"Then you should try the east coast!" Liam exclaimed.

"But...I haven't given myself the time to really think about it. Part of me thought this day wasn't going to come."

"Seriously? Why?"

Another shrug. "I don't know. I think I was still considering just staying in so I wouldn't have to decide. And with no family to go home to..."

"Well, that's just stupid. I'm telling you, Will, you need to at least come home with me and just spend a few weeks in Laurel Bay. It's not like you've got anything else planned. Just check it out and come with me to look at property—both for the project and for my own personal home purchase—and if you totally hate it there, I'll let it go."

It wasn't the worst idea, but...

No, wait. It *was* the worst idea. It wouldn't matter if he went with Liam for a few weeks or a few days or even a few hours. Being around Arianna would be torture and there was no way he'd be able to avoid her.

Hell, he wasn't even sure he wanted to.

Maybe if he could just see her and explain why he did the things that he did...

She'd still end up hating him.

Probably more than he hated himself for it.

"Plus, I have a huge family!" Liam went on. "I guarantee you, once my mother meets you, you'll be one of us!"

Yeah, that so wasn't the way he wanted to become a Donovan...

But...it also had merit.

Maybe if the rest of the Donovan family saw that he was a decent and trustworthy guy, it wouldn't be such a bad thing for him to start dating Arianna properly. They could have the kind of relationship they should have rather than cramming a month's worth of dating into a single day.

Okay, maybe he could get on board with this plan of Liam's. He just had to make sure he didn't appear too eager.

"What about financing?" he asked casually. "You don't know anything about my financial situation, just like I don't know anything about yours. How is all of this going to work? Especially if you're also looking to buy a house."

"I've had the down payment for a house put aside for years and I've lived very frugally during my time in the service. So the house is a non-issue. As for a business loan, I don't see that being an issue either. If we present a solid business plan, there shouldn't be any problems. As veterans, we're covered and eligible for plenty of programs. And with a veteran business loan..."

Will nodded. Of course his friend would have this all figured out. Everything in him wanted to say yes, but...what if Arianna had moved on?

And why wouldn't she? You never kept in touch.

Yeah. That.

There were so many variables in play here that it wasn't such an easy decision to make.

Actually, it was downright difficult.

"Tell you what," Liam said, interrupting his thoughts. "Just take tonight to think about it. Tomorrow we've got a lot to do with packing up and all that. Promise me you're going to seriously think about it."

"I will. I promise," he said, and hoped this conversation was over. What he wanted most right now was some time to himself to actually think without Liam yammering on and pressuring him.

As if reading his mind, Liam picked up his phone and stretched. "Now if you'll excuse me, I need to call my baby brother and threaten to strangle him if he keeps on setting out sisters up with his friends." He clapped Will on the shoulder. "I'll see you in the morning."

"Night," was all he said before putting his attention on his own phone. Once Liam was gone, however, he pulled up his photos and found the ones of him and Arianna. Just looking at her beautiful, smiling face made his heart ache.

Seeing her again would be both pleasure and pain, and he had to be realistic. It wasn't going to be some big romantic reunion. What he did—while right at the time—was still really unfair to her. Knowing how stubborn her brother was, Will had a feeling it was a family trait. If she couldn't forgive him or—worse—if she'd moved on, could he really stay in their tiny town and make a life for himself there?

His gut told him no. It would be too hard and it didn't matter that they'd only had the one day, he knew Arianna was perfect for him.

But could he possibly convince her and her family that he deserved a chance?

That was the million dollar question he wasn't sure he could handle the answer to.

Get DARE ME now:
https://www.chasing-romance.com/dare-me

And meet the rest of the Donovan family here:
https://www.chasing-romance.com/the-donovans-series

Also by Samantha Chase

The Donovans Series (Sweetbriar Ridge):

Loving You

Teasing You

Wanting You

The Donovans Series (Laurel Bay):

Call Me

Dare Me

Tempt Me

Save Me

Charm Me

Kiss Me

The Wylder Love Series:

Irresistible Love

Indescribably Love

The Montgomery Brothers Series:

Wait for Me

Trust in Me

Stay with Me

More of Me

Return to You

Meant for You

I'll Be There

Until There Was Us

Suddenly Mine

A Dash of Christmas

A Merry Montgomery Christmas

The Magnolia Sound Series:

Sunkissed Days

Remind Me

A Girl Like You

In Case You Didn't Know

All the Befores

And Then One Day

Can't Help Falling in Love

Last Beautiful Girl

The Way the Story Goes

Since You've Been Gone

Nobody Does It Better

Wedding Wonderland

Always on my Mind

Kiss the Girl

Meet Me at the Altar:

The Engagement Embargo

With this Cake

You May Kiss the Groomsman

The Proposal Playbook

Groomed to Perfection

The I Do Over

The Enchanted Bridal Series:

The Wedding Season

Friday Night Brides

The Bridal Squad

Glam Squad & Groomsmen

Bride & Seek

The RoadTripping Series:

Drive Me Crazy

Wrong Turn

Test Drive

Head Over Wheels

The Shaughnessy Brothers Series:

Made for Us

Love Walks In

Always My Girl

This is Our Song

Sky Full of Stars

Holiday Spice

Tangled Up in You

Band on the Run Series:

One More Kiss

One More Promise

One More Moment

One More Chance

The Christmas Cottage Series:

The Christmas Cottage

Ever After

Silver Bell Falls Series:

Christmas in Silver Bell Falls

Christmas On Pointe

A Very Married Christmas

A Christmas Rescue

Christmas Inn Love

The Christmas Plan

Life, Love & Babies Series:

The Baby Arrangement

Baby, Be Mine

Baby, I'm Yours

Preston's Mill Series:

Roommating

Speed Dating

Complicating

The Protectors Series:

Protecting His Best Friend's Sister

Protecting the Enemy

Protecting the Girl Next Door

Protecting the Movie Star

7 Brides for 7 Soldiers:

Ford

7 Brides for 7 Blackthornes:

Logan

Standalone Novels:

Jordan's Return

Catering to the CEO

In the Eye of the Storm

A Touch of Heaven

Exclusive

Moonlight in Winter Park

Waiting for Midnight

Mistletoe Between Friends

Snowflake Inn

His for the Holidays

About Samantha Chase

Samantha Chase is a New York Times and USA Today bestseller of contemporary romance that's hotter than sweet, sweeter than hot. She released her debut novel in 2011 and currently has more than ninety titles under her belt – including THE CHRISTMAS COTTAGE which was a Hallmark Christmas movie in 2017 and WEDDING SEASON which was a Hallmark June Wedding movie in 2023! She's a Disney enthusiast who still happily listens to 80's rock. When she's not working on a new story, she spends her time reading romances, playing way too many games of Solitaire online, wearing a tiara while playing with her sassy pug Maylene...oh, and spending time with her husband of 34 years and their two sons in Wake Forest, North Carolina.

Sign up for my mailing list and get exclusive content and chances to win members-only prizes!
https://www.chasing-romance.com/newsletter

Start a fun new small town romance series:
https://www.chasing-romance.com/the-donovans-series

Where to Find Me:

Website:
www.chasing-romance.com

Facebook:
www.facebook.com/SamanthaChaseFanClub

Instagram:
https://www.instagram.com/samanthachaseromance/

Twitter:
https://twitter.com/SamanthaChase3

Reader Group:
https://www.facebook.comgroups/1034673493228089/

Made in the USA
Middletown, DE
26 August 2024